Downward
Facing Death

Downward
Facing Death

MICHELLE KELLY

MINOTAUR BOOKS

A THOMAS DUNNE BOOK

NEW YORK

This is a work of fiction. All of the characters, organizations, and events portrayed in this novel are either products of the author's imagination or are used fictitiously.

A THOMAS DUNNE BOOK FOR MINOTAUR BOOKS.
An imprint of St. Martin's Publishing Group.

www.thomasdunnebooks.com
www.minotaurbooks.com

Designed by Omar Chapa

Library of Congress Cataloging-in-Publication Data

Names: Kelly, Michelle (Romantic fiction writer), author.
Title: Downward facing death / Michelle Kelly.
Description: New York : Minotaur Books, 2016.
Identifiers: LCCN 2015037861 |
    ISBN 978-1-250-06737-1 (hardback)
    ISBN 978-1-4668-7566-1 (e-book)
Subjects: LCSH: Homecoming—Fiction. | Murder—Investigation—Fiction. |
    England—Fiction. | Mystery fiction. | BISAC: FICTION / Mystery &
    Detective / Women Sleuths.
Classification: LCC PR6111.E5226 D69 2016 | DDC 823/.92—dc23
LC record available at http://lccn.loc.gov/2015037861

Our books may be purchased in bulk for promotional, educational, or business use. Please contact your local bookseller or the Macmillan Corporate and Premium Sales Department at (800) 221-7945, extension 5442, or by e-mail at MacmillanSpecialMarkets@macmillan.com.

First Edition: January 2016

10   9   8   7   6   5   4   3   2   1

For the real Ben. Who taught me what real love really looks like, just when I thought it only happened to other people.

Acknowledgments

Turning a story idea into an actual, tangible book requires the work of more than one person. A big thank-you to my wonderful agent and editor, Isabel Atherton of Creative Authors, and to Anne Brewer, my editor at Thomas Dunne Books.

A shout-out to my children, Alannta and Callum, for putting up with Mum being completely cuckoo during the writing process. I love you rug rats; you make it all worthwhile.

A nod to all the people who have inspired me over the years in the areas of writing, yoga, and cooking. Being able to bring my biggest passions together in this story has made it a joy to write.

Downward
Facing Death

Chapter One

Baking bread and horse manure.

They were the first things Keeley could smell as she stepped off the train at the metal stop sign that passed for a station in Belfrey, Derbyshire. Home.

Except that, after she had been away for so long and adapted so eagerly to city life, it didn't feel like a homecoming at all. Nevertheless, she remembered these smells as she bumped her luggage up the stone steps leading to the High Street. The horse manure wafted down from the surrounding farms that were tucked away in the lines and folds of the hilly landscape. The bread came from the High Street itself, with its various craft stores, coffeehouses, and "olde worlde" sweet shops, all jostling with each other for supremacy.

Her mouth was dry. Ignoring the fancy coffee shop, and even the traditional eatery with its selection of local produce, Keeley made her way to the pub, the Tavern, halfway up the street. It was a run-down place that stuck out like a nicotine-stained thumb against the vintage shop fronts and cobbled streets, which were still strung with bunting from the Easter Festival.

The soles of her sneakers stuck to the threadbare carpet as she walked in, and she breathed a sigh of relief that she had remembered to change out of her pumps. Satin and the beer-sodden floor of the Tavern did not mix.

Keeley tugged her zebra-print luggage inside and straightened up as the bar door swung shut behind her, leaving her blinking in the suddenly dim light. She grinned into the darkness, waiting for her enthusiastic welcome home.

One that never came. One solitary, gruff voice piped up from the corner.

"All right, duck? Are you lost?" The man's face showed genuine concern, though his expression was nearly lost amid the sun-beaten lines of his face. He was small but wiry, with that lean strength and straight back that characterized men of a certain age and type in Belfrey.

Keeley squinted at the familiar face, struggling for a name, then hurried over and sat down opposite the man as it came to her.

"Jack Tibbons?" Keeley beamed at him, wondering how she could have forgotten the old man. Not only was he sitting at the very same table he always sat at when she had frequented the Tavern with her father, but he was also her father's best friend. "It's me, Keeley. George Carpenter's daughter."

Her father had been the local butcher—the only butcher within a ten-mile radius, in fact—around Belfrey for years, having inherited the business from his father and grandfather and great-grandfather before him. Everyone in Belfrey knew George Carpenter. The day of his funeral, it seemed as though the whole town had turned out.

Jack's face showed surprise, then recognition as he looked Keeley up and down. She could hardly blame him, she supposed, for not recognizing her straightaway. Eight years of living in London, then an ashram in India, then a two-year sabbatical in New York teaching hot yoga to classes of sleek and streamlined professionals had left her slimmer, more tanned, and with a poise that she certainly hadn't possessed when she left Belfrey.

"So it is. Well, I suppose I had better buy you a drink. Tom!" he shouted at the empty bar, "Get the girl a drink, will you?"

A guy about her own age, with long hair and a beard, and a metal ring through his nose that made her wince just looking at it, came out from a door behind the bar, looking bored until he laid eyes on Keeley. He did a double take, and Keeley realized she wasn't the only one who had changed in her absence. Tom, the manager's son, had been a short-haired, cherub-faced teenager the last time she saw him. He was also, she noticed as she stood up and went to the bar, nearly twice the height he had been. Craning her neck to look at him, she almost wished she had kept on the heels.

"Small white wine please," she said.

"You're back, then?" He sounded almost disgruntled, as if annoyed she had been away so long. "I thought you'd gone off to some fancy place in India?"

"I was studying yoga and nutrition," Keeley told him, thinking that the ashram she had stayed in could hardly be described as "fancy." For six months, she had slept on a mattress on the floor and gotten up at five every morning. "I'm a qualified teacher and nutritionist now. I've been working in New York, and I'm about to open a lifestyle café." She allowed herself a smug smile at the last two words. The Yoga Café would be an entirely new concept for the small English town, and she was rather proud of the idea even if it wasn't entirely her own, but rather inspired by the local juice bar she had frequented in Manhattan.

"In New York?" Jack looked puzzled, while Tom reached up for a glass and started wiping it with a grimy-looking tea towel. His face was carefully blank. Keeley sighed. He obviously wasn't going to be rushing to one of her classes or popping over to sample a tofu burger with quinoa.

"No," she explained patiently to Jack. "Here in Belfrey. Right here, in fact." She waved an arm in the direction of the street outside. "In my father's old shop."

Carpenter's Butchers was her legacy, one that had been left in her mother's less-than-loving hands over the years. Hands that had more or less washed themselves of not just the shop but Belfrey, too, whisking Keeley away to London the day after her father's funeral. The store had carried on being a butcher's for a while, managed by Jack Tibbons himself until his arthritis set in and he could no longer handle a cleaver; then the premises were rented out as an embroidery shop until the recent recession hit and left it empty and abandoned for nearly a year. "Do something with that shop," her mother had snapped during one of her monthly phone calls to Keeley in New York (her mother made no pretense of wanting to be "close" to her only daughter), "or I'm going to sell it." And so here she was.

The irony of turning a former butcher's into a vegetarian café wasn't lost on Keeley, but she liked to think her father would have encouraged her to follow her dreams.

"I'm going to be selling vegetarian dishes, healthy and tasty foods, and in the evenings, I'll be holding yoga classes. . . ." She trailed off from her proud sales spiel when she saw both Jack and the barman looking at her in horror. She had expected some confusion, distaste even, perhaps indifference—but abject horror? That seemed a little extreme, even from a former butcher and a metal-head bartender who looked as though he occasionally bathed in pigs' blood.

"You don't know, then, duck? I thought that's what you were back for." Jack patted her arm in sympathy. Keeley frowned at him.

"Know what?"

Before Jack could answer, the door opened, bringing in a swath of light that temporarily blinded Keeley as she turned to see the newcomer. Whoever it was had made both Jack and Tom suddenly spring to attention. A male figure stood like a silhouette in the flash of sunshine, slowly becoming more distinct as the door creaked shut and Keeley blinked to clear her vision. Before her stood a guy who was most certainly the finest specimen of a male she had seen in a long time. With close-clipped dark hair, a perfectly honed physique, and a dimpled chin coupled with a strong jaw, he was a poster boy for the alpha male. It was a shame he was also a jerk.

Not that she knew whether or not he actually was a jerk, of course, but looking like that, it was inevitable. He was precisely the type of guy she had avoided for most of her adult life, preferring arty, sensitive types that she could have conversations with about philosophy and the like. She always prided herself on not being shallow, not falling over her feet for a man just because he happened to raise her estrogen levels. She had slipped up, with her first serious boyfriend, at the tender ages of eighteen to twenty-one, and he had been reason enough for her to avoid his type ever since. Before her ill-fated first love, she'd had a crush on that same type of guy, but that was way back in her first year at Belfrey High School, when she had mooned over Benjamin Taylor from afar, hoping he would notice her. He never did, no matter how many times she walked past his table in the canteen, hoping to catch his eye, or moved her chair closer to his in Maths class. While other boys at school had teased her, dubbing her "Lardypants," Ben Taylor never showed the slightest indication that he was even aware of her existence.

As this new vision of masculinity approached, Keeley noted how Jack nodded at him with obvious respect and Tom seemed to shrink into himself, almost as if he expected chastisement. Who was this guy?

"Hello, Ben," Jack said in the same tone he might have said, "Greetings, Your Highness," and Keeley experienced a moment of confusion, then an ominous dawning clarity. How could she not have realized it was him? The dimple in his chin should have given it away instantly.

Benjamin Taylor! Immediately, Keeley felt like that shy, plump eleven-year-old and blushed from the roots of her hair to her shell pink–painted toenails. She took a deep breath and let it out through her lips in increments, curling her tongue. It was a breathing technique designed to cool unwanted emotions. For the first time, it didn't work; only made her cheeks flame hotter as she accidentally let out a low whistling noise that sounded very much as if she had appraised Ben and liked what she was seeing.

Ben turned to her and raised an amused eyebrow.

"I wasn't whistling at you," she said hurriedly. "I was, er, doing my breathing exercises."

Now Ben looked both amused and perplexed. Jack jumped in before Keeley could embarrass herself any further.

"This is George Carpenter's girl. It's her that's taken on the old shop."

Was Keeley imagining things, or had there been a meaningful tone to Jack's voice? As if they all knew something she didn't. Ben looked at her, his expression grim, and Keeley felt her stomach sink. Something was very definitely wrong here. Ben held an object up to her face, and it took a moment for her to register what it was. A police badge.

"I'm Detective Constable Taylor," Ben said, "and I'm going to have to ask you a few questions."

"Er, about what?" This homecoming was rapidly turning into an episode of *The Twilight Zone*. Ben looked surprised.

"She doesn't know," Jack said, shaking his head.

"Miss Carpenter," Ben said, his words dropping like stones, "someone tried to burn down your shop last night."

SITALI—COOLING BREATH

To soothe and calm the nervous system in times of stress or anxiety. Such as being confronted with your high school crush in less-than-optimal circumstances. Also useful for hot flashes.

Method

- Purse your lips as if blowing a kiss.
- Curl up the sides of your tongue.
- Let your tongue "float" so it doesn't touch the roof or floor of your mouth.
- Inhale and exhale slowly, using your tongue like a straw to draw the air in and out.

Recommendation

Try not to whistle. Particularly at your former crush!

Chapter Two

Keeley sank farther into her chair, her legs trembling.

"Burn it down?" she parroted, her mind skittering in a hundred different directions, trying to get a grasp on this new information and failing. She had a sudden and vivid craving for a bacon-and-sausage sandwich—for years, her favorite comfort food.

Breathe, she told herself. *Find a focus point and breathe into your center.*

Taking a deep breath, she focused on a point on Ben's shirt directly in front of her and noticed how it skimmed over obviously defined pectorals to tuck neatly into the waistband of his dark trousers, which fit his lean hips and strong thighs in a way that reminded her more of a catalog model than of the quintessential country cop. . . . Okay, maybe this wasn't helping.

"Miss Carpenter?" Ben looked more than a little bemused, and Keeley's eyes snapped back up to his face.

"Yes. Sorry. It's just a shock."

Jack patted her arm in sympathy again, and Tom pushed a glass of water over the counter toward her. Keeley went over and took it from him with a smile, grateful for the small kindness. This, as well as her father's shop, had been one of the things that had pulled her back to Belfrey; the sense of community and of looking after their own that had felt so suffocating to her at the age of seventeen was like a balm ten years later.

Except that when she looked again at Ben, his eyes didn't seem kind at all. They looked suspicious.

"I've been trying to call you all day, Miss Carpenter. We spoke to your mother, and she told us you should have arrived in Belfrey two days ago."

Keeley froze as the meaning of Ben's words sank in. He thought *she* was to blame for this. She took a sip of water to calm the stab of anger in her belly.

Which she then spat all over that well-fitting shirt. As Ben jumped back, cursing, Keeley turned horrified eyes to Tom.

"What on earth was in that water?"

"Water? That was vodka," Tom said, grinning. "It's good for shock." Across from her, she heard Jack starting to chuckle. Keeley slammed the glass down onto the table, spilling the offending vodka, and stood up, glaring at Ben, who was now wiping his shirt with a bar towel and looking less than pleased.

"Can I see the premises?" Only now did the full implications of the news hit her. If the damage was severe, then her plans to open the café would go up in smoke along with the building! There was no way she would convince her mother to pay for a full renovation.

Ben cocked his head to one side a little, as if weighing up both her words and the possibility that she was responsible for the fire.

"I'll take you over there now."

"It's my shop," Keeley pointed out. "I hardly need a chaperone."

"It may be your shop," Ben said, unfazed by her curt tone, "but it's also a crime scene."

He placed a hand on the small of her back, the briefest of touches, as he guided her toward the door. Keeley flinched away at the heat of his palm through the thin fabric of her blouse, an image of him in the school canteen flashing through her mind unbidden. He hadn't given any sign of recognizing her, though he must know who she was by the name; everyone in Belfrey knew everyone else. Ignoring the outstretched hand ready to take her luggage, Keeley stepped out into the warm air, blinking as the bright spring sunshine hit her. While she followed Ben down the meandering hill of the High Street, her heart thudded as she waited to see what damage had been done. Thankfully, the front of the shop at least looked fine. Fumbling for her keys in her handbag, she noticed her fingers shaking. A few openly curious faces peered out of shop windows nearby, but Keeley ignored them, swung open the door, and stepped inside, Ben close behind her.

A wave of nostalgia hit her. Although the shop itself was empty apart from a small counter, she immediately pictured her father behind his rows of meat, a smile on his adorably fat face, and felt again like a schoolgirl running in to embrace her dad on her way home from class. He had never judged her, never made her feel less than adequate or pinched the roll of puppy fat at her waist with a pursed mouth and disapproving eyes—unlike her mother.

Darla Carpenter's dissatisfaction with both her husband and her daughter had been evident pretty much every day that Keeley could remember.

Pushing the memories and sting of tears aside, Keeley strode through to the small kitchen at the back of the shop, aware of Ben's keen eyes upon her. The smell of charred wood and brick hit her instantly, and she surveyed the damage with an unsettling mixture of emotions. Relief that it wasn't as bad as she had feared—though the back door and frame were all but burned to a crisp and the back wall was seared black—and horror that someone, anyone, could deliberately do such a thing. It seemed almost a macabre joke that it should happen here, in this very room, defiling her father's memory.

"Was it kids, maybe?" she asked hopefully. Teenagers perhaps, hanging around, playing a silly game, a prank that had gotten out of hand. Ben paused, obviously unsure how much to tell her, and Keeley felt like stamping her foot with frustration.

"It's my shop," she pointed out. "I have a right to know what happened."

Ben shrugged. "As I said, Miss Carpenter"—she wondered why he didn't call her Keeley and concluded that he didn't remember her at all—"we have been trying to reach you. Your mother seemed to be under the impression you were arriving here before today. You're renting Rose Cottage from Mrs. Rowland, I believe."

"My mother," Keeley said with impatience, "barely remembers I exist, never mind keeps track of my plans. I had my things sent up to the cottage two days ago, but I've been staying in London with a friend. I wasn't due to arrive until today, as I'm sure Mrs. Rowland will be able to confirm."

Ben didn't respond to that, and she had a suspicion that Mrs. Rowland had already been questioned.

"Your phone?"

"I had no signal on the train, and the battery was going anyway, so I turned it off. See?" Keeley pulled her phone from her bag and thrust it in Ben's face. He looked at her calmly.

"Thank you."

Feeling foolish, she returned her phone to her bag and walked toward the back door. Ben followed, placing a hand on her arm. He was very close, standing over her so that she had to tip her chin to look at him, and she could smell the musky scent of his cologne and the faint tang of male skin. Her mouth felt dry as he gazed down at her and lifted those full lips into a half smile.

"It's still a crime scene, so I'm going to have to ask you not to touch anything. We've cordoned it off round the back, and upstairs." He nodded toward the stairwell in the far corner of the kitchen that led up to a small studio flat.

Stepping away from him, Keeley felt her cheeks burning with a combination of embarrassment, desire, and anger. Even so, she didn't miss the mysterious way he had said the last two words, hinting at darker things. Things he wasn't sharing with her.

"Why upstairs? You didn't say the damage was that bad," Keeley accused. "I'm supposed to be opening in two weeks! I'm going to be delayed as it is, sorting this mess out."

"Don't you want us to find out who it was? These things take time, Miss Carpenter."

His constant use of her surname was getting on her nerves. "It's Keeley, or at least *Ms.*," she snapped. "As for uncovering the culprit, it would help if you told me exactly what has happened. Like I said, couldn't it just be kids?"

Ben looked serious.

"I'm afraid not. Thankfully, the fire services were alerted almost as soon as the blaze started, thanks to Jack Tibbons's dog barking its head off, but it was no prank. There's evidence that gasoline was poured all around the back door. 'Kids,' as you put it, don't tend to go to those lengths. If help hadn't arrived so quickly, you may not be opening at all."

Keeley blanched as the reality of the situation began to hit her. Ben went on, seemingly oblivious to her distress.

"Forensics will be back tomorrow to see what—if anything—they can find in the way of evidence to identify the perpetrator. It wasn't a particularly professional arson attempt, but it was definitely deliberate."

"But who would do such a thing? And to an empty shop?" Keeley shook her head. Whatever she had been expecting upon her return to Belfrey, it wasn't this.

Arson. It sounded so, well, sinister.

Ben looked at her intently.

"Unfortunately, arson is often one of the easiest crimes to commit and one of the hardest to prove. But there are usually two reasons: revenge for some kind of grudge, or an insurance scam."

"Well, I certainly had nothing to do with it." Keeley drew herself up to her full height—just under five foot four—and glared at him. As gorgeous as he might be, she wasn't going to stand here in her own shop and be accused of something so heinous. Or at least, he was making it sound heinous. She wondered if he really was hiding something, or if the mysterious air was just part of his ego trip.

Ben didn't bat an eyelid at her indignation.

"If you say so. In that case, Miss Carpenter—Keeley—you

need to ask yourself this: Who carries enough of a grudge to attempt to derail your business?"

Keeley couldn't answer him. There was no one—how could there be? She hadn't set foot in Belfrey for ten years, and everyone had loved her father. Perhaps her mother hadn't been quite so popular, but Keeley couldn't think of any reason why anyone would want to do this to her. And besides, who carried a grudge for ten years? She shook her head mutely at Ben, who continued to regard her with an intensity that made her uncomfortable. To think, for years at school, she had longed for him to look at her.

"You're absolutely certain," Ben said slowly, "that you only arrived in Belfrey today?"

"Yes!" she snapped, exasperated. "I told you, you can check."

He went on as if he hadn't heard her. "And you have no quarrel with any of the residents in Belfrey?"

Keeley was becoming seriously annoyed. She took a deep breath, trying to remember everything she knew about staying calm in the face of anger. It seemed the ancient yoga masters of India had never had to deal with the likes of Benjamin Taylor.

"How about a man named Terry Smith? Remember him?"

His question confused her enough that she momentarily forgot her fury at him. Clearly, his questions were leading somewhere.

"No, I don't think so. My mother might. Why, do you think he did this?" If that was the case, why insist on interrogating *her*? Then Ben's next words took all the breath from her body, like a sucker punch to her stomach.

"Hardly. Considering that he was found dead upstairs." Ben jerked his head up to the ceiling, indicating the studio flat above the shop, where Keeley had planned on holding evening classes.

Her gaze followed the direction of his movement with a kind of morbid curiosity.

"Dead?" she echoed.

Ben nodded, his full mouth flattened to a grim line.

"Not just dead. Murdered."

Keeley stepped back and away from him, pressing her hand to her chest and feeling her eyes widen in disbelief. She groped for the kitchen counter and leaned against it, forcing herself to relax. Ben just continued to look at her with no trace of sympathy. Surely he didn't think her responsible for *that*?

"Murdered . . . but why?"

"Well, that is precisely what I intend to find out. You're certain you don't recall him?"

Keeley shook her head. Then she began to feel angry again as he continued to regard her with that level gaze. Despite the neutrality of his tone, there was an obvious implication that she knew more than she was telling him. She let go of the counter and stood straight, if not tall. (Expressions such as "drawing oneself up to one's full height" didn't tend to work very well when the one in question was only five feet four inches, she reflected wryly.)

"I can assure you, Detective Constable, I have no idea who, how, or why anybody was murdered or my premises vandalized. I came back to open a successful business, and certainly wouldn't be involved in anything that would jeopardize that." She glared at him, feeling quite proud of her little speech. Ben lowered his eyebrows, still looking at her, then gave a slight nod as if he had reassured himself about something. Keeley, whose muscles were quivering because she was so tense, let her shoulders drop and exhaled with relief, though she wasn't entirely sure what she was relieved about.

"Okay," Ben said. "But I have to advise you that I'll most likely be in touch with further questions."

Keeley swallowed down a retort, not wanting to crank up the tension between them any further. She motioned toward the stairwell.

"Has everything . . . been cleaned?" She felt suddenly queasy. A corner of Ben's mouth twitched as if he was amused again, though she certainly couldn't find anything funny about the situation.

"Yes, it's all been taken care of, but as I said, I can't let you up until forensics have finished. But there's no noticeable damage upstairs."

Thank God, Keeley thought, her overactive imagination having conjured up visions of having to clean up puddles of blood— or worse.

"How did he die?" she asked, her natural curiosity kicking in once more. Ben looked suspicious again and hesitated, as if wondering how much to tell her, before he said in a quiet tone:

"Hit over the head with a blunt object, by the look of things, though our postmortem guy couldn't determine with what, exactly."

Which meant they hadn't found the murder weapon, Keeley realized. She began to wish she had paid more attention to the reruns of *CSI* that her flatmate in New York had been constantly watching.

"Maybe he just banged his head?" she offered. Ben's lips quirked again in that half-smile she was sure meant he was laughing at her. "Or maybe he interrupted whoever was trying to set the fire?" That was a viable suggestion, she thought, but when the smile vanished and he looked suspicious again, she wished she hadn't said anything.

"We're working on that assumption," he said carefully as a thought hit Keeley with a jolt of anxiety.

"How did they get in? It should have been all locked up."

Ben gave her another nod. "The estate agent reports that none of the keys were missing. Before you give me the 'it wasn't me' speech, an inspection of the back door lock does suggest it was picked. Honestly, I'm surprised the place was left so unsecured."

Keeley bit her lip, feeling guilty—though in all truth, up until now, security had been her mother's responsibility. The back gate was bolted and the back door fitted with a standard Yale lock. There had never been a burglar alarm installed. In a small, sleepy town like Belfrey, who would want to break into an empty shop?

Perhaps Belfrey wasn't as sleepy as she had thought.

Once she had locked the shop back up, Ben offered to drive her to Rose Cottage, and after a moment of hesitation, Keeley agreed. As much as she didn't relish the prospect of spending any longer than absolutely necessary in the detective constable's company, considering that she seemed to be Suspect of the Moment, neither was she looking forward to the twenty-minute, predominantly uphill walk to Rose Cottage on legs that were now decidedly shaky. Buses in Belfrey came only a few times a day, and even then were rarely on schedule. It was high time she got herself a new car.

Keeley sat stiffly in the passenger seat of Ben's Saab, hoping he wouldn't continue to question her. She had no idea who could be responsible for the fire or the alleged murder of a man she didn't know, and right now wanted nothing more than a cup of soothing herbal tea and some deep stretching. She pushed any thoughts of bacon-and-sausage sandwiches firmly to the back of her consciousness. An hour in Belfrey, and she was already reverting to the chubby teenager of ten years ago. Perhaps it was a good thing Ben didn't remember her.

"You've changed since school," he said, making it clear that in fact he knew exactly who she was. Keeley felt herself cringe.

"I suppose so," she said, aiming for nonchalance and ending up with sulky instead.

"When I spoke to your mother, she said you were opening a vegetarian café. Seems kind of funny for a butcher's daughter," he remarked, his earlier reticence seemingly forgotten. Keeley was wary of his desire to chat. No doubt some tactic meant to trip her up and get her to confess to murdering the poor man found in her café. She shrugged to suppress the chill that came over her and sat staring out the window.

"Not really. I want to show that food can be tasty as well as good for you, and ethical to boot."

"You think it will catch on? In Belfrey?" Ben sounded doubtful. Keeley nodded, any grudge against Ben momentarily forgotten in her usual enthusiasm to talk about her favorite subject.

"I'm not pushing some New Age fad here; there are proven benefits to a nonmeat, organic diet. And yoga itself is booming— the yoga classes at the local gym are packed full, I checked."

"So what has one got to do with the other?" He actually sounded interested, and Keeley twisted in her seat toward him. If she could get the local detective on board, that would certainly help her credibility.

"Yoga isn't just a form of exercise, although it can be used like that, it's actually a whole lifestyle system, of which diet is a big part. Not that you have to eat a vegetarian diet to practice yoga, it's a personal choice thing, but they definitely reinforce each other.

Lots of people come to yoga as a means to lose weight too—something else a nonmeat diet can assist with."

Ben glanced over at her, taking his eyes off the road for a moment to trail them down her body. Keeley shifted in her seat self-consciously; the temperature inside the car seemed to have kicked up a few notches.

"Is that what got you into it? The weight loss?"

Instantly Keeley felt herself morphing into the girl he would have remembered; the shy, overweight girl with frizzy hair and buckteeth, and she shrank back away from him.

"Well, I certainly got fed up with being called Lardypants," she said tightly. Ben snorted in amusement.

"People called you that, really?"

"You were there," she said in a small voice. At that, Ben slowed the car, a funny expression on his face.

"I'm quite sure," he said slowly, as if offended, "that I never called you that name."

"Not you," Keeley amended, "but some of the kids in your crowd did." She heard the bitterness in her own voice and winced. She had spent many hours on the yoga mat learning to let go of both old grudges and poor body image; half an hour in the company of Ben Taylor, and it all came flooding back.

Next to her, Ben was quiet.

"Well," he said after five minutes of increasingly uncomfortable silence, "I'm sorry about that. If I had known, I would have said something. I never have been able to stand bullies."

"It doesn't matter," she said, although all of a sudden it did matter, and very much so. She would have preferred him not to remember her at all than to see her as some poor victim. An overweight victim, at that. Still, she supposed it was marginally better than him viewing her as a murder suspect.

They drove the rest of the way to Rose Cottage with Keeley's eyes firmly on the landscape. Amber Valley truly was a beautiful part of the country, and one of the things she had missed most during her ten years away was the views. In every direction lay a visual feast of rolling green and gold hills, merging into a blue and gray horizon dotted with the inland cliffs and heights of the Peak District. There was such unspoiled beauty, it seemed almost inconceivable that anything bad could ever happen here.

Ben finally turned onto Bakers Hill and paused outside the cottage. Keeley breathed a sigh of relief and, in spite of the day's revelations, felt her heart leap at the sight of her new home, a postcard-pretty quintessential country cottage, complete with blush roses climbing around the arch of the doorway and a thatched roof. When she had shown a picture of it to her friends in New York, they cooed with delight. Her mother, more used to the practicalities of living in the country, shook her head with disdain. "You'll get squirrels," she had said, wrinkling her nose at the thatch. When Keeley was younger, they had lived in one of the more modern town houses in the center of Belfrey, but Keeley always secretly wished to live in one of the more traditional cottages, even those at the end of the High Street that were so old and uncared for, they had subsided into triangular shapes as if the ground were about to swallow them up.

Ben got out of the car with her, lifting her luggage out of the boot. The cottage had been let fully furnished, and the rest of Keeley's things been delivered the day before, so there was little for her to do except unpack a few boxes.

"Thank you," she said to Ben, feeling awkward and wondering if she should invite him in.

"Call me," he said, and Keeley frowned, momentarily misreading his intention until he continued. "If you think of anything that might help me figure out who torched your shop, or you remember anything relevant about Terry Smith, let me know straightaway. Otherwise, I'll let you know when the forensics have finished."

"Yeah, sure," she mumbled, all but snatching her suitcase away from him. She didn't look back as his car purred its way down the hill away from her. Seeing Ben Taylor again, and in such circumstances, was certainly not the homecoming she had expected. That, nor her shop being turned into a crime scene.

The key was under the mat as Mrs. Rowland had promised it would be, so it surprised her when the front door turned out to be open. Nervous, Keeley pushed open the door and peered around it. In the kitchen, a small, plump woman with a chestnut-colored bob was arranging flowers in a large, brightly colored vase on the table. Annie Rowland. Keeley let her breath out with relief and wheeled her luggage into the cottage, shutting the door behind her. The scent of freesias filled the air as her landlady turned to her, a large and welcoming smile on her face, her small blue eyes shining.

"Keeley! Look at you," the older woman exclaimed, wrapping Keeley in a warm, comforting hug that had her blinking back unbidden tears. Finally, someone who seemed pleased to see her back in Belfrey. Although Keeley had not really known Annie in her younger days other than as a customer in her father's shop, she was so relieved to see a friendly face that she returned the hug as if greeting a long-lost friend.

"You look amazing," Annie exclaimed, then rather ruined the compliment by adding, "so much like your mother."

Keeley grimaced. After her weight loss, she had indeed seen her mother's more angular features appear from underneath the puppy fat, like a sculpture emerging from a dollop of clay. With the addition of a deep tan from her time in India and some shockingly expensive New York highlights, Keeley had hoped the resemblance had somewhat softened.

"I've made it all as nice as I can for you, dear, made the beds up and everything," Annie trilled, then picked up her coat from the peg it hung on and started to shrug it on. Keeley felt a little stab of panic. She had been so looking forward to her first day back in Belfrey and to moving into Rose Cottage; had envisaged herself puttering around on her own, arranging her things the way she wanted them and maybe even uncurling her yoga mat in the garden and moving through a few Sun Salutations in the crisp spring sun. Now she felt as though being alone were the last thing she wanted, and wondered if she wasn't having some kind of delayed reaction to the shock.

"There was a murder at my father's shop—well, my café now," she blurted out, "and someone set it on fire, or tried to." Annie's mouth dropped open, and she promptly hung her coat back up.

"Oh, dear. Do you know, I saw something on the front of the *Belfrey Times* this morning on my way into Ripley, but I didn't think to stop and have a look. I didn't realize it was your place. You poor lamb, did you know the victim?"

Shaking her head, Keeley filled her in on the morning's events, sitting down at the kitchen table with weak legs. Definitely a touch of shock.

"Ben—DC Taylor—suggested maybe the victim interrupted

whoever tried to set the fire. He seemed to think it was someone with a grudge." *Or me, setting up an insurance scam,* she thought bitterly but didn't want to say that to this kind-faced woman. Keeley didn't think she could take another suspicious look.

Annie waved a hand dismissively. "That Taylor boy, he's been watching too many detective shows on TV, fancies himself as a star in one of them. Not enough going on in Amber Valley for his liking, he should transfer over to Derby. Who would have a grudge against you, or your father? He was a well-liked man. Most likely whoever set the fire got caught in it themselves." Annie nodded decisively, as though her word were the final say on the matter. Keeley didn't share what Ben had told her about blunt objects. She wondered how much information had been released to the newspapers, and if this Terry Smith was a popular person in Belfrey. What if the whole town thought it was her? Or down to some kind of family feud—but that was preposterous, surely?

Then a cold curl of doubt began to unfurl in her chest as something Annie had said niggled at her. There certainly seemed to be little reason why anyone should wish to target Keeley herself, or her late father, but there was one member of her family who made a habit of getting people's backs up.

Her mother.

Chapter Three

A phone call to Darla Carpenter proved unfruitful. As Keeley had expected, her mother was suitably offended at the thought that there could possibly exist anyone who didn't find her utterly amazing.

"Did you know the victim? Terry Smith?"

"Not very well," Darla admitted. "He was a ratty little man, always stank of ale and always in the betting shops. He came in your father's shop a few times, and he always tried to haggle about prices. Quite unpleasant, really."

"So you don't know what he would have been doing in our shop?" Although Keeley had been thinking of the shop as *her café* for weeks now, somehow it didn't seem right to describe it like that to her mother—who, after all, still owned the premises.

"No idea. Besides," Darla went on, a chill to her voice that could freeze lava, "I haven't been back to Belfrey in years. I arranged everything to do with the leasing of the shop through the estate agents."

"Was there any mention of anyone wanting to buy?" Keeley asked. Perhaps if the fire had been set with malicious intent, it had more to do with business reasons than personal ones. Perhaps her plans for the building had seriously derailed someone else's entrepreneurial dreams? If this Terry Smith was some kind of drunk, as her mother implied, perhaps he had just been looking for a place to sleep and caught the arsonist unawares? Keeley blinked as if to ward off the macabre images that filled her mind, along with a wave of pity for a man she didn't even know, but who had come to such a gruesome end.

"No, I don't think so. Honestly, Keeley, you sound like that detective who keeps ringing me up. I do believe he thinks *I* had something to do with it."

Keeley suppressed a giggle at the thought of Ben Taylor and her mother at loggerheads. The policeman would certainly have met his match in Darla.

"So, I suppose you're going to need money for the repairs?"

"Possibly." Keeley sighed. Darla had already made it clear that if Keeley's idea for the Yoga Café wasn't profitable within the first year, she would be selling. At the moment, Keeley's meager savings didn't stretch to buying the property. Most of the savings account she gotten access to at the age of twenty-one had been spent on her travels to India and then the lease on her New York flat.

She rang off before Darla could make her feel any worse. Without bothering to change or even rummage through her things for her yoga mat, she ran through a quick series of postures that were designed to balance and reenergize her. That was the beauty of her yoga practice; it could be done anywhere. Although the industry itself was big business—and in New York especially, she had seen just how commercialized it could become, with the elite paying a small fortune for classes in heated, mirrored studios and handwoven mats that cost an average month's salary—when one got down to the bare bones of it, none of the expensive trappings were necessary. It was just the body and the breath, and a combination of both movement and stillness that could relax or invigorate, depending on the practitioner's needs. What had initially attracted Keeley was just that; how it became so personal. There was none of the competitiveness she had found in gyms full of sweaty, struggling bodies each trying to lift more than the next, or the sidelong glances in aerobics classes from women who reminded her of her mother, sleek and vindictive.

Keeley moved through her workout with her mind as blank as she could make it, the soothing rhythm of the postures keeping her thoughts away from both her mother and the murder. As she bent and stretched, breathed and reached, she felt a peace that she hoped would remain with her after she finished.

Instead, she just felt restless and hungry. After discovering little in the cottage other than blocks of tofu, packets of herbal tea, and some spices, she decided to take a walk down to the shop on the corner of the hill. It was, if she remembered rightly, next door to the Baker's Inn, a more upmarket version of the Tavern. A nice cool glass of wine sounded like the perfect remedy. Although she usually drank very little, if ever a girl deserved a pick-me-up, it was today.

Keeley emerged from the local newsagents with a grocery bag containing a few vegetables and a carton of soup that looked to be about a hundred years old. Although she hadn't expected the only shop outside of the High Street to have much in the way of vegetarian produce, she had assumed it would at least have *some* produce. The shelves had been all but empty, and the ancient-looking shopkeeper glared at Keeley as she came in, apparently angry at the interruption.

The Baker's Inn stood to her left, and that glass of wine was becoming more and more tempting. Perhaps they would be a touch more welcoming there than the Tavern was at least. The mock Tudor front and trailing flower baskets hanging around the wooden front doors gave the inn a homey, comforting look.

Her hopes died as she entered the inn to an indifferent glance from the barman and a few curious looks from the customers. There were none of the warm greetings and friendly camaraderie that she remembered from her childhood in Belfrey. In fact, Keeley was beginning to wonder if Belfrey had ever truly been as she remembered it, or if ten years away had added a rosy tint to her nostalgia. She had regaled her American friends with stories about the pretty English village she grew up in but was beginning to think they had been just that, stories. Made up by a girl desperate to feel she had actually belonged somewhere.

"A small, sweet white wine, please," Keeley ordered. The barman poured her wine and pushed her glass over the counter without making eye contact. Still, at least he hadn't spiked her drink with vodka.

Keeley sat down at a booth, looking around for a friendly or at least familiar face and not finding one. Eyes that had been appraising her with curiosity now slid away from her as if she weren't there. It couldn't be because of the murder, for no one had even bothered to ask who she was or what she was doing there. Feeling a little nauseated, Keeley understood why she was being treated like an outsider.

Because she was one. Even if there had been anyone here she recognized, she had been away from Belfrey for ten years. Not only did she look different, but she *was* different as well. And she no longer fit in.

Keeley was staring glumly into her glass of wine when a shadow fell across her table. She looked up to see a woman and man about her own age beaming down at her. The woman had long blond dreadlocks and wore what Keeley could only describe as a purple chiffon sack. She was pretty, although Keeley couldn't help but think she had marred her looks a little with the scattering of small stars that were tattooed across her right cheekbone. The man next to her, in contrast, was a vision of perfection, with shiny hair curling onto his collar and a deep tan that set off his obviously whitened teeth. His toned form was encased in a vest and cut-off jeans. He wouldn't have looked out of place back in Manhattan, Keeley thought, especially with those teeth. She wondered if he was gay. Either that, or a gym instructor.

"I'm Duane," he said, offering her a smooth, brown hand. "I work at Belfrey Leisure Center." He gave her a flash of those sparkling teeth, and as he slid into the seat opposite her, his eyes lingered for a moment on her breasts. Her latter assumption was right, at least.

"And I'm Megan, Duane's cousin. I own Crystals and Candles on Belfrey High Street."

Keeley's ears perked up at that. Perhaps she would have something in common, if not fashion sense, with another young female shop owner in Belfrey. She introduced herself and explained about her plans for the café, gratified to have found at least two people who seemed to think it was a good idea. They also didn't mention the murder, either out of tact or because they hadn't heard about it yet.

Megan freely admitted that although her only customers that tended to be residents of Belfrey were teenagers and the odd eccentric spinster, she also had plenty of customers coming over from the nearby towns of Ripley and Matlock. Keeley thought that ironic, considering the two towns couldn't be more different. Ripley was generally regarded as "rough" by the residents of Belfrey, who considered their own town a cut above. Whereas Matlock was Amber Valley's main tourist attraction, thanks to its seaside town vibe and beautiful, illuminated caves and cliff faces.

Megan's words cheered her. If a shop selling crystals purported to "clear the pathways to angelic influence" and candles that smelled like marijuana could flourish in Belfrey, then her Yoga Café should do just fine. She was even more cheered when Duane encouraged her to seek customers at the leisure center.

"We have only one yoga instructor at the minute, she comes in from Derby, and the demand for classes is more than she can manage. Perhaps you could run an evening class up at the leisure center?"

Keeley nodded, thinking it over. With the opening of the café delayed, she wouldn't be able to hold classes upstairs in the flat yet either. A regular class at the local gym would pull in some extra money as well as help her drum up some interest in her business. She smiled at Duane with genuine enthusiasm.

"That sounds like a great idea." Keeley reached for her glass only to find it empty. Duane took it from her, his fingertips brushing hers. His fingernails, she noticed, were perfectly manicured.

"I'll get you another," he said smoothly. Keeley blinked at him.

He was definitely flirting with her, she decided, but as tempting as another glass sounded, all she really wanted to do was get an early night. She shook her head.

"Thank you, but I had really better go. Some other time," she suggested, her gaze taking in Megan as well as Duane so that he didn't misread her intentions. Duane was handsome, very buff, and obviously interested, yet Keeley hadn't experienced that immediate and all-important spark of attraction from being in his company. *Not like with Ben,* spoke an impish voice inside her, one that Keeley mentally and firmly told to shut up.

Duane followed her to the door and opened it for her, standing far closer to Keeley than he needed to so that she had to brush past him as she exited the inn. Megan waved at her, her dreadlocks bouncing.

"About that drink," Duane said, flashing Keeley what was obviously meant to be a seductive smile, though the whiteness of his teeth against the shadows creeping in the doorway made it more eerie than alluring, "how about Wednesday night? I could meet you in here, say about seven? Just me and you," he added.

Keeley hesitated. Then she thought about Ben and the charred frame of the back door of the café. *What the hell,* she thought, it was only a drink.

"It's a date," she said with a smile of her own, then ducked under Duane's impressive biceps and hurried off up the hill before she could change her mind.

The night air hit her, making her feel decidedly tipsy, and an owl hooted, making her jump and then laugh at her own foolishness. As she let herself into Rose Cottage, she felt happier than she had all day, and optimistic about her future in Belfrey for the first time since stepping off the train. The police would resolve the murder, she was sure, and the damage to the café would be repaired. She even had a date! And with a man who had never witnessed her being called Lardypants or accused her of murdering poor homeless alcoholics and then setting fire to her own shop.

Keeley climbed into freshly laundered sheets, courtesy of Annie Rowland, and drifted off into a dreamless sleep. Yet the last face she saw on the inside of her eyelids before oblivion took over wasn't Duane's, but Detective Constable Ben Taylor's.

Chapter Four

Keeley spent the next day sorting out the little unpacking she had to do and flicking through her recipe books, making plans for the opening of her café. She was determined to go ahead, murder or no murder. A deep yoga practice that morning had strengthened her resolve and given her a fresh perspective on matters. Standing on your head for ten minutes tended to have that effect on a girl.

When Ben phoned to let her know that the café would be hers again as of the next day, she felt even more cheered.

"So, do you have any leads?" she asked, the thought of a murderer wandering around Belfrey unnerving her more than she cared to admit.

"Nothing concrete," Ben replied tersely, his voice down the phone line sounding very deep and masculine. Sexy, if you liked that kind of thing.

Which I don't, she reminded herself as Ben went on.

"No thoughts as to why Terry Smith was on your premises?"

"Like I said, none." He really was like a dog with a bone, no matter how delicious his voice might happen to be.

"If you say so," he said, making no effort to hide his disbelief. Keeley could just imagine that handsome face closed with suspicion, his eyes narrowed in her direction. "You'll be pleased to know I spoke to your friend in London, and your alibi checks out."

As if she herself had ever held any doubt. Keeley muttered a good-bye and replaced the phone with a curse, then immediately picked it back up to ring Carly, the friend in question, who would no doubt be wondering what the hell was going on.

"Keeley? How is everything? I had this guy phone me earlier—it sounded like there had been some trouble?"

"No, no, everything's fine," Keeley reassured her. Her friend didn't sound convinced.

"Are you sure? He said he was from the police."

"Yes, he was, and yes, I'm sure. Some guy was found dead at the café, but I'm certain they will sort it all out soon." Her voice had a false ring even to her own ears.

"Dead?" Carly shrieked, sounding both appalled and excited at this unexpected gossip. Of Keeley's London friends, Carly had been the most critical of her plans, insisting that "nothing ever happens in the country." Keeley pretended she could hear someone at the door and cut the call before Carly could wring out the details from her.

Ten minutes later, she was considering calling her back. With her unpacking and her daily routines done, she was restless and even a little bored. When the doorbell did ring, revealing a red-cheeked Annie Rowland, Keeley ushered her landlady in gratefully, only to feel her heart sink when Annie flourished the day's local newspaper at her. MURDER AT THE YOGA CAFÉ the headline screamed, obviously channeling a national tabloid. Keeley shook her head in frustration. This was publicity she didn't need—and wherever had they gotten the name from? She was sure she hadn't mentioned it to anyone.

"It's a much bigger story than yesterday," Annie said with disapproval, sitting her plump frame down at the kitchen table.

"I'll have chamomile, dear," she said to Keeley's offer of tea.

Keeley made two cups and sat with her, pulling the newspaper toward her for a closer inspection. Thankfully, there was little about her in particular other than that she was the owner of the building that had become a murder scene and the daughter of a former local businessman. There was plenty about Terry Smith, however, and it was apparent that he wasn't the pitiful, homeless drunk that Keeley's imagination had conjured up. Described as a local businessman—apparently, he now owned the local betting shop her mother had accused him of frequenting—Terry Smith was also a well-known local personality. Keeley felt her heart sink even as her curiosity was piqued. What on earth had he been doing in her café?

"Any idea why he was there?" Annie asked, echoing her own thoughts. Keeley shook her head.

"None at all. I can't even say I remember him. My mother said he used to come into Dad's shop, but she painted him as a bit of a waster, to be honest."

"Well," Annie said, her voice dripping with tact, "your mother wasn't really known for being the friendliest of women, or for giving people the benefit of the doubt. But," she went on hurriedly, "the paper *has* made Terry sound a lot more likable than he really was."

Keeley turned to page five, where the story continued, and saw a picture of the man himself. Although well dressed and trim—certainly not a down-and-out—he had a pinched look to his face, coupled with a sly look in his eyes that fit with Darla's description of "ratty." Then Keeley thought about the man's terrible end and felt uncharitable. She of all people should know to look beneath the surface and not judge on appearances.

"Why wasn't he liked?" she asked, continuing to scan the page. There was very little factual detail about the murder, other than that he had been found dead at the scene of an attempted arson, which rather made it sound as if he were responsible for the setting the fire. Although local police were described as treating his death as an open murder investigation, there was no indication of how the man had been killed or any mention of a murder weapon. Keeley wondered if Ben had been telling her the truth about Smith's cause of death or if he was trying to catch her out.

"How shall I put it?" Annie was saying, trying to be diplomatic, which made Keeley smile. "He always came across as rather a mean man. Too quick to laugh at another's misfortune, you know? He was a regular in the Tavern, but people put up with him rather than liked him."

"Do you go to the Tavern, then?" Keeley asked, surprised at the image of the gentle Mrs. Rowland in the shabby pub. Annie smiled.

"Not often, but now and then if I'm shopping on the High Street. Donald—that was my husband—preferred the inn down the road, but I don't go in there now he's dead. Too many memories, you see. I do miss him; we never were able to have children, so we just had each other, really." Annie looked sad, and Keeley felt a rush of warmth for her.

"When did he die?"

"Oh, a few years ago now. He had a heart attack. Too much red meat and too many cigars, if you ask me. We could have done with a place like yours."

Keeley gave her a grateful smile, though she doubted the opening of her café would tempt too many middle-aged men away from their vices. She felt moved by Annie's obvious affection for her late husband. She had never heard that kind of warmth in Darla's voice when her father was mentioned. In fact, Darla rarely mentioned him at all. Pushing away a wave of her own sadness, Keeley handed the newspaper back to Annie and plastered a smile on her face.

"Well, I'm sure the police will sort it all out. Ben—DC Taylor—certainly seems very thorough." Keeley blushed when Annie eyed her astutely and raised an eyebrow at Keeley's use of his Christian name.

"We went to school together, you know," she blurted, and Annie gave her a little nod. There was no mistaking the mischievous gleam in the woman's eyes.

"He is handsome, isn't he?" she said before tucking the paper under her arm and standing up. "I have to go, I said I would make cookies for the church ladies' meeting tonight. Why don't you come along? You would be most welcome. Everyone remembers your father."

Keeley smiled but shook her head. With the news of the murder no doubt having reached most people in Belfrey by now, she wasn't quite ready to face everyone yet. Tomorrow, after a good night's sleep, would be a new day.

The next morning, however, dawned gray and unwelcoming, the balmy spring weather having given way to a chill in the air and some ominous-looking rainclouds that hung low over the hills, obscuring the landscape in swirls of fog. After a fractured sleep, Keeley woke up not feeling very motivated at all, in spite of the previous day's plans to make a start on cleaning up and preparing the shop for its transformation. She went through her morning stretches rather sluggishly, then performed five minutes of an invigorating breathing exercise—known in yoga as a *pranayama*—and then jumped into a cool shower. As she dried her unruly hair afterward, she felt physically more alive but was still filled with an eerie trepidation about the day ahead. No matter how much she tried to tell herself the whole thing was coincidental, she couldn't ignore the fact that a man had been killed in the very place she hoped to birth a thriving business. Keeley wasn't especially superstitious, but nevertheless, a murder was hardly anyone's idea of an auspicious omen.

She walked the mostly downhill route into the town center, relieved not to encounter too many locals on the way and to engage in no longer a conversation than the general "All right, duck?" which made her smile in remembrance of her childhood. Funny how one forgot the little things. The feel of the cobbles under her feet when she reached the old roads leading to the center, the lowing call of cattle drifting down from the hills, and the smell of wildflowers and freshly cut grass lifted her spirits and lightened her step. By the time she reached the High Street, Keeley felt almost at home. She found herself looking at the shop front that would soon be her café with fondness rather than trepidation, picturing the bare, Windex-smeared glass awakened with the bright curtains she had ordered and the faded signs replaced with her own. Keeley had had an artist friend in New York draw up her design; the *Y* and *C* of the café name would be shown as small silhouettes in yoga poses, the *Y*, of course, reaching its hands to the heavens, and the *C* showing a kneeling back bend. A stylized red and green pepper came before and after the letters. The sign itself, she remembered, was due to be installed in a week's time. She thought of Terry Smith then and sighed, coming back to reality as she let herself in and walked through to the damaged back wall.

The crime scene tape around the back had been removed, and Keeley made a mental note to ask Ben what, if anything, forensics had discovered. Although he probably wouldn't tell her. She wondered again about the blunt object that had killed poor Terry Smith, a piece of the puzzle that hadn't been released to the local press. If the suspicious detective hadn't been feeding Keeley false information, then he must have kept the nature of the murder weapon back from the townsfolk because he suspected them too.

Which meant one of the residents of Belfrey, many of whom Keeley knew or was at least familiar with, could be behind the murder at her café. It made sense, she supposed; after all, wasn't it a well-known fact that you were most likely to be killed by someone you knew?

Stop being so morbid, Keeley chided herself as she went round opening the drapes in the shop, letting the weak sun trickle in. It did little to light up the interior other than expose the thin layer of dust on the counter. She pulled the cleaning products she had brought out of her hemp-woven tote bag and got started, scrubbing at baseboards and shining windows as though she could wipe the place fresh of any grisly memories. As she cleaned, she tried to envision the shop as it would be when it was finished, with the pretty wooden furniture that she had ordered and the colorful drapes and wall hangings she had bought back in New York. She had gone for bright, fresh colors against soft lemon walls and blond wood furniture, aiming for a happy yet relaxed vibe, the colors reflecting the freshness of the food.

She pictured the little counter stacked with fresh fruit and selections of herbal teas, and a salad and wrap bar from which customers could help themselves to a range of her simple salad recipes. Cake stands filled with delicacies—who said vegetarians couldn't indulge themselves?—and her pride and joy, her top-of-the-range smoothie maker, so that customers could watch their drinks being made up right before their eyes. Keeley imagined it full of customers, laughing and chatting while she moved from the shop front to the kitchen, serving and cooking. She would need to advertise for a waitress, of course, and maybe someone to help out with drinks on busy days. They would need some training on how to prepare her recipes for tasty smoothies and fresh fruit juices. On the weekends, perhaps she could even run workshops on healthy living and cooking simple, tasty dishes. Living in America had taught her the importance of branding, and she was soon mentally designing everything from Yoga Café T-shirts to napkins for the place settings.

Keeley was so lost in her daydreams that she had finished scrubbing the two downstairs rooms before she knew it, and as she straightened up, she was almost surprised that the café remained bare and empty, in direct contrast to her musings. *In time,* she reassured herself.

Then, downstairs done, she looked at the small staircase that led upstairs and took a deep breath. That was where it had all happened, not even three days ago. As she climbed the stairs, her legs felt like lead even as she told herself not to be so silly. A yellow piece of crime tape, still stuck to the corner at the top of the staircase, made her jump as it fluttered when she walked past it, and she peered round the doorway as though she expected to see the ghost of the man himself.

The room was empty, of course, looking perfectly bare and unoccupied, as if nothing had ever happened here. It was a large space with a small kitchenette counter at one end and an adjoining bathroom that had just enough room for a toilet and shower. Her father had leased it out a few times over the years, but mostly the space had remained unused. It was perfect for Keeley's needs, just the right size to hold small yoga and relaxation classes. She would replace the thin carpet with laminate floor and have the walls freshly painted a cool, serene blue. A few mirrors, some posters showing various yoga poses, and a stack of mats and props in the corner, and she would be good to go. The small kitchenette would add a relaxed vibe where she could sit and chat afterward with her classes and, hopefully, make friends. Yet knowing what she now knew, she couldn't quite call up the positive visualizations that she had for the café space downstairs. A horrible thought struck her: What if the tragedy that had occurred here put people off attending? Her business would be scuppered before it had even begun. A gruesome murder was hardly in keeping with the fresh and friendly vibe she was aiming to evoke.

Perhaps that was the point. Ben had certainly seemed adamant that it may be the work of someone with a grudge against her or her family. *No,* she mentally shook her head, letting out a dry chuckle. It was beyond egotistical to think someone had gone so far as murder just to derail her business plans. Unless, as she had originally thought, Terry Smith was simply in the wrong place at the wrong time. . . . Now that she was lost in less positive thoughts, the sound of the front door downstairs opening and closing made

Keeley literally jump with shock, and her heart pounded against her ribs. She held her breath as she heard footsteps downstairs. Ben, perhaps? But whoever it was didn't bother to call to announce their arrival. Creeping downstairs as quietly as possible, Keeley heard the footsteps go into the kitchen area, where the smoke damage was visible, and she knew it couldn't be Ben.

Not unless he had taken to wearing stilettos, anyway. Could it be the perpetrator, returning to the scene of the crime? Her heart felt as though it were thumping in her throat as she reached the bottom of the stairwell and looked around it just as the figure of a woman loomed in the doorway that joined the kitchen to the main area.

"Can I help you?" Keeley asked as she straightened up and took the last two stairs, aiming to sound assertive and a little annoyed but ending up with a frightened squeak.

A glamorous young woman around her own age looked at Keeley with a flash of disdain; then her glossed lips opened in a very wide—and very insincere—smile.

"Keeley Carpenter, it *is* you!"

Keeley blinked in confusion; then recognition dawned. Her breath came out in a rush of relief as she smiled back at her old friend.

Raquel Philips. They had been inseparable at junior school, bonding over the fact they both came from flawless but distant mothers who had seen one another as rivals, being alike in many ways, even down to their shared Christian name, Darla. Keeley had always been slightly in awe of Raquel, who was possessed of both beauty and poise and the natural arrogance to ensure she was always at the center of someone's attention. In high school, their friendship had cooled somewhat, mainly due to Raquel's leaving

Keeley behind for the "popular" crowd, but Keeley had remained a shoulder for Raquel to cry on and someone to help with her homework. They hadn't kept in touch after her father died and Darla whisked her away, and so the last time Keeley had seen Raquel was at their high school leaving disco, where the other girl had largely ignored Keeley in favor of her more adoring hangers-on.

"How are you?" Keeley gushed, taking in Raquel's appearance. Her voluptuous figure was poured into a beige dress that Keeley was certain was real silk; her dark hair tumbled over her impeccably made-up face in a style that looked casual but must have taken hours to create. With a fur stole around her shoulders—which Keeley fervently hoped was fake—she looked like an old-time movie star. In fact, Keeley acknowledged with a stab of jealousy, she looked like the sort of daughter Darla longed for Keeley to be.

"You look great," Keeley told her, feeling slightly ashamed of her envy. Raquel nodded, the fact of looking great clearly something she took for granted, and her eyes raked Keeley up and down in a slow, leisurely way that left Keeley feeling she had somehow been found wanting. She was suddenly acutely aware of her lack of makeup and the duster in her hands, which she shoved into the back pocket of her jeans defensively as she fought the urge to fix her hair.

"You look . . . different," Raquel allowed, and in a flash, Keeley remembered just how catty her old friend had always been.

"You've lost that weight, anyway," Raquel went on, "you were always quite chunky, weren't you? Do you remember that nickname you had at school? Lardypants, wasn't it? Too funny." Raquel gave a thin laugh, a malicious glint in her eye that Keeley now remembered all too well.

"Hilarious," Keeley mumbled through gritted teeth. It was becoming apparent just exactly why she hadn't bothered to stay in touch with Raquel after her move.

"Exactly what is it you're planning on doing here?" Raquel asked, abruptly changing the subject. "I own the diner just around the corner, you see, and I do hope we aren't going to clash. My customers are absolutely devoted to me, of course, and I'd hate to think of your little enterprise failing to get off the ground because of *me*."

Obviously, this wasn't just a social call. Keeley eyed Raquel in surprise. "A diner? Wow, that's great." Somehow the image of the silk-clad Raquel working behind a café counter didn't fit.

"Yes—well, I went to university, of course, and went to Europe for a while, then Mummy and Daddy bought me the diner as a little gift. I have people in to do the cooking and serving and everything, naturally."

"Naturally," Keeley echoed, trying to suppress a grin. No doubt Raquel, who had never been at all academic, didn't do very well at university and also clearly failed to land a rich husband, one of her often-stated ambitions. It would be just like the Philipses to buy her a little business to keep her occupied. She wondered if they were also bankrolling her wardrobe.

"Anyway," Keeley offered, feeling a little more charitable now, "I doubt we will clash at all. I'm serving vegetarian food mostly, and fresh juices, that kind of thing."

"How quaint. Still watching your weight, then, I take it?" Raquel gave her a sickly smile, and Keeley sighed to herself. It didn't look as though she and Raquel would be renewing their friendship anytime soon.

"No, I'm a yoga teacher. My café will reflect that: healthy, fresh food that's good for body and soul." She gave a genuine smile, impressed at her own sales pitch. "I'm quite sure there's room on the High Street for both of us." Perhaps it was only natural that Raquel should be worried, Keeley thought, trying to be understanding. After all, there were quite a few eateries on the High Street as it was, and they must all be in at least indirect competition with each other.

Raquel's response, however, banished any warmth that Keeley might have felt. The other woman narrowed her eyes at Keeley in a way that was almost certainly designed to be menacing.

"There had better be," she said before sweeping past Keeley and letting herself out with only a flick of her hand to signal a good-bye. Keeley stared after her, feeling a chill that came from more than just the swinging shut of the door after Raquel's departure.

Raquel's last words had sounded very much like a threat. Almost against her will, Keeley's head turned toward the stairwell, her gaze focusing on the shadows from the room above. She wondered if Raquel had known Terry Smith.

After finishing her cleaning and calling the kitchen installation crew to arrange a new date, Keeley realized she was more or less at loose ends until the interior work began. She rather tentatively walked across the road to the Tavern for a very late lunch. The first face she saw as she walked into the smoky gloom was Jack's, again in his usual spot. His patronage must have kept the Tavern going through the recent recession, she thought with a smile as he nodded toward the empty chair next to him. With another grateful smile, Keeley ordered a sandwich and pot of tea from a glassy-eyed Tom and then slid into the offered chair. A large Irish wolfhound sat next to Jack, wagging his tail as Keeley sat down and fixing her with dark and mournful eyes that looked almost comical peeping out from under the shaggy gray fur that covered him. He smelled vaguely of mud. This must be the dog that scared off the would-be arsonist, thereby saving her shop. Keeley stroked his huge head, acknowledging her debt, and was rewarded with a slobbery lick to the hand.

"He likes you," Jack commented as Keeley surreptitiously wiped dog saliva from her hand onto her jeans.

"He's lovely," Keeley said, then asked, "What's wrong with Tom?"

Jack snorted.

"Too much of that whacky-baccy the youngsters smoke. I hope you're not into all that"—he peered at her disapprovingly—"what with all that hippie stuff you're into nowadays."

Keeley suppressed a smile. "I'm not sure yoga qualifies as 'hippie,' but no, a glass of wine is about my strongest vice." She eyed the large and sour-smelling tobacco pipe that Jack was happily puffing away on. It appeared that the indoor smoking ban hadn't reached Belfrey.

"Did you know him?" she asked suddenly, not realizing she was going to speak the words until she did so. "Terry Smith, I mean?"

Jack eyed her for a moment, taking a long inhalation from his pipe and then coughing out a stream of smoke that made the dog sneeze.

"Aye, I knew him well enough. Most of us did; he came in here for the football sometimes. Ran the betting shop, you see. Ben told you what happened, then?"

Keeley nodded. "I think he suspected I had something to do

with it," she confided. Jack just nodded, not at all surprised, and Keeley couldn't help but wonder if that was because he thought Ben likely to suspect anyone in the vicinity, or because he thought of Keeley as an automatic suspect as well.

"I wasn't even in Belfrey at the time of the murder," she said, her words coming out more defensive than she would have liked.

Jack shrugged. "Got nothing to worry about, then, have you?"

Keeley wasn't quite sure what to say to that, but was saved from responding by the arrival of Tom with tea and a limp-looking sandwich. Keeley smiled at him and he stared at her for a minute, then gave her a slow, unfocused smile of his own before sloping off. Jack shook his head at Tom's retreating figure.

"Course, it could have been anyone," he said suddenly. Keeley swallowed her bite of sandwich—which, in spite of its limp appearance, had the texture of cardboard—and looked at him in puzzlement.

"Terry's murderer," the old man clarified. "No one liked him, you see. Mean man, had a nasty streak in him, I reckon."

Keeley nodded. Annie had said as much, albeit more diplomatically. Although she wouldn't wish his end on anyone, the fact that Smith didn't seem to be well liked did hint that his unfortunate demise was due to someone's having a grudge against him, rather than against Keeley or her family. Perhaps rather than Terry interrupting the arsonist, the killer had attempted to cover the evidence with a fire. It made a great deal more sense, considering that the murder must have happened first. The burning of her shop then would have been a cover-up attempt that had unfortunately just happened to be on her premises.

Of course, that didn't explain why on earth Terry Smith and his killer had been there in the first place. Keeley sat back in her chair, deflated that her theory didn't stack up quite so neatly after all.

"Do you have any idea who might have done it?" she asked Jack. He shook his head sharply, looking around as if afraid of being overheard, though there was no one else in the pub other than a few youths by the pool table in the far corner and two middle-aged men drinking bitter in the other.

"No," Jack said, "and it wouldn't do for people to go around accusing people, either. Belfrey's a small town, you see. Gossip gets around."

"Does everyone think it's me?" Keeley blurted. Jack seemed to think about his answer for a few moments, which didn't reassure her.

"I reckon not," he said finally. "Though it's a bit strange, all the same."

Keeley shifted in her seat uneasily. If Jack Tibbons, who had known her since she was tiny and who had been a dear friend of her father's, didn't seem completely convinced of her innocence, then what could she expect from anyone else? She thought about Raquel's less-than-friendly welcome. Although the other woman hadn't even mentioned the murder, seeming more interested in the prospect of Keeley setting herself up as a business rival. She told Jack about her encounter with her old friend, leaving off the part where Raquel had spitefully alluded to her high school nickname. Jack pulled a face.

"She's a right sort, that girl. All fur coat and no knickers, if you ask me."

Keeley laughed in surprise at the old saying, coughing on the piece of sandwich in her mouth. She took a sip of tea to wash it down and grinned at Jack, who smiled back, a wicked glint in his rheumy eyes.

Looking at the clock, Keeley remembered she had a date with Duane in a few hours and had wanted to visit Megan's shop before returning home. She swigged the last of her tea and said goodbye to Jack, who gave her an affectionate wink, and waved at Tom, who, although he was apparently looking right at her, appeared not to notice.

As she made her way to Crystals and Candles, she had to walk past Raquel's Diner, a pretty-looking place with a cheerful poppy stencil in the window and red-checked drapes that matched the cloths on the two small tables outside. Through the window that made up the shop front, Keeley could see the interior was busy, though Raquel herself sat in the corner, drinking from what looked like a champagne flute, with two young male customers hanging on her every word. Like a queen holding court. The menu boards outside offered traditional food: a full English breakfast, steak and ale pie, and the famous Codnor cod. There was unlikely to be fierce competition between the traditional diner and her own Yoga Café, but Keeley did remember Raquel as being highly competitive at school. Not that any rivalry had included Keeley back then, as she hadn't been high enough on the social scale to matter.

Keeley smelled Crystals and Candles before she saw it. The door was open, and the heavy smell of a musk-based incense wafted down the street. Keeley entered, pushing through the velvet strips that lined the doorway, into a shop that looked more like a fairies' grotto. Crystals of all shapes, sizes, and colors lined one wall; candles, the other. A selection of the candles was lit, causing the crystals to twinkle a rainbow of colored lights. In the middle of the shop, a large table offered all manner of New Age knickknacks, from tarot cards to angel statuettes. Megan sat behind a velvet-draped counter, perched on a stool, though she jumped up with a shriek of delight when she saw Keeley, coming round from behind the till and giving her an enthusiastic hug, which Keeley returned awkwardly.

"So nice to see you again! Would you like anything to drink?" Megan waved at a selection of herbal teas in front of her, and Keeley nodded, picking a brand she recognized from New York.

"Yes, thank you. I just thought I'd pop by."

"Make yourself at home. It's been quiet today, so I may as well lock up. Are you meeting Duane tonight? He's done nothing but talk about you!"

"Really?" Keeley blushed, feeling more embarrassed than flattered. Megan thankfully didn't seem to require an answer as she disappeared into the back room to make the tea, chattering all the while. Keeley sat down, the incense making her feel light-headed.

"I suppose you've heard about the body?" Keeley asked as Megan came back out, then winced at the abruptness of her own words, which somehow sounded harsher in the otherworldly atmosphere of Megan's shop.

Megan pursed her lips and nodded.

"Yes, of course, but we didn't want to mention it. You must be terribly upset. I always did say that man had a very dark aura, but karma catches up with us all, you know." Megan nodded sagely. Ignoring the other girl's slightly strange conception of karma, Keeley leaned forward over the counter.

"You knew him, then?"

"Only by sight. He was hardly the type to come in here, and to be honest, I wouldn't have wanted him to." She shuddered as if the very thought of Terry's dark aura had poisoned the serene atmosphere she was trying to create.

"Was he really that bad?" Keeley wondered aloud. In spite of the sympathetic article in the local press, so far no one seemed to have a good word for the man. Megan sipped her tea and gave a worldly wise sigh.

"Some people just have a darkness around them, a negativity. It makes you feel drained being around them. Psychic vampires, they're called. Terry always struck me as that sort of person."

"Right." Although Keeley wasn't sure she bought into Megan's spiritual beliefs, she knew exactly what the woman meant about people's ability to leave you feeling emotionally drained. She often felt that way when she was around her mother.

"Why in your café, though?" Megan pondered. Keeley took a long gulp of her tea, completely unable to answer the very question she had asked herself for the last two days. Why indeed?

KAPALABHATI—INVIGORATING BREATH

Will reenergize you when you're feeling lethargic. Also great
for clearing the sinuses.

Method

- Sit comfortably, and consciously relax the abdominal muscles.
- Inhale and exhale slowly through your nose.
- Inhale deeply, then exhale through your nose in short, sharp
  bursts as you contract your stomach muscles—almost as if
  you are "pumping out" the breath through the nose.
- Continue inhaling deeply and pumping out the exhalation,
  up to twenty times. Then take a long, slow inhalation, and
  exhale through the nose to finish.
- The whole exercise can be repeated three times if you are
  feeling very sluggish or "bunged up" or both. *Kapalabhati*
  literally means "shining skull" because of its invigorating
  effect. It is also sometimes referred to as "bellows breath,"
  due to the pumping motion and sound of the exhalation.
  Probably not one to try in public.

Chapter Five

After leaving Megan to lock up, Keeley took the bus back to Rose Cottage, trying to head off thoughts of the unfortunate Terry Smith by pondering a more mundane question. What to wear? Her impending "date" with Duane wasn't filling her with as much excited anticipation as perhaps it should. Every time she tried to picture his handsome, almost pretty face and undeniably buff body, she instead saw Ben Taylor's intense green eyes with their cool, uncompromising gaze. When it came to the inevitable trying-on of outfits, somehow Keeley found herself wondering what Ben would think. Holding up a red fitted dress that clung to every yoga-toned curve, she thought with a flash of rare pride that there was no way he could fail to notice her now.

She settled for her new jeans and a checked blouse. After all, she hardly wanted to give Duane—or the villagers—the wrong idea. After curling her hair and applying a touch more eyeliner than usual, she found herself pacing the cottage restlessly, waiting until it was time to leave. What had seemed a good idea the other night after a glass of wine was less appealing now, but it would feel rude to back out. What was the harm in a quiet drink?

As soon as she walked into the inn, she wanted to run back out. It was busier than it had been last time, and she could feel the gazes raking over her as she walked up to the bar. The barman made eye contact with her for a change, but only to ask, loudly enough for anyone in the small room to hear:

"You're the girl who took Rose Cottage on? Same as owns the place Terry was killed? Bad business, that."

Keeley smiled, attempting to look as friendly and nonthreatening as possible, though she could feel a tightness in her jaw. Out of the corner of her eye, she saw more than a few heads turning their way.

"Yes, it's horrible. I only hope they catch whoever was responsible."

The barman shrugged.

"Your place, though, isn't it. How did they get in?"

Keeley opened her mouth to protest her ignorance when a deep voice came from behind her shoulder, startling her.

"Picked the locks, by the looks of things. Ms. Carpenter is lucky she was elsewhere at the time, or it could have been incredibly dangerous for her."

Ben. She turned and nearly bumped her head on his chest. He placed a steadying hand on her arm.

"Would you like a drink?"

Keeley blinked at him, more than a little shocked. He was the last person she'd expect to champion her innocence. He was smiling at her almost kindly, though she couldn't be entirely sure the expression had made it to his eyes, then looking at the barman expectantly.

"Thank you. A small white wine, please," Keeley asked, her eyes still on Ben. Out of his work clothes, he looked younger and even more like a catalog model, in jeans and a casual T-shirt that defined his frame to perfection. He was taller and stockier than Duane, with the sort of physique that suggested sports rather than posturing in the gym. Rugby, maybe. With effort, she pushed away a vision of him in shorts and covered in mud, reminding herself that Ben Taylor was exactly the sort of man she would usually avoid. Although Duane was both handsome and rather shallow, there was a sort of naiveté to him, in spite of his obvious charms, that didn't leave her feeling so unsettled.

The barman served her almost deferentially now, nodding at Ben with obvious respect. As soon as the bartender had moved down the counter to serve the next customer, Keeley gave Ben a relieved smile.

"Thank you."

Ben shrugged one shoulder in a movement that was almost graceful.

"No worries. It certainly doesn't help my investigation to have the locals jumping to conclusions or stirring up unrest."

Keeley raised her eyebrows. There she was, thinking he was being gallant, but of course, he was just doing his job. In fact, she recalled now he had displayed the same focus at school, whether in class or in sports. Certainly he had always been too engrossed in the task at hand ever to notice her attempts to engage him.

Clearly, not a great deal had changed.

"What brings you here?" Ben asked, his tone abrupt. Keeley went to answer him, and as she did so, saw Duane enter the inn.

She closed her mouth and waved at him, giving Ben a grin that felt false even to her.

"I'm with Duane," she said, then winced when she realized how that could be misconstrued. Ben glanced from her to him, his face devoid of expression. Was it her imagination, or had his eyes become even more guarded?

"I see. Well, I'll let you get on with your night, then." He turned and left as Duane hurried over, and Keeley watched him retreat to the other side of the room, craning her neck to see who he had sat down with. She felt oddly surprised when she saw him sit next to a young blond woman. She hadn't even thought about his having a girlfriend—but then, why wouldn't he? In any case, it was none of her business.

"Are you okay?" Duane was looking at her with concern. Keeley realized with a jolt of embarrassment that she had been so busy watching Ben, she hadn't even greeted her date.

"Yes, yes, wonderful. I saw Megan today," she gushed. Duane's face brightened.

"Yes, she told me. You've got things moving with the café, then?"

As they carried on talking and Duane steered her over to a small table—mercifully out of sight of Ben Taylor and his companion—Keeley felt herself relax. Duane was pleasant, if unchallenging company, and certainly seemed eager to help Keeley establish herself as a local yoga instructor.

"We need some fresh faces up at the leisure center. Especially one as pretty as yours."

Keeley blushed at the compliment. Although the mirror didn't exactly show an old hag, she still found such compliments difficult to accept. Six months in New York surrounded by the beautiful people had left her feeling decidedly plain. But then, judging by the easy way the words rolled off his tongue, she suspected Duane gave out compliments like other people gave bread to ducks. He had an easy charm that she imagined must make him very attractive to women, and she wondered if that was the reason for her lack of enthusiasm.

. . . Nothing to do with Ben Taylor, who didn't even look in her direction when he went up again to the bar. Keeley twisted in her seat and turned her attention fully to Duane.

However, after twenty minutes of listening to a breakdown of his workout regime and his battle against body fat, her eyes were beginning to glaze over. As much as she was interested in healthy living, she liked to think there were other topics of conversation to be had.

"But, of course, you will know what I mean, with your yoga practice, won't you?" Duane said. Keeley had no idea what point he was referring to, but nevertheless, she opened her mouth to speak, eager to talk about it with someone who had a genuine interest. But before she could formulate a word, Duane was talking again, about his superior flexibility or something. Keeley sat back in her chair and sighed, then looked up as two women around Annie's age approached the table. One, who looked familiar, was tall and thin, and her companion was shorter and a great deal plumper. Keeley couldn't help but be reminded of the fat and thin aunts from *James and the Giant Peach,* a favorite book from her childhood that her father had read to her over and over again.

"You're Keeley, aren't you?" the taller of the two asked. They each gave Keeley a genuine smile, and she sat up, relieved both for a break from Duane's monologue and at the chance to make more friends.

"You're staying at Rose Cottage? George Carpenter's girl? My, look how pretty you are, your dad would be so proud."

Keeley blushed, pleased at the mention of her father. She recognized the shorter woman, she realized, from her father's shop. Maggie, she thought. Her mother hadn't liked her much, but then, Darla didn't like anyone much.

Maggie and her companion sat down at their table. Duane shot Keeley an annoyed look.

"I'll go to the bar," he said in a sulky tone. Maggie looked at him in approval.

"Why, that's kind," she said. "We'll have two gin and tonics. In fact, make them doubles."

Keeley stifled a smile at Duane's look of horror and turned her attention to the women. She started to tell them about her plans for the café, only to be interrupted by the taller woman, who introduced herself as Norma.

"Yes, your café. You're not still opening it after that poor man was killed, surely?"

"I am," Keeley said, trying to sound assertive in an attempt to convince herself as much as the woman. "It's a tragedy, of course, but I'm going ahead with my plans. It's what my father would expect," she added quietly. Norma nodded impatiently.

"But aren't you scared? Who do you think did it?"

"Yes, you must have some idea," Maggie said, leaning over the table. There was a greedy, almost predatory look in her eyes, and Keeley remembered why her mother hadn't liked her. The woman was notorious as the village gossip. They hadn't come over to welcome her at all, but to press her for details that—had she any to give—would no doubt be all round Belfrey by the morning.

"If you'll excuse me," she said, standing up and joining Duane at the bar, where he was now talking to a pretty redhead who seemed to be hanging on his every word. She gave Keeley a less-than-friendly look as she joined them.

"I've got a bit of a headache," she said to Duane, which wasn't altogether a lie, "so I'm really sorry, but I think I'll get going."

Duane winked at her. "I'll walk you home."

Keeley went to protest, then saw Ben watching her out of the corner of his eye. She smiled at Duane.

"That would be lovely, thank you."

She was acutely aware of Ben's eyes on her as she walked out, Duane close behind her with a proprietary hand on her lower back. Outside, it was gloomy and overcast, the clouds pulling the night in early. She shivered and then regretted it as Duane moved his arm up around her shoulders. Sidestepping neatly, she quickened her pace. If he noticed her reluctance to get too close to him, he gave no sign, but launched instead into a description of his latest workout class. By the time she had reached Rose Cottage, Keeley was sure her partly feigned headache would be all too real. As she turned to say good-bye to Duane, he had a hopeful look in his eyes that made her wish she hadn't agreed to let him walk her home. Damn Ben Taylor.

"Are you inviting me in for coffee?" he asked in a low voice, pulling her toward him, his gaze fastened on her lips. Keeley felt her face flame, the nearness of him embarrassing rather than arousing her. In the half light, his handsome features looked almost ghoulish, and as his lips started to descend toward hers, she felt a stab of panic. She stepped back, bumping into the doorframe as she raised her clutch bag in front of her as if to ward him off, reaching for her keys.

"Like I said, I've got a really bad headache," she gabbled. "Perhaps I could call you tomorrow?"

She gave him a swift peck on the cheek and darted inside the door, leaving him looking confused. Once inside and listening to the sound of his footsteps going down the hill, she leaned back against the solid oak and sighed with relief. So much for her date. She wondered if there was something wrong with her. Duane was attractive, fit, and certainly available, even if not the greatest conversationalist in the world. After her months of celibacy, and recent shock, an uncomplicated fling could be just what she needed. She was a modern woman, after all, even if deep down, part of her yearned for the full-on Disney romance. But she just couldn't muster up any interest in Duane or the comforts he was so obviously offering. All she wanted right now, in fact, was a cup of chamomile tea and a hot bath, and then bed.

As she took off her shoes, she saw an envelope lying on her interior doormat, with her name neatly typed across the front. It was hand delivered; there was no stamp and no address. Frowning, Keeley reached down and picked it up, feeling a creeping sense of foreboding. She opened it, holding her breath.

The letters jumped out at her, stark and crude against the paper. They were typed in bold, as if the author had been determined to hammer the point home. Keeley swallowed, her chest constricting as she tried to calm the mounting tide of panic. No matter how hard she stared at the words, willing her eyes to be playing tricks on her, they remained the same:

IT SHOULD HAVE BEEN YOU.

Chapter Six

The next morning, Keeley hesitated before pressing the intercom outside the police station. If you could even call it a station, as Belfrey's local police department seemed to consist of a tiny redbrick building sandwiched between the library and the local community center. Through the glass doors, she could see a small reception space with an unattended desk. The doors were locked, with a small typed sign asking visitors to please press the button and report to reception. *Which would be easier if there was someone around to report to*, Keeley thought as she shifted anxiously from one foot to the other. The anonymous letter sat in the back pocket of her jeans, seeming to grow heavier with each passing second.

Her first thought—after the initial shock subsided and she finished locking all the doors and windows to the cottage, trying not to scare herself with visions of a psychopathic murderer lurking in the shadows—had been to throw the letter away. It was probably no more than some spiteful village gossip with too much time on his or her hands. Why would a cold-blooded killer waste time on such things? It made no logical sense.

Yet a long night of tossing and turning and jumping out of her skin at every owl call and creak had convinced her she needed to report it. Still, she had been on the verge of changing her mind a few times on the walk down to the High Street and was thinking again of just walking away, when a figure finally emerged behind the reception desk and looked at Keeley through the glass with what she was sure was annoyance. She recognized the young woman in police uniform as the blonde whom Ben had been sitting with at the inn the previous night. Perhaps just a colleague, then, rather than a girlfriend.

The woman police constable buzzed Keeley in and then fixed her with what was definitely an impatient look as Keeley approached the desk.

"Can I help you?" she snapped. She looked flustered, and Keeley couldn't help but look around her to the door she had come through, which must lead into an office. Was Ben in there? She didn't particularly want to see him, what with his suspicious eyes and abrupt manner, yet she also found herself not wanting to confide her fears to anyone else, especially not this hard-eyed young woman.

"I hope I'm not interrupting anything," Keeley said, flushing as she realized her voice sounded more sarcastic than apologetic, which only made the WPC look more annoyed.

"I'm up to my ears in paperwork, and the bloody photocopier's broken," she said by way of explanation. Keeley smiled at her, then hesitated, reaching for her back pocket and fingering the edge of the letter.

"Well, what is it?"

Keeley dropped the letter onto the desk in front of the police-woman and smoothed it out to show the message. She touched it gingerly, as though afraid it would go off like a bomb in her hands. The other woman squinted at it, puzzled, then rolled her eyes.

"Trouble with the neighbors, is it?" she said, sounding bored. Keeley felt her own spark of annoyance flame in her chest at the girl's dismissiveness.

"I've hardly been here long enough to warrant any. I'm Keeley Carpenter. I own the premises that Terry Smith was killed in."

The WPC snapped to attention at that, straightening her back and looking at Keeley and then again at the letter with rather more interest.

"So you think this message is referring to the murder. A threat to yourself?"

"I can't think of anything else it could be," Keeley admitted. She had ruminated long into the early hours, looking for any reason, however small, that a Belfrey resident could have to post her a poison pen letter, and had come up with precisely zero.

"Well, the murder is DC Taylor's case, but as he's Local CID, he's actually based in the main station at Ripley. I suppose I had better give him a ring."

"Give me a ring about what?"

Ben's voice, along with a gust of wind from the suddenly opened door, made Keeley jump and turn to face him, startled. Out of the corner of her eye, she saw the blond woman hurriedly smooth down her hair and lean over the counter toward him, her expression no longer annoyed at all but now that of an eager puppy.

"DC Taylor," she cooed, fixing him with what was clearly meant to be an alluring smile, "I have something here that may need bringing to your attention."

I just bet you do, Keeley thought. Ben seemed not to notice the blonde's demeanor at all, giving her only a cursory nod as he crossed the small reception area in one long stride and stared down at the letter. No doubt, he was used to women fawning all over him. His expression darkened as he looked up at Keeley.

"When and where did you find this?"

"Er, on my doorstep," she stammered, feeling wrong-footed by him once again, "last night. Do you think it has something to do with the murder?"

Ben ignored her question, answering instead with one of his own.

"So why didn't you report it last night?"

Keeley was saved from answering by the blonde, who cut in on her behalf. No doubt it was purely to get Ben's attention, but nevertheless, Keeley gave her a grateful smile.

"We wouldn't have been open. And it hardly qualifies as an emergency."

"You could have phoned me. You have my number." Ben glared at Keeley as if she had personally insulted him. She swallowed hard, meeting his glare with one of her own, even if she did feel like squirming inside. Why was he so hostile? Surely he couldn't still think her responsible? *He probably thinks I sent it to myself.* She opened her mouth to accuse him of precisely that, but Ben had already turned his attention back to the letter.

"Kate," he addressed the policewoman, "get this bagged up and tagged, please."

Keeley watched the woman reach under a counter for a pair

of gloves before picking up the letter and taking it into the office, giving Ben a last simpering smile, which he seemed to ignore.

"Ms. Carpenter," he said, looking and sounding suddenly tired, "if you could just come in here for a few minutes." He waved toward a door marked INTERVIEW ROOM, and Keeley felt a wave of anxiety and stayed where she was. Ben sighed and pushed a lock of hair out of his eyes.

"Just for a chat. You're looking at me like I'm about to arrest you."

"You do seem rather suspicious of me." Keeley decided to be frank. Ben, however, just looked surprised.

"Really? Occupational hazard, I suppose. Would you just come and sit down? I'm exhausted."

Keeley followed him into the interview room, sitting opposite him in an uncomfortable plastic chair. Under the sickly lighting, she saw there were indeed shadows under his eyes.

"Rough night, then?" She tried and failed to keep the sympathy out of her voice, fighting the urge to come over all nurturing and offer him a cup of chamomile.

"There was a bit of bother in Matlock, in one of the biker bars. Not by the bikers themselves—they're generally a very polite bunch of guys—but a couple of local youths causing trouble. Problem was, there were about fifty witness statements to take, and half the officers at Ripley were out investigating a vandalized tractor."

Keeley stifled a giggle. It certainly wouldn't be funny to the poor farmer whose vehicle had been damaged, but even so, the situation struck her as so bizarre, she couldn't help smiling. Ben's mouth twitched a little at the corner; then he let out a low laugh that made Keeley's stomach flip.

His whole face changed when he laughed, she noticed, making him look boyish and far more approachable. Dimples that she only now remembered having spotted at school appeared in his cheeks, and his eyes danced at her. She ducked her head as she realized she was staring, and Ben stopped laughing abruptly and gave her a strange look.

"Would you like a drink? I really need a coffee. Then we can try to figure out what's going on here."

Keeley nodded, avoiding his gaze as he got up to leave the room, brushing past her in its small confines as he did so.

He returned quickly with a tray and two mugs, and Keeley took hers with gratitude, the warmth of it comforting between her hands.

"So, you found it last night? What time? Was it delivered when you were out?"

He was all business again, a small notebook and pen having appeared in his hand from the lining of his jacket.

"It must have been. I would have noticed if it had been there when I left. It was on the doormat when I came in. Which was about half past ten."

"Were you alone?" His voice was clipped again, and when Keeley met his eyes, he looked back down at his notebook, an eyebrow raised expectantly. He was asking about Duane, she understood.

"Yes," she said quietly, then louder when that eyebrow nearly disappeared into his hairline, although he didn't look up at her. "Yes. Duane—that's the guy I was with at the inn—walked me home, but he didn't come in. I saw the letter when I was taking my shoes off."

"Why?" he asked, and Keeley frowned at him, puzzled.

"Because I crouched down to pull them off and I saw it on the mat?" Ben had gone very still, and was staring at his notebook intently, although he hadn't written down anything except the time. With a not unpleasant surprise, Keeley realized what he had meant.

"Duane didn't come in," she clarified, "because I didn't want him to. I had a headache."

Ben did look at her then, with what she was certain was relief. Keeley felt a little surge of triumph. Was he, after all this time, finally interested in her?

"A headache," he repeated, looking amused.

"Yes." Keeley nodded firmly. "A headache."

Ben stared at her for a long minute; then his gaze dropped, just for a second, to her lips. Keeley felt her tummy tighten. Was that desire in his eyes? But it was gone as soon as she wondered about it, leaving her berating herself and looking away. Letting old feelings from high school distract her was the last thing she needed to do. He sat back in his chair, picking up his notebook again. There was a sudden, heavy tension in the room that she didn't quite understand, and Ben seemed to be studying his notebook intently. The change in atmosphere made her feel testy, and when she spoke, her voice came out sounding more irritated than she'd intended.

"Do you have any more questions for me, or is that it?"

Ben frowned at her tone.

"I need to know who you were with and at what time if you want me to investigate this letter."

"I was alone, I told you," Keeley snapped.

"Did anyone know you were going to be out yesterday evening?"

"Only Megan and Duane. I was with him all evening, of course."

"Of course," Ben said with just the barest touch of sarcasm. "I take it you mean Megan Powell, the owner of the New Age shop."

Keeley nodded, a chill settling over her as she wondered if he suspected Megan.

"How well do you know Miss Powell?"

Keeley shook her head.

"It wasn't her." When Ben just looked at her coolly, Keeley found herself examining her statement. Intuition told her Megan wouldn't harm a fly, but how well did she know her? She shook her head again, irritated. Too much time in Ben Taylor's company, and she would be suspicious of her own shadow. There was another uneasy silence; then Ben leaned over the table with a swift smile that showcased the dimple in his chin.

"Look," he said, pocketing his notebook and pen, "do you want to do this over lunch? I haven't eaten since yesterday, and you've obviously had a shock. There's a little Italian place around the corner, does the best bowl of comfort pasta you could eat."

Keeley grinned in spite of herself, feeling suddenly at home.

"You mean Mario's? I used to go there with my friends every Saturday."

"Did you?" Ben looked confused. "I forgot for a moment you grew up here. Silly. Considering we went to school together."

"I don't expect you to remember me from school," she said, surprising herself at how clipped and tight her voice sounded. She really must stop bearing a grudge over her unreciprocated crush. If his reaction to Kate's simpering was anything to go by, Ben seemed to be one of those rare men who were genuinely oblivious to how hot they were.

"Of course I remember you; I told you that in the car. You've . . . changed, though." His tone was so obviously diplomatic that she looked away, thoroughly deflated. He meant, of course, that she wasn't fat anymore. She stood up, wondering now if she should refuse his offer of lunch, mysterious letter or no mysterious letter. But she did need his help, and a bowl of Mario's cheese and spinach pasta rolls sounded too good to resist.

Mario himself remembered her, throwing his arms around her in delight. He was a small blond man who, although authentically Italian with a thick Florentine accent, couldn't have looked less so if he tried. He kissed both her cheeks, then pinched her waist disapprovingly.

"Where have you gone?" he demanded as he ushered her and Ben to a table. "Do people not eat in London?"

"Actually, I've been in America." Keeley gave him a quick history of her travels, gratified by Mario's interest in her plans for the café.

"Ah, we can share recipes. We should help each other, no?"

Keeley nodded, enthused by his warmth, then saw Ben looking at her curiously as Mario bustled off.

"You really went to India? That must have been amazing."

"It was," she admitted. And it had been, if only for the initial relief of getting away from her mother. And of course, it had started her off on her path to becoming a yoga instructor. Which conversely had led her right back here, to Belfrey.

"Did you always want to be a policeman?" she asked, wondering now why Ben himself hadn't left the small town for pastures new. He nodded.

"Once I stopped dreaming of being a professional footballer, yeah. Dad was in the army, wasn't he, so he always wanted me to follow in his footsteps. The police force seemed a reasonable compromise. I'm hoping to make detective sergeant this year. If I can nail this case—" He realized what he was saying and grimaced. "Sorry, that was insensitive."

"It's okay. It's not as if I knew him. You must have, though?" Keeley hadn't really considered that before, how personal a murder case must be for the authorities concerned when it occurred in such a small community, where everybody knew everybody. It was fairly short odds you would know either the victim or the perpetrator, if not both. No wonder he was so snappy about it.

"I can't say I liked him all that much," Ben admitted, "but he definitely didn't deserve that."

"Is it your first murder?"

"Not quite. But certainly my first in Belfrey. It's just not a place where things like this happen very often. The odd domestic maybe, or a pub brawl that gets out of hand, and of course, any violence is bad enough, but this is different."

Keeley nodded. As a pretty red-haired waitress brought over their food, Keeley looked down at the huge bowl of fresh, steaming pasta and didn't feel hungry anymore. This murder was different, though not in the way Ben meant. But because it seemed to concern her, and she had no idea why.

"I think whoever wrote that letter was the murderer," she blurted, admitting it for the first time as much to herself as to him. Ben nodded slowly, his expression hardening again into that of detective.

"What makes you say that?"

Keeley shrugged. "I don't know." Maybe she just didn't want

to think of two psychopaths on the loose in Belfrey. "Don't you think so?"

"Logically?" Ben shook his head. "They seem very different acts. A murder and an arson attempt, followed by a nasty anonymous letter. They seem like entirely different modi operandi. Not to mention that if you didn't know Terry Smith, there's no reason why his killer would want to taunt you. Yet gut instinct tells me that yes, it could be the same person."

Keeley stabbed her pasta repeatedly with her fork, unable to face actually eating any of it. The implications of Ben's words had been gnawing at her all night and could no longer be ignored.

"So if the murderer wrote that letter, and they were implying it should have been me who died in the café, not Terry . . ." She was unable to finish the sentence, her tongue thick in her throat. Ben reached over and closed his hand around hers.

"Then you could be in danger, Keeley."

His hand felt hot and heavy on hers, and Keeley found herself staring at their enjoined fingers, at the contrast between his rougher, darker skin and her own softer, paler digits. When he saw the direction of her gaze, he removed his hand and sat back. Keeley felt suddenly cold.

"That's why you should have contacted me last night. Whoever posted that letter may still have been lurking around."

She could have walked right past the killer, she thought with a stab of horror.

"Perhaps, with your opening delayed anyway, you could stay elsewhere until this is sorted?" Ben looked at her hopefully, which made Keeley at once both more alarmed and annoyed.

"I'm not being run out of town," she protested. "That's probably what they, whoever 'they' are, want."

"But why? Have you given any more thought to who in Belfrey could have reason to dislike you? Or if not you specifically, then your plans for the café?"

Keeley went to say no, then paused. It seemed far-fetched, but there had been no mistaking the animosity from Raquel yesterday.

"Maybe—" she began, only to be interrupted by the arrival of a dark-haired woman smelling strongly of expensive perfume, who leaned over their table with a squeal and threw her arms around Ben, her scarf trailing in Keeley's pasta.

Raquel.

"Benny!" she cooed. "How lovely to see you!" Her face looked flushed. Did every woman in town turn into a simpering idiot around Ben Taylor? Keeley sat back, crossing her arms and looking pointedly at Raquel, who took no notice of her at all as she squished herself onto the seat next to Ben, her large breasts practically in his face. Although Ben wasn't staring at Raquel with the same rapt attention paid by the other male customers, he wasn't exactly pushing her away either, Keeley thought, with a sour taste in her mouth that immediately made her feel ashamed. She really must spend more time on her yoga mat before both Ben and Belfrey destroyed all her hard-won equilibrium.

"What are you doing in here?" Raquel asked Ben, still ignoring Keeley. In response, Ben jerked his head across the table toward her so that Raquel had no choice but to finally acknowledge her presence.

"Oh," she said flatly, her perfectly made-up face a mask of disdain. "Didn't take you long to get your claws into our last eligible bachelor, did it?" She laughed, as if to indicate her words were nothing more than a lighthearted joke, but there was nothing lighthearted about the cold flash of malice in her eyes as she looked at Keeley directly. Oblivious, Ben just looked amused, with that wry half smile that seemed to be his default expression. Other than glaring at her suspiciously, of course.

"It's a work lunch, actually," he said, leaning back so that his arm was almost draped over Raquel's shoulders. Raquel took it as an invitation, leaning into him and giggling.

"I suppose I should leave you to it, then," she said, making no move at all. When Ben didn't answer but looked at Keeley, she let her breath out in barely disguised exasperation. What did he want, her permission for Raquel to join them?

"Perhaps we should do this another day," she said stiffly, reaching for her jacket and trying her best to ignore Raquel's look of triumph. Ben looked puzzled.

"We really need to talk about this, Keeley." He turned to Raquel. "Perhaps you could join us later?"

"I'm actually on a lunch date." Raquel indicated a much older, nervous-looking man hovering a few feet away. He looked old enough to be their father, Keeley thought, but he also looked very well off, with a beautifully tailored suit and a watch on his wrist that had likely cost more than the entire six-month lease on Annie's cottage.

"Still chasing the dream, I see," Keeley said, regretting her catty remark as soon as it left her lips. Raquel narrowed her eyes at her, reminding Keeley of a cobra about to strike. As Ben looked from one to the other, it finally seemed to dawn on him that not all was well between the two of them.

"Weren't you both friends at school?"

"Yes," conceded Keeley, trying to inject a note of friendliness into her voice, as Raquel said at the same time, "Not really. Not close like *we* were," the last obviously referring to herself and Ben. Keeley frowned. She didn't remember Ben and Raquel being particularly friendly at school, but judging by the way Ben averted his eyes at Raquel's comment, she had missed something. After Raquel wriggled away to join her "date"—leaving Ben with a lingering kiss on the cheek and Keeley with a glare—Keeley sat looking down at her hands, her appetite destroyed and her self-esteem more than a little deflated. At least it had taken her mind off the murder. She took a sip of her drink and avoided Ben's eyes.

"She's a bit much, isn't she?" Ben said, surprising her into looking up.

"She's very pretty," Keeley said, blushing as she heard the question in her words.

"I suppose," he said, which made her feel about a hundred times worse. "Anyway, where were we?"

I was about to suggest Raquel was behind the letter—and possibly the murder, Keeley thought bitterly, thinking now that her suggestion was completely ludicrous and would only look make her look jealous. A few snide comments did not a murderer make, and if Ben and Raquel had indeed been as "close" as the other girl intimated, then he wasn't at all likely to treat her suggestion with any seriousness. In fact, the more she thought about it, the more Keeley didn't think it had anything to do with Raquel at all. A poison pen letter, typed and hand delivered, just didn't feel in keeping with what she knew of Raquel—the woman would deliver any poisonous remarks to her face; she was sure of that much. And what could Raquel possibly have to do with Terry Smith?

Unless, a thought niggled at her, she had been dating him, or leading him on, perhaps. Raquel obviously still had a penchant for older, richer men, and though no Casanova, as a business owner, Smith would hardly have been destitute. She looked at Ben, who was waiting for her to answer him, and shook her head.

"Only that I didn't have any idea who would want to send me something like that," she said, unable to stop herself glancing over at Raquel, who was sitting at a table with her long-suffering date but currently draped around one of Mario's better-looking waiters. She looked back at Ben, who was drumming his fingertips on the table.

"Well, if it was the killer who sent that letter, then he's showing his hand. Which is a good thing from the point of view of catching him, but not so great for you. I would be a lot happier if you could at least get someone to stay with you, Keeley."

Although she knew his concern was as much out of his duty as a police officer than anything else, his anxiety over her well-being touched her.

"I'll ask Carly if she can come and stay," she conceded, thinking that a little company might be just what she needed.

"Brilliant. I don't want to alarm you unnecessarily, it may turn out to be no more than a nasty prank, but you can never be too careful. Are you not eating that?"

Keeley blinked in confusion at the change of subject, then looked down at her pasta and pushed it toward Ben.

"I've lost my appetite. Have it, please, or Mario will never forgive me."

Ben chuckled and took the bowl, tipping the pasta onto his plate along with his lasagna and eating it quickly. He hadn't been lying when he complained of not having eaten all day. He was probably a typical pie-and-potatoes man, she thought, glancing over toward Raquel and wondering how often Ben frequented the diner.

"Do you think," she said slowly, not wanting to implicate Raquel directly, "it could be a business-rivalry thing? It seems far-fetched, but"—she shrugged—"I can't think of any reason why anyone should have a personal grudge against me."

Ben wiped his mouth, looking serious as he set down his cutlery. Very precisely too, Keeley noticed, thinking of her mother, who had always been a stickler for such things.

"It's not far-fetched at all. People go on about 'crimes of passion' because I suppose they're deemed more interesting—though I doubt the victim would agree—but money is often the biggest factor in crimes of all kinds."

"Hence why you thought I set the fire."

"Did I?" Ben looked far too innocent, then shrugged as Keeley shot him an indignant look. "I'm a police detective, Keeley. I have to consider all angles. If your alibi hadn't checked out—"

"I'd still be in the frame." She finished the sentence for him. At least he was honest, but the cloud of suspicion that met her when she had arrived in Belfrey still rankled. As Raquel's high-pitched laugh floated across the room, Keeley sighed and pushed her chair back.

"I really am tired," she said, rubbing her forehead, "and there's honestly nothing I can tell you."

Ben nodded.

"I'll walk you out. In fact, I'll take you home, if you like, maybe have a look around the outside of the cottage and see if anything has been disturbed."

Keeley hesitated and was about to accept when she heard Raquel calling from across the room.

"You're not going, are you, Benny?"

"No thanks," Keeley said, shrugging on her jacket and pushing her chair under the table with more force than warranted. She walked away while Ben was still protesting, waving vaguely at Mario and letting herself out into the dull afternoon light. It started to rain as she shut the door behind her, and, cursing her lack of foresight in not bringing an umbrella, Keeley pulled her jacket over her head as she hurried over to the bus stop. She prayed Ben wouldn't follow and insist on taking her home, only to feel disappointed when he didn't. No doubt talking to Raquel and her over-friendly breasts.

As she stepped onto the bus, Keeley heard her name and turned, her stomach doing a treacherous flip only to sink when she saw it was Duane, emerging from the library, of all places. She gave him a small wave before hurrying to her seat, thankful when the bus driver pulled off quickly. As it meandered its way through the back streets of Belfrey, Keeley found her thoughts turning to the morbid, wondering in which of the pretty cottages or small stone houses a murderer lurked. Or the person—if they weren't one and the same—who had pushed that awful letter through the door. As she peered out the grimy windows through the now heavy rain, a thought occurred to her. Ben was working on the assumption that the person responsible for the letter could be the same person responsible for the murder and arson. Implying, of course, either one or two culprits. But what if the initial assumption was wrong? If the murder and arson had in fact been separate events, committed by two different people? That might explain why there seemed to be no clear motive, because there was not one, but two. Keeley sat up in her seat, excited at her sudden brain wave and wondering if she should phone Ben, then deflated again as another thought occurred to her.

The police would have been able to determine times and things like that, so the two incidents couldn't have occurred too far apart. Even so, she was sure she had heard somewhere that establishing time of death wasn't an exact science, so the scenario could still be possible. But then that meant the possibility of three different perpetrators, and her theory still didn't answer that pivotal question: Just what was Terry Smith doing in her flat?

If she wanted the answer to that, she would need to know more about the man.

Keeley thought again about Raquel and wondered if Jack Tibbons would be up on the local gossip. He was the kind of man who knew everything about everyone, though not necessarily the kind who would be free with his information. Perhaps she should ask him a few questions. In fact, she decided that doing some sleuthing of her own could be a good idea. If Ben was right about her being in danger, then the sooner this case was solved, the better, and playing the part of the interested newcomer might help her uncover details that the police might miss. Between Ben's official investigation and her own, the murderer could be caught and safely locked up before this whole mess derailed her plans for the café.

Because if it wasn't solved before the author of the letter decided to make good on their threat, then Belfrey's first vegetarian café wouldn't be opening at all.

Chapter Seven

Putting her amateur theories to rest, however, didn't come as easily as Keeley hoped. She had scheduled a night in, planning and trying out recipes, but instead found herself thinking more about alibis and motives than marinating and seasoning. Feud or not, she was still certain Raquel had something to hide. After yet another sleepless night, Keeley had resolved to get started on her own investigations and was up early in an attempt to make notes on what she knew so far. Which, she had to admit, wasn't a great deal. Instead, she made a list of the things she needed to know, and the people she could ask. The former was a good deal longer, but it certainly beat sitting around waiting for her own head to be bashed in with a mysterious blunt object. The police didn't seem to be getting anywhere, so maybe a fresh pair of eyes was just what was needed.

Her resolve was strengthened when Kate, the young WPC

from the station, arrived just after breakfast on Ben's request, to have a look around the exterior of the cottage.

"Shouldn't this have been done yesterday?" Keeley asked, somewhat annoyed at being interrupted in the middle of mastering a complicated headstand. She had gotten up so fast to answer the doorbell that the blood had rushed straight to her face.

"Well, I believe DC Taylor attempted to talk to you yesterday, but you weren't very forthcoming," Kate replied, looking less than happy herself. No doubt she disapproved of Ben taking a former suspect out to lunch. Keeley was immediately apologetic, remembering the way she had rushed off yesterday and then ignored a call from him later on in the day.

"I wasn't feeling very well," she muttered. The policewoman looked unconvinced, and after asking her a few questions, really just going over the same ground she had covered with Ben, asked to see the back garden.

"Why? The letter came through the front door."

"I know that"—Kate looked cross at Keeley's statement of the obvious—"but the sort of person who sends nasty anonymous letters is just the sort of person who snoops through windows."

Keeley tried to push away the thought of someone spying on her as she went about her daily routines. She really must stop wandering around in her yoga pants and remember to pull the curtains, she admonished herself. As she let Kate in through the back gate, she looked around at the small garden warily, half expecting an intruder to jump out of the bushes.

"It's funny, though," Kate went on, her earlier hostility seemingly forgotten, "but you could say the same about the victim."

"Sorry?" Keeley felt confused, having a sudden mental image

of Terry Smith wearing her yoga pants and wondering if she had spoken aloud.

"Terry always struck me as that sort of person. You know, the type to go snooping through windows. He always seemed to know things about people; nasty stuff, you know. Dirty laundry."

"He doesn't sound like a very nice man," Keeley said, wondering if there was anyone in Belfrey who had something nice to say about the unfortunate Terry Smith. It seemed almost sad that the man should meet such an abrupt end and yet have no one grieve for him. "Did he have a girlfriend or anything?" she asked, thinking back to her suspicions concerning Raquel.

"Not that I know of. I don't think he had anybody, really. Which makes things a bit harder for us, considering that people are most often killed by someone close to them. In any case—" she frowned at Keeley, looking suspicious, "—why do you want to know?"

"Just curious." Keeley shrugged, looking away. She sensed the other woman looking at her; then Kate turned away and finished her cursory inspection of the back door.

"Nothing looks out of place or unusual?"

"Nothing."

"I didn't see anything by the front door either. Oh well, I suppose it was too much to expect the anonymous author to leave a calling card. And looking for things like fibers or hairs on bushes by the front door is fairly pointless; lots of people could pass by."

Keeley thought again of all those episodes of *CSI*.

"Isn't forensic evidence crucial, though? If you could match something to the murder scene?"

Kate gave her a withering look and seemed on the verge of rolling her eyes.

"This isn't *CSI.*"

Keeley blushed.

"We have no real evidence that this is even connected to the murder as yet. Who owns the cottage—you?"

"Annie Rowland." Keeley hoped that the WPC wasn't planning on telling her landlady. Although she felt sure the older woman would be concerned on Keeley's behalf, she didn't want her thinking that she had brought trouble with her to Rose Cottage. Although it was probably a little late for that, being that half the town seemed to think she had something to do with the murder.

Thankfully, Kate seemed to decide there was nothing more to be gained here and took her leave, telling Keeley as she got into her car, "DC Taylor advised you to be careful, he said something about you having a friend over? And to call him—"

"If I think of anything else," Keeley finished for her. "Got it." Kate smiled tightly and drove away while Keeley glanced up and down the hill, hoping none of her neighbors had seen the police car parked outside the cottage. That would hardly lift the finger of suspicion from her.

As for Carly staying, the truth was that Keeley had all but forgotten the idea. Thinking through her theories about Terry Smith's demise had indeed proved a distraction from her own fears. So much so, she decided there was no better time than the present to begin asking a few questions. After a belated breakfast of her own apple and cinnamon smoothie and a large portion of tofu scramblies, she changed into her jeans and left for the town center. This time, she took her umbrella.

As she passed the inn, she remembered Norma and Maggie, the voracious gossips, and wondered if they should be her first port of call. Then she remembered their almost predatory manner the other evening and decided against it. Perhaps as a last resort. Although Keeley didn't doubt that the pair would be more than happy to let her in on any juicy bits of information they may have at their disposal, she was also under no illusions that they wouldn't then do exactly the same to her, wasting no time in letting the other residents know that she was asking questions. No doubt with an embellished spin on things. No, she would need to be feeling a little sharper and more self-assured before she tackled those two.

Her first potential informant, as she had decided the previous day, would be Jack. She had thought of Annie too, but remembering the landlady's valiant attempts to be diplomatic when it came to discussing the personalities of both Terry Smith and Keeley's own mother, she thought Jack her best bet. He wasn't one to mince his words.

For once, though, he wasn't alone as she stepped into the dingy half-light of the Tavern, but sitting with two other men, both as craggy and hard-bitten-looking as Jack himself. He looked up and nodded at her as she came in, his nicotine-stained fingers clutched as ever around his pipe. The other two men eyed her with a curiosity that didn't seem entirely friendly, but Jack's dog at least was pleased to see her; sitting up and wagging his tail in an excited motion that caused his whole body to shake—no mean feat, given the size of him. Again Keeley thought about the fact that if it wasn't for the wolfhound, the arson attempt on her café may well have succeeded. She crouched down by the dog and rubbed behind his ears, and he rewarded her with an affectionate butt to the side of the head that nearly had her sprawling on the floor. Jack tutted and yanked the dog away.

"Behave yourself, now, Bambi," he admonished, the name eliciting a surprised squawk of a laugh from Keeley as she stood up.

"Bambi? That's his name?"

"Aye. It were the wife's idea. When he was a puppy, he had these long spindly legs and these big eyes, see. And she always was a soft 'un, so Bambi he became. She had just gotten ill then, and the dog was a comfort to her like."

"It suits him," Keeley said kindly, remembering Jack's wife had died just a year before her father, of a cancer that had taken a long, painful time to reach its inevitable end. Jack had been by her side throughout.

"Can I get you a drink?" she asked him, glancing at the other two men, who had made no move to introduce themselves. Jack shook his head and Keeley made her way to the bar, ordering a tonic water from a vacant Tom. As she walked back over to the table, she realized that Jack hadn't actually invited her to sit with him and hesitated, wondering if she was interrupting something.

"Jack, have you got a minute?" She hovered uncertainly at the edge of the table. Jack looked up at her, frowned for a moment, then waved his hand toward a free stool.

"Sit down. This is the Carpenter girl," he said to the two men, who gave her a brief nod in unison. They looked alike, one just being a little fatter than the other, with a red nose that spoke of a life spent working outdoors and a touch more homemade liquor than was healthy. Brothers, perhaps.

"Ted and Dan Glover," Jack introduced, confirming her assumption. "They own the big farm at the top of the hill."

"Oh, of course, I remember," Keeley said, giving them a warm smile. "We used to get our milk and eggs from you."

The skinnier of the two men—Ted, she remembered now—

regarded her with an even look that froze the smile on her face. Definitely not friendly.

"That's right, and your father got a lot of his meat from us, too, you know, just over the road."

Keeley nodded in encouragement but felt her stomach sink a little. She had a feeling she knew where this conversation was going.

"I hear you've got plans to turn it into a vegetarian café now," the brother chimed in, saying "vegetarian" the way another person might say "cockroach." Trying to pretend she hadn't noticed their obvious hostility, Keeley nodded, her smile now not so much frozen as having succumbed to rigor mortis.

"That's right." She sensed that launching into her usual mini sales pitch about a healthy diet and lifestyle wouldn't be advisable in the face of the Glover brothers.

"You don't think that's a bit of a daft idea? In a farming town?"

Keeley took a long, slow swallow of her drink, her smile finally wiped off her face, and eyed Dan calmly, although inside she was cringing. Jack sat silent beside her, making no move to defend her. Not that she really expected him to. He had made his own dismissal of her business just as apparent, if not quite so rudely. Bambi at least offered some support, pushing his great head into her lap and looking up at her with his mournful eyes. She combed her fingers through the fur between his ears, grateful for small comforts. Perhaps she should get a dog—she had read somewhere that people with pets showed decreased stress levels and better immunity to disease.

"I'm sure Belfrey, and Amber Valley as a whole, is big enough for us both, Mr. Glover," she said politely. The conversation reminded her of her earlier one with Raquel. She wondered if every newcomer who tried to set up a local business that was perceived as a bit different from the norm was treated like this, and made a mental note to ask Megan how Crystals and Candles had first been received.

Dan Glover nodded curtly, as if the matter was settled, but his brother wasn't done. He leaned over the table toward her, a mean glint to his eyes that Keeley thought looked almost fanatical.

"Do you know what people like you have done to the business of farming?" he demanded, each word rapped out sharply like a strike against her. "As if things aren't bad enough, what with the floods and the bloody economy." A drop of spittle had gathered at the corner of the man's mouth as he spoke. His brother had nodded along throughout, his piggy eyes fixed on Keeley.

She sucked in a deep breath before she answered, trying her best not to show she felt intimidated. Bambi had raised his large head and was looking at Ted Glover from under his shaggy fringe, his large body tense. No doubt he too had picked up on the man's barely contained rage.

"I'm sorry if you're having problems, I really am, but they're none of my making, Mr. Glover. And I'm not sure what you mean by 'people like me.'"

"Bloody do-gooders!" he snapped, the whole of his face now as red as his nose. "Traipsing around the countryside, moaning about the way things are done, letting out the livestock, damaging machinery. Going on about animals' rights as if we don't have any ourselves."

"I don't reckon Keeley here's into any of that," Jack cut in. His tone was amiable enough, but Keeley was sure she detected an edge of steel to it. Bambi must have sensed it too, for he let out a soft growl and narrowed his eyes at the farmer, who sighed and finally sat back on his stool.

"Sorry," he said grudgingly to Keeley, not looking or sounding one bit sorry, "just a sensitive subject, that's all."

"It's all right," she said stiffly, sipping her drink—though it wasn't, really. How on earth could her opening a little café have any impact, in the larger scheme of things, on the Glovers and their livelihood? She suspected Ted Glover was, quite simply, a bit of a bully, and his brother not much better. She should ask her mother about them too. Assuming her mother would tell her what, if anything, she knew.

Thinking about Darla brought her attention back to the real reason she was here: Terry Smith. Now, though, she didn't want to ask Jack questions, not in front of these two, who clearly thought her a blight on the local community, in any case.

To her surprise, however, right on cue, it was Dan Glover who brought it up, but without the hostility she might have expected.

"How's the police getting on with finding the killer, anyway? They must have some idea by now who it is, surely."

Keeley shrugged, not wanting to share any confidences with this pair. Or to admit that she didn't think Ben had any more idea than she did.

"Bloody useless, the local police. Can't find their arse from their elbow," Ted muttered sullenly into his beer. Clearly a man angry at the world, Keeley thought, still trying not to take his comments personally.

"It's not like it's any great loss, though, is it?" his brother said, and Keeley looked at him, interested now.

"Did you know him?"

The Glovers shrugged, again almost in unison.

"Only for the betting," Dan said.

"But he would always try and cheat you, if he could. Never liked paying up, either."

"Though he was quick enough to complain if you owed him money."

They both nodded at Keeley, her sins obviously forgotten for the moment while they had a new target. Then Ted, clearly the more dominant of the two, drank back his beer in one long gulp and nudged his brother.

"We need to go. Be seeing you," he nodded to Jack, not even bothering to address Keeley. Dan at least nodded at her before he drank back his own beer and left. Keeley watched them go, suppressing a shudder of distaste.

"Don't mind them," Jack said, as if reading her thoughts, "they don't like most folks."

Keeley turned to him, placing her palms flat up in her lap as if beseeching. Bambi sniffed them, licked one of them, and then looked disappointed when he realized she wasn't offering a tasty tidbit.

"Jack, is everyone going to be like this? Honestly, I thought . . ." She trailed off, embarrassed to feel tears stinging her eyes.

"Don't go upsetting yourself." Jack patted her knee awkwardly. "Most of the younger folk will probably come flocking to you. It's the older ones, we've got set in our ways, that's all."

Keeley nodded, though she didn't feel convinced. Her enthusiasm for questioning Jack about Terry had waned in the face of the Glovers' rudeness, and she suddenly felt she didn't want Jack to think she was snooping. He was one of the few friendly faces she saw.

Instead she excused herself and took her tonic water over to the bar, feeling glum. She had discovered precisely nothing about Terry Smith so far other than the fact she already knew: that he was pretty much solidly disliked by every other resident of Belfrey. A distinction Keeley herself felt close to acquiring. Tom was polishing glasses, looking as faraway as usual.

"I think it sounds pretty interesting," he announced, surprising her, "this yoga stuff."

"Really?" Keeley perked up a little. Though she did have to suppress a giggle at the thought of Tom doing an inversion or upside-down pose. Would his beard get tangled in his nose ring?

"Yeah, I saw this clip on YouTube of a naked yoga class. It was hot."

Keeley nearly choked on her tonic water. "That's not quite the same as what I do," she said, but Tom continued, his eyes becoming even more glazed over.

"There was this one girl, she did this thing with her hips—"

Keeley finished her drink in one quick gulp.

"Fascinating. But I'm not sure that's yoga you were watching, Tom. I'd better be going." She slid off her barstool, only to pause at his next words.

"Terry was in the diner last week."

"Oh?" Keeley slid back onto the stool, although given her height, or lack thereof, getting back on was rather less graceful than getting off.

"Yeah, I heard you asking Jack about that too, the other day."

"Is that unusual, though? I mean, it is a diner."

"I reckon so. The thing is—" he lowered his voice and leaned over the bar toward her, "—she was giving *him* money. Out of the till. Not like change, but a wad of notes."

That did seem odd. It didn't fit with Keeley's theory that

Raquel could have been dating Terry for his money either. Could they have been in business together? Some venture that, for whatever reason, Keeley's plans for the café had derailed? Although that didn't really explain why Raquel would want to kill him. And if either of them had intended to either buy or lease the premises, then Darla would surely have known. It didn't make sense.

As Keeley said good-bye to Tom and Jack and stepped out into the High Street, a realization struck her—one so obvious, she couldn't believe she hadn't made the connection instantly.

Terry had been blackmailing Raquel. Why else would a notorious gold digger be giving her money away? Either that or she had a gambling problem, which didn't fit with what she knew of Raquel Philips. But what could Raquel be hiding that she would be willing to pay to keep secret? Or even to kill?

Keeley paused in the middle of the street as she turned over the new possibilities Tom's bit of information had turned up. There was only one way to figure out Raquel's connection to Terry. Ask. Keeley looked across the street to her café as if for luck. It still looked empty and abandoned, as indeed it had been for so long, and it was hard to imagine that in just a few weeks, it would be open for business and, she hoped, thriving. She tried to picture it in her mind, but instead the image now burning bright behind her eyes was a memory rather than a visualization. The memory of the times when it had indeed been thriving and busy, when her father was behind the counter. She felt sure that George Carpenter would have encouraged her in her plans, yet locals such as the Glovers acted as though she were somehow betraying his memory, an attitude that upset her. It wasn't even accurate, she thought as she turned away and began to make her way down the hill toward the diner, to describe Belfrey as a "farming town."

Traditionally, it had always been a milling town, and the historic cotton mills still stood, now turned into museums or office space. Those who hadn't chosen to work in the mills had gone instead to the mines in nearby Heanor. Of course, they were all closed now too. Farming was, she supposed, one of the few traditional large-scale industries left.

Other small towns in Amber Valley had succumbed to unemployment and the recent recession and were a shadow of their former selves, but Belfrey had remained afloat and was still sought after as a place to live. That was due in large part to its flourishing small businesses and various tourist attractions, such as the lush Water Gardens near the river and the country's oldest working windmill. Keeley had half hoped the locals would be glad of her revamp of the shop, of her own small attempt to keep local trade booming. The Glovers at least had given the impression they would rather she shut up shop and left town. They were so hostile, it had been tangible. Hostile enough to send her an anonymous letter or set her shop on fire? It was possible. Passions certainly seemed to run deep here.

As she reached Raquel's Diner, she took a deep breath, not sure she was ready for another showdown with its glamorous proprietor. She decided not to confront her directly with her blackmail theory, which would surely just cause Raquel to clam up.

The diner was empty of customers when Keeley walked in to see Raquel sitting in a corner, filing her nails and looking bored while a thin, pale girl in a red apron cleaned the counter, her expression listless. Raquel looked surprised when she saw Keeley, setting down her nail file and eyeing her warily.

"Come to check out the competition, have we?" she said, although her comment was lacking the level of sarcasm Keeley had come to expect. Keeley tried what she hoped was a warm smile on her, only for Raquel to ignore her and go back to her nails. Well, she hadn't expected it to be easy. She ordered a cup of tea from the girl at the counter, waited for her to pour it, and then took it over to the table where Raquel sat. She pulled out a chair opposite the diner's namesake, who watched her with a frown.

"Mind if we have a little chat?"

Raquel looked surprised again; then her perfectly glossed lips curved into a catlike smile.

"Is this about Ben? I wouldn't get too attached, darling, every single woman in Belfrey has had her eye on him for years."

Keeley felt herself flush from the neck up as she recalled her own crush and lifted her mug to her face in an attempt to cover it. Thank God she had grown out of it.

"No, of course not. It's not like that. Ben's just investigating the murder at the café."

"Oh yes, the murder," the Raquel said, her voice light. Her motions with the file, however, became quicker and firmer. Keeley sat her mug back down, watching Raquel carefully. At least her gibe about Ben had led nicely on to the subject of Terry Smith.

"It's been quite unnerving, coming back to such tragedy."

Raquel paused in her filing for a few seconds before resuming with even more furious movements. If she wasn't careful, she would have no nails left, Keeley thought.

"Hardly a tragedy," she said in clipped tones.

"You weren't a fan of his either, then." Keeley made it a statement rather than a question. Surely the poor man had had some friends.

"I didn't really know him, but I've heard from my customers that he wasn't a nice guy."

"He wasn't a customer himself?"

Raquel stopped her nail filing then, setting the tool down on the red and white checkered tablecloth and looking evenly at Keeley.

"Maisie," she said, addressing the girl behind the counter but keeping her eyes fixed on Keeley, "go and finish that washing up, will you."

The girl scuttled into the kitchen without hesitation, no doubt used to being ordered around by her boss.

"Okay," Raquel said, drawing out the second syllable, "what's with the questions?"

Keeley took a sip of her tea, which was far too weak and full of sugar she hadn't asked for.

"I'm just trying to get a better picture of the man. I mean, he did die on my premises"—she felt a chill as the reality of the situation hit her once again—"and I don't even really know anything about him."

"He's dead. What does it matter?" Raquel's bluntness shocked Keeley into blurting out, "But you did know him, didn't you?" She cringed at her complete lack of subtlety.

"Exactly what are you getting at?" Raquel snapped. Seeing what she was sure was a flash of panic in the other woman's eyes, Keeley felt her confidence return a little.

"I just got the impression he came in here quite a bit," she said, trying to be casual but feeling a weird flicker of excitement when Raquel again looked perturbed. She was hiding something; Keeley would bet her last pound on it.

"Now and then."

Raquel stood up, placed her nail file back in her designer handbag, and looked at the clock. "We're closing," she said, although it was only a quarter past one. Knowing when she was being dismissed, Keeley got up. She wanted to ask her about the money, but had no idea how to bring it up without dropping Tom in the proverbial manure.

"He was something of a businessman I heard, had his fingers in a few pies. I wondered if you had any financial dealings with him?" She stressed the word "financial," her eyes searching Raquel's face.

Raquel glared at her, opening the door of the diner and holding it for her, a nonverbal *get out.*

"He owns a betting shop," she said with disdain. "What possible dealings would I have with him?" She looked angry now, and Keeley admitted defeat to herself and made her way out the door, feeling that she had begun to uncover something, but had no coherent idea what. The door half closed behind her; then she heard Raquel say her name in a quiet voice. Keeley turned her head, just for a moment wondering if she was about to hear some kind of a confession.

"Don't cross me," Raquel said. Her eyes held such menace that Keeley physically recoiled as if she had been struck. Not a confession, then, but a threat.

"Or you will regret it," Raquel finished, before closing the door firmly in Keeley's face.

Chapter Eight

Keeley walked away with her heart beating faster than was comfortable in spite of her efforts to use her breathing exercises to calm her central nervous system. The truth was, she had to admit to herself, that there was a nastiness in Raquel that really quite scared her, and what had seemed a wild theory now seemed more than fitting: that her old school friend was indeed capable of a gruesome act of violence. Although she tried to tell herself her questions had obviously hit a nerve, confirming that Raquel indeed knew Terry Smith a good deal better than she was letting on, Keeley also had to admit that her questioning technique left more than a little to be desired. In fact, she had been downright clumsy, and had made even more of an enemy of Raquel.

Although it hadn't been her intention, she found herself going into Crystals and Candles, seeking a friendly face and a comforting cup of herbal tea. The heavy smell of incense and various aromatherapy oils hit her as she went in, the flickering candles casting sinister shadows around the brightly colored shop. Keeley gave herself a mental shake; she really must get a grip on herself.

Megan, at least, seemed pleased to see her, enveloping her in a patchouli-scented embrace and waving her to a seat.

"What's happened? You do look pale." She peered at Keeley in concern. Keeley hesitated, wondering how much to tell her, reflected that she didn't really know her all that well, and then recounted her conversation with the Glover brothers, leaving out any mention of her plans to discover what she could about Raquel and Terry's murder. Megan listened with a sympathetic expression, then leaned over and patted her hand.

"Try to ignore them. People are set in their ways here, they don't like anything that's different or new. Especially if you're a newcomer like us." Megan had told her before that both she and Duane originally came from Derby, which might be their nearest major city but was worlds apart from the closed-in community of Belfrey.

"But I'm not a newcomer," Keeley said with a sigh, "I was born and bred here. I know I've changed, but even so, I expected to fit back in more easily than this." All the time she had lived in London and New York, she thought of herself as quintessentially a country girl, even though she had embraced city life, and she had imagined settling back into Belfrey would be as natural as a duck sliding back into water. To not feel welcome was disconcerting, for if she didn't belong here, then where would she, ever? She gave Megan a weak smile.

Megan gave a sharp nod, as if deciding something, and went over to a small segmented box of crystals on display by the till. The sort of cheap lucky charms Keeley had never set much store by. Nevertheless, she tried to look grateful when Megan handed her a small mud-colored stone.

"Keep this by you at all times, preferably close to your skin," Megan directed her with a sudden air of authority that seemed unlike her. This was her domain, of course, just as yoga and nutrition were Keeley's, and police work was Ben's. Keeley squashed that thought before she could acknowledge its obvious conclusion—that detecting should be left to the experts. She may not have known Terry Smith, but his murder was becoming personal, and Keeley needed to be proactive.

It was either that, or be terrified.

"Bitten off more than you can chew," Megan said, causing Keeley to blink with guilt and confusion before she went on, "is that how you feel? Moving back here? You should have more confidence in yourself—you have a very capable aura, you know."

"Do I? Thank you. Is that what the stone is for?" She looked down at the stone, which had warmed in contact with her skin.

"Oh no. That's a smoky quartz. It's for protection."

Keeley felt herself grow cold, as though the stone in her hand were leaching all the warmth from her body.

"What makes you think I need protecting?" She also wanted to ask *from whom,* but instead Megan answered solemnly:

"There are dark forces around you, trying to attach themselves to your energy flow. This will help strengthen you."

"Oh. Right." Keeley slipped the stone into the back pocket of her jeans, then remembered Megan's advice and took it back out, tucking it inside her bra instead. It didn't hurt to be careful, and the gesture certainly made Megan happy, judging by the beaming smile she now wore on her face.

"I could get my spiritual circle to go to your house—or

perhaps the café—and do an energy-clearing and protection ritual, if you like. It could do a world of good. Things like murder,
they leave an imprint on a place."

"Er, maybe. I've got the decorators and kitchen fitters coming
over the next few days, so I might be a bit busy. But we'll see after
that," she added as Megan looked crestfallen. The shopkeeper was
so eager to help that turning her down was rather like kicking a
puppy. Keeley wondered for a brief moment if Megan really was
psychic, and if it would be worth showing her the poison pen letter.
But if that were the case, then she would have been able to deduce
who killed Terry Smith. Keeley could just imagine Ben's face if
she asked him to give her the letter back before it had even been
processed for fingerprinting and whatever else the police did with
such evidence, so that Megan could read its "aura."

"How did things go with Duane?" Megan asked, changing
the subject. "He wants to get in touch with you, I saw him this
morning."

Duane. With everything else going on, he had been the last
thing on Keeley's mind.

"He's a lovely guy," she said, feeling awkward now, "but I'm
not sure I'm ready to start dating."

Megan gave her a sympathetic look. "Still pining for an old
flame? I have crystals and even spells that can help with that, you
know. But I think he wanted to ask you about the yoga class tomorrow, if you were still going to take it over? The usual instructor has been cutting her hours, and the center really needs someone
to take the Saturday lunchtimes—they're absolutely full. He said
you seemed really keen, and of course, it might help you feel more
welcome."

Keeley blinked and nodded, trying but failing to recall when she had apparently had this conversation with Duane. It must have been on their "date" at the inn, when she had tuned him out. Obviously, he hadn't just been talking about himself. She should have given him more of a chance, she thought, trying not to think about Ben and the way he had questioned her about Duane's walking her home.

"Yes, I'm looking forward to it. It's the twelve o'clock class, isn't it?" She had no idea, of course, but Megan didn't seem to notice.

"One o'clock, actually. It's the beginners, so it should be simple enough for you. I might go myself, I've heard yoga is brilliant for opening up your spiritual pathways."

"It is good for body and soul," Keeley agreed, thinking she shouldn't be so quick to dismiss Megan's off-the-wall beliefs. Not everyone had understood her need to take herself off to India and do two hours of yoga postures every day before dawn, after all. Each to their own. Plus, it would be nice to have a face she knew at her first class here.

The wind chimes that served as a door alert went off behind her, and Keeley looked over her shoulder as Megan rose to greet her new customer. She obviously knew him, and in fact, seemed to know exactly what he had come to purchase, as she went straight over to a small cabinet on the far side of the shop, next to the tarot cards. It was filled with mysterious-looking jars and pots with handwritten labels wrapped around them. Megan reached inside for one of them and placed it into the newcomer's hands. He was a thickset man who looked to be in his early fifties or so, with thinning, sandy hair and the kind of face that could only be described as "jolly." He would have been handsome in his youth, she decided, but that had been eclipsed by a love of good food and no doubt good wine. There was an air of affluence about him, not least because of his well-tailored blazer, adorned with rather flashy gold buttons, and slacks, but a nervous air too, as if he were agitated about something. He beamed at Keeley as he moved toward the counter with the pot of lotion clutched in his fleshy hands, but it was a smile that didn't quite reach his eyes.

"This is Gerald Buxby." Megan introduced the man in the tone of voice that suggested Keeley should recognize the name, but it didn't sound familiar to her. "The mayor of Belfrey," Megan clarified as Gerald reached a hand for Keeley to shake. It was a surprisingly firm shake, she thought, as she realized that for some reason, she had expected it to be limp. He gave Keeley another broad smile that didn't quite meet his eyes.

"This is Keeley," Megan continued her introductions, "she's opening the vegetarian café I was talking about the other day. Where that awful murder happened, of course."

Gerald's smile wavered for a moment on his face, sliding over his features before settling into a wider beam than before.

"Of course, you're George Carpenter's girl. I knew your father well, he was a wonderful man."

Another apparently known-to-her-father person whom Keeley had no recollection of whatsoever. She tried to remember if Buxby had been the mayor before she moved away, but it wasn't the kind of thing a seventeen-year-old girl paid attention to.

"I'm sorry, I'm not sure I remember you." As she said that, she could have sworn she saw a hint of relief in his eyes.

"Oh, I wouldn't expect you to, my dear. You were a slip of a thing when I saw you last. I didn't live in Belfrey then, you see, I'm a Bakewell boy born and bred, but I used to see your father on a weekend for the bowls. Quite the player, old George."

Keeley nodded in fond recollection. Her father had always said bowls was a "proper country sport," along with fishing and fox-hunting, the latter of which thankfully, to her vegetarian sensibilities at least, was now outlawed across the land.

"Your mother too, she was an amazing woman. How is Darla?" Keeley wasn't sure which struck her as the more odd: the fact of anyone who knew her mother well describing her as amazing, or the idea that Keeley would have any real idea of whether her mother could currently be described as "well" or not.

"She's the same as ever," she said, settling for an evasive truth.

"Good, good. Well, listen, if there's anything I can do to help you get yourself started up in business or settle back in, just let me know. I live just up the road from here, the big white house, you can't miss it."

"Thank you." Although Keeley should have been gladdened by his offer of help, for being on good terms with the town mayor couldn't do any harm to her rather dismal social standing, something about his offer felt hollow.

Or perhaps she was just being paranoid, after the open hostility of both the Glovers and Raquel. Keeley fancied she could feel her "protection" stone growing warm where it nestled at the side of her bra. She watched as Gerald handed his pot of cream to Megan, who wrapped it in hemp paper and began to ring it through the till. Her curiosity about its contents distracted her for a moment from Gerald.

"Is that something you've made yourself?" She was so certain Megan would tell her it was a potion designed to ward off evil, or commune with the fairies at the bottom of the garden, or something, that she felt almost disappointed when Megan said, "Yes, it's a foot lotion."

"My feet swell something terrible in the hot weather," Gerald explained, looking a little shamefaced to be discussing the state of his feet with her, "and Megan's cream is the only thing I've found that soothes them for any length of time."

"I'm trying to develop my own line. Moisturizers, hand creams, that sort of thing, using herbs and natural ingredients, locally sourced where I can."

Keeley was impressed, again thinking she had been too quick to write Megan off as flaky. Herbs and ethical ingredients—now, that was something she could understand. Not to mention the fact that it dawned on her Megan might well be able to offer her some useful business advice, for she was an outsider and had managed to successfully run a small business in Belfrey that may seem rather "different" to some of the locals. She had the town mayor as a regular customer, no less.

"I'd like to try out some of your products one day, they sound great," she said honestly. Megan looked happy.

"They're doing really well, actually. Even Gerald's housekeeper has some of my soothing headache balm, doesn't she?"

"Yes, Edna gets quite overwrought sometimes, tends to suffer terrible migraines. She swears by your balm; in fact, I wouldn't be surprised if she was needing some more soon, she seems more agitated than usual lately." As the words left Gerald's mouth, he closed his mouth almost comically quick, as though he thought something may escape without his meaning to, then flushed. Odd, Keeley thought, and even more so when his color deepened as Megan went on, oblivious to his sudden discomfort, "I'm not surprised. Terry being killed has the whole town feeling out of sorts. It's not a nice thought, is it, knowing there's a murderer in our midst."

Gerald's color went from red to a sickly white in an instant. "Yes, yes, it's really quite awful. Well, I've got a lot to do, girls, so good-bye, now." He gathered up his hemp bag and rushed out of the shop, setting the wind chimes off loudly. Keeley watched him go, puzzled.

"Well, that was odd."

"Yes, I thought so too." Megan looked thoughtful. "But it is an unsettling subject and he must feel sort of responsible for it all, being the mayor. There's the food festival coming up next week, and it's not good publicity."

"That's true." Keeley remembered the annual food festival, held in the Town Hall, where various stall holders showcased some of Amber Valley's traditional and best cuisine. Pies, battered fish, and the finest sausages abounded. Her father had always done a roaring trade on food festival weekend, and it did pull in people to Belfrey for the day. Even so, the possibility of some bad publicity didn't warrant the man's demeanor. She had thought him nervy even before Megan explicitly referred to it.

"Did he know Terry well?" Keeley tried to sound as casually interested as she could.

"Well, I suppose he knows everyone, it's his job. But I wouldn't have thought he knew him on a personal level. Maybe he did, and that would explain why he seems so upset."

"Maybe," Keeley echoed, still looking at the doorway from which he had so quickly made his departure.

She left Megan with an invitation to share a bottle of wine with her at the weekend, and went to the local supermarket before catching a cab back to the cottage to stock up her all-but-bare cupboards. She hadn't been feeding herself very well, and also wanted to practice a few recipes. It was high time she started concentrating on menus, or she wouldn't leave herself time to get in all her stock. Although she hadn't had a formal word from Ben yet regarding her being able to start work on the café, she couldn't see what else the police were going to find from the scene that they hadn't already. She should have asked him about it yesterday, but of course had been distracted by that horrible letter. The altered date for the decorators and shop fitters to come in and work their magic was close, and so she should really make sure she had the all clear. Keeley thought about calling him but didn't, remembering Raquel's words and the way the other woman had sneered at her. Had implied she was one in a long line of women who had had a crush on the man.

Still, as Keeley squeezed an apple to check its firmness, or inspected a box of free-range eggs to make sure none were cracked, her thoughts kept straying back to both Ben and the killing of Terry Smith, which were now inextricably linked in her mind. Reason enough to stay away from the detective constable. As for her attempts at uncovering the truth, she felt as though she had uncovered something, but that something seemed to lead only to deeper mysteries. Raquel was certainly guilty of something, and her undisguised threat had shaken Keeley; even so, now that she was away from her and in more everyday surroundings, engaged in such an ordinary pastime as shopping, the idea that her old schoolmate could be behind arson and murder seemed far-fetched. The whole scenario, in fact, seemed so bizarre that it couldn't be true—but of course, it was. *Someone* had done it. Keeley thought about the mayor, and the way his face had changed at the mention of Terry Smith and the way he had rushed off. But Gerald had seemed such a genial, amiable kind of guy. Not to mention the fact that he had offered her his support, which was hardly conducive to his having tried to burn down her business just a week beforehand. She hadn't been convinced of his sincerity at the time, but given some of the other reactions she had experienced so far, Keeley thought she needed all the help she could get.

At least there was one area she felt sure of her own expertise, she thought as she unpacked her bags and surveyed her purchases stacked up on the kitchen side, and that was in providing her future customers with good food. If she could just get them through the door, she felt sure she could keep them returning. Cooking was something she enjoyed as much as her yoga practice, if not more; after all, any form of exercise could feel like a chore on tired days, but cooking she always found a pleasure. It was a character trait most definitely inherited from her father. Her mother preferred her food made for her, had even employed a cook to make use of the choice cuts of meat her father brought home.

Keeley's interest in cooking for others came from the months she had spent in India, where the kitchens were communal, with all visitors expected to take turns serving everyone else, and supplies had consisted mostly of vegetables and rice. There are only so many things that could be done with vegetables and rice, but Keeley had found she enjoyed rising to the challenge and creating new recipes, and when her fellow travelers had started clamoring for her dishes, she discovered a new love: creating food for other people. Now, thank God, she had more to work with than vegetables and rice.

It had occurred to her too, thinking about local dishes and appetites, that she was going to need a good selection of hearty dishes if she was going to tempt the locals in, especially the older residents of Belfrey such as Jack Tibbons, a pie-and-potatoes man if ever she saw one. Smoothies, wraps, and salads weren't going to cut it. But hearty stews with plenty of root vegetables, warming curries and casseroles, and traditional desserts, those might just do the trick. Although with it coming up to summer, she would need to think about lighter recipes too, perhaps some pasta dishes and omelets, and various summer fruit puddings. Perhaps she should have seasonal menus made up, rather than a standard "one size fits all."

Thinking about food made her feel both happier and hungry, and she was soon humming to herself as she chopped an aubergine in preparation for one of her staple meals, vegetable moussaka. She would make a good amount, she thought, and then she could take some round to Annie to sample, and save some for Megan too.

The knocking at her door was so loud, Keeley nearly sliced through her own finger, instead just nicking it slightly so that a tiny bead of blood bubbled up. Pressing her finger to her lips and sucking on the wound, Keeley went to the front door, a little nervous. Whoever it was didn't sound happy. She opened it just a few inches, even though she immediately felt cross with herself for feeling so apprehensive. Whoever had written her that letter, no doubt this was exactly the feeling they wished to instill in her. In defiance of her own fear, she then flung the door open, causing the man who stood there to step back rather than have the oak door hit him in the face.

"Oh! Ben, I'm sorry." Keeley felt a smile spring immediately to her face at the sight of him, before she arranged her face into one of wary curiosity, an image of Raquel fawning over him at Mario's coming unbidden to her mind. Even so, his unexpected visit made her hopeful.

"Have you found out anything about the café? Or the letter?" She stood away from the door as she spoke, motioning for him to come inside, but Ben shook his head and stayed where he was. Only then did Keeley notice how serious his face was, his mouth set in that grim line she recognized from her first day back in Belfrey. When he informed her that her café had so nearly been burned down. Keeley put a hand to her mouth.

"Has something else happened?"

"No," he said, his voice curt, "but it will if you continue going around the town asking questions like you did today. What on earth did you think you were doing?" Although he didn't raise his voice, fury was coming off him in waves. Keeley felt shocked. Yesterday he had seemed so attentive, had relaxed in her company for the first time, and now he was ruder than ever.

"I don't know what you mean," she said, although of course, that wasn't strictly true. "I did talk to a few people about the man who was killed, but I don't see how it could cause any harm."

"Don't you." The way he said it, it was more a statement than a question, and so Keeley made no answer, but folded her arms and waited for him to speak.

"It could cause plenty of harm, Keeley, in fact, you could seriously impede an ongoing murder investigation, not to mention ruffle feathers in the community you claim you want to settle into. Like I said—and I would appreciate an answer—what on earth did you think you were doing?"

Chastened but also angry, Keeley wrapped her arms tighter around herself; whether to ward him off or contain her own hurt at his manner toward her, she wasn't sure.

"I was curious. The man was killed at my shop, the same one someone tried to burn down, possibly the same someone who sent me that letter. Are you so surprised that I would want to know more about him?"

"No. But I would have thought your safety came before your curiosity. I don't remember you being foolish, Keeley."

No, thought Keeley, *you barely remember me at all.* And how dare he call her foolish? "If I'm in danger," she pointed out, trying to keep her voice level, though she was gritting her teeth at his words, "then that's already true. I don't see how a natural curiosity about things makes it any more acute."

Ben made a sound that was almost a snort. His derision was evident.

"Natural curiosity? Is that what you call it? You practically accused Raquel of being the culprit."

"I did no such thing," Keeley snapped, praying she wasn't blushing, because this was exactly what she suspected had happened. Then the implication of his words washed over her. It was Raquel who had complained to him, who else? Reinforcing her hints that she and Ben were close, or at least friendly. Why else would she raise it with the local detective, who might otherwise think it suspicious? Keeley glared at Ben, angry that he either couldn't or didn't want to see Raquel's obvious manipulation.

"That's not the way I heard it. And I'd appreciate it if it didn't happen again."

His words were clipped and measured, dropping between them like stones, and Keeley sighed. It probably wasn't a good idea to mention her theories about multiple culprits, or that she thought the town mayor himself had something to hide. As for the money Tom had seen changing hands, if Ben was so friendly with Raquel, he could find out for himself, she thought with more than a touch of spite.

"Duly noted, Detective Constable," she said with no small

touch of sarcasm, "I see freedom of speech is alive and well in Belfrey."

Ben shook his head at her in seeming exasperation, the way someone might to a disobedient child.

"Just concentrate on doing your own job, Keeley, haven't you got enough to worry about? And let me do mine."

Keeley nodded, just once, unwilling to show that she indeed felt like a naughty child caught in the act. Her indignation slipped away as quick as it had come, leaving her feeling contrite. It must be difficult enough for him and his colleagues without her blundering around, making things worse. She wanted to say sorry, but Ben had already turned away. He got into his car and drove off without looking at her again, and Keeley went back into her house, shoulders drooping, still unsure whether she should feel angry or remorseful. She went back into the kitchen and picked the knife back up only to find her finger was still bleeding. Looking down, she saw she had smeared her top with blood where she had folded her arms. The sight of it made her think both of Terry Smith and her father with his carcasses, and she swept the food off the counter, her appetite having wholly disappeared.

Chapter Nine

Belfrey Leisure Center was both bigger and better equipped than Keeley had been expecting. It was a thoroughly modern building, with a plush reception dotted with palm trees and relaxing Muzak filtered through that didn't disguise the whir of exercise machines in the adjacent gymnasium. A pretty receptionist of indeterminate age greeted Keeley and handed her the relevant paperwork to sign. Keeley would hire the room for a fixed fee and keep the individual payments from those who attended. As she was taking over someone else's class, she didn't have to worry about finding participants, only keeping them.

The receptionist showed her to a small studio with the typical mirrored walls and air-conditioning that was too cold for comfort.

"Could I have the temperature up?" Keeley was sure her tone had been nothing but polite, yet the girl pouted at her as if she had demanded something outrageous, and walked off with a curl of her heavily glossed lips that didn't really answer the request one way or the other. Keeley was about to go after her, to explain that a cold room was hardly conducive to helping the muscles and joints warm up, and she wasn't teaching such a strenuous class that her clients would be glad of the chill. A man's laugh rang out, then said something she didn't catch, but was still loud enough that she recognized Duane. Not quite ready to face him after dismissing him the other night, she stayed in the room, turning her back to the doorway and making a fuss of arranging her yoga mat.

By the time she looked up, three ladies had come into the room and were hovering at the back of the class. Smiling, Keeley straightened up and went over to introduce herself, taking a note of their names and any ailments or injuries she needed to know about, as well as collecting her fee. Keeley had always felt uncomfortable asking for the money, something she knew she needed to get over pretty quick if she was going to make a success of things. Back in Manhattan, she had had little choice but to charge exorbitant prices, but had made herself feel better about the commercialization of the practice by teaching a free class every Saturday at a youth center downtown. It had touched her the way the teenagers, typically disaffected, had seemed so grateful for her time. She had always been "too soft" according to Darla, "just like your father." Indeed, George Carpenter had been known for his generosity, for extending credit to his poorer customers and slipping an extra sausage or dollop of mince to a mother with more mouths to feed than she could cope with. Keeley thought that was something to be proud of.

More women trickled in, mostly middle-aged or over, but none she recognized, although one thin, birdlike woman with thinning dark hair looked familiar. After going through her introductions, it was time to begin. Keeley was on her yoga mat facing the class when one last woman came rushing in, with a loud apology and a beaming smile. When she saw it was Maggie, the local gossip who had tried to question her at the inn along with her friend, Keeley's smile wavered. She hoped the woman wasn't about to continue her line of questioning.

"Keeley, dear! How are you?" Maggie cooed. Keeley gave her a brief smile and waved toward the pile of mats.

"You're only just in time, Maggie. Grab a mat; we're about to start." Maggie's face fell, her beady little eyes looking mean without that wide smile, but she did as she was asked without trying to start a conversation, for which Keeley was grateful. Small mercies, and all that. She turned to face the class, who were watching her with expectant faces, and took a deep breath.

"Okay, ladies. If you can stand tall, with your feet hip-width apart, and raise your arms over your head like this. . . ."

Keeley led the women—and it was all women, she noticed, not one man had attended, although the class was open to all—through a set of modified Sun Salutations as a warm-up. Sun Salutations were a series of linked poses, with the movement linked to the breath, which warmed up the body and were designed to complement any form of yoga practice, from the slowest and most relaxing to the most challenging. After the third round, she taught the class a form of breathing that also linked with the movement, and made a slight whooshing sound on the exhale. By the time they were on their ninth Sun Salutation, the class was moving and breathing in unison, the sound of their breath like the roar of the ocean, but coming from a distance. Like when you go on holiday and you first hear the sea, usually right after you taste its tang on the air. Even Maggie was joining in wholeheartedly, and Keeley allowed herself a bubble of pride that rose up in her stomach and bobbed in her throat. She had missed this.

As she took the class through a series of simple standing postures, then down on the mat for more reclining stretches, she moved around the class, helping each woman individually. Learning who had a stiffness in the hips or a tight shoulder, who got short of breath easily or found it hard to slow down. Keeley thought back to Ben's words the previous night. *You do your job.* This was her job, or one of them, and she felt like she was somewhere she belonged for the first time since she had set foot in Belfrey and been confronted with the horrible news.

As the class wound down, finishing with some abdominal work and rejuvenating poses, Keeley was feeling as serene as a goddess. Even without the smiles and praise of the class, she knew it had gone well. She was feeling so much happier that even when Maggie approached as she was rolling up her mat, Keeley gave her a genuine grin.

"That was wonderful," Maggie enthused. "I can't wait until next week."

"Thank you. Me neither." Behind Maggie, she noticed that the wiry little woman who had seemed familiar was hovering, rubbing her hands together in a nervous gesture.

"Can I help? Diana, isn't it?"

Diana nodded, and without taking her eyes from Keeley's, her head gave an almost imperceptible jerk toward Maggie. Obviously, she didn't want to talk in front of her. Maggie, however, clearly wasn't ready to leave now that she had Keeley alone.

"So how is everything? Has there been any word on the murder yet? Surely they must know something by now?" Presumably, "they" indicated Ben and his colleagues at Amber Valley Police

Department. Keeley saw Diana turn her gaze to Maggie, curious now, and immediately felt irritated. Now no doubt the whole class would soon know who their new yoga instructor was, and the little haven she had just found would be well and truly interrupted.

"Not as far as I know," Keeley said, her voice cool, hoping that Maggie would get the hint. She saw that predatory gleam in the woman's eyes again and for an uncomfortable moment wondered if that was how she had appeared to Raquel the day beforehand. She hoped not.

"To be honest, Maggie," she said, deciding the best course of action was to be blunt, "I'd rather not talk about it." The woman looked annoyed, though her voice was honey-lined with contrition.

"Of course you don't, you poor dear. Are you finding it awfully hard to cope?" Maggie's words dripped sympathy. Laced with arsenic. For now, no doubt all of Belfrey would soon be hearing that the killing had rendered her a nervous wreck.

"I'm fine, Maggie, honestly. I'll look forward to seeing you next week." She gave the woman a smile as insincere as her own, relieved when she gave a soft little snort and turned away, knowing when she was being dismissed. *I'll pay for that,* Keeley thought. But at least she was gone for now. She turned her attention back to Diana, who looked at the door Maggie had just left by and shook her head.

"Dreadful woman, isn't she? You're right not to tell that one anything."

"There's nothing to tell," Keeley mumbled, aware she was being less than honest, and having never been a comfortable liar.

"Anyway, I wasn't sure it was the same Keeley, but Maggie just confirmed it, so that's something, I suppose. I wanted to apologize for my husband?"

"Your husband?" Keeley echoed her words, confused.

"Yes, I understand he was quite rude to you in the Tavern yesterday? I heard Jack giving him a bit of gip about it this morning. Very fond of your father, Jack was."

Clarity dawned. Her husband must be one of the Glover brothers. Ted, most likely, as he had been more openly hostile than the other. Keeley felt sorry for Diana even though, for all she knew, Ted Glover could be a pussycat behind closed doors. Looking at the woman, though, who even after an hour of yoga had a twitchy, anxious air about her, Keeley doubted it.

"Oh, don't worry, it's not your fault, and I suppose I should have expected a few raised eyebrows." Keeley downplayed the fact that Mr. Glover seemed convinced she was solely responsible for the difficulties the farming industry had faced in the past few years. As if she were setting up shop on purpose to annoy him. Some people were like that, she knew from experience, in thinking that everything was a personal slight, from economic recession to inopportune weather.

"Well, as long as he didn't upset you. He doesn't mean it, you know, he's just quick to anger, and the farm's not doing so well as it has been. He doesn't mean it," she said again, and her hand twitched up near her face as though to ward off a blow. Seeing the movement, Keeley felt sick, and reached out a hand to the woman before realizing what she was doing. Diana stepped back, hoisting her gym bag up onto her shoulder to create a barrier between them and hurrying off with a mumbled good-bye and her eyes averted. Keeley watched her go, resisting the urge to call her back and offer her some words of comfort. There was nothing she could say, and there might not be any need to say anything at all, but that involuntary movement had instinctively struck her as the sign of a woman who was scared of her husband.

Keeley was engrossed in thought as she walked back to the reception, and so nearly jumped out of her skin when she heard a male voice close behind her.

"So how did it go?"

Duane. Keeley turned to find him so close, she nearly bumped into him. He had crept up on her like a cat. Flustered, she stepped back, then blinked to see him half naked, clad in only a tiny pair of Lycra underpants, his perfectly honed torso on show. Surely he didn't teach his gym classes like that? The housewives of Belfrey would have heart attacks on the spot.

"I'm on break, I was just having a sunbed," he explained with a slow smile that indicated he took Keeley's appraisal as evidence that she liked what she saw.

"I see. Yes, it went really well. I'm really grateful to you for getting me this opportunity." Which was true, Keeley thought, aware that by avoiding him, she may well have seemed ungrateful.

"Thankful enough to let me take you to dinner?" He flashed his perfect white teeth at her in a smile that struck her as rather sharklike. Keeley hesitated, unsure what to say. She *was* grateful, and a little guilty she hadn't expressed that sooner, and she didn't want to offend him. Not just for altruistic reasons either, but also because he had been her link to getting classes at the center and she didn't want to jeopardize that relationship. Neither did she want to lead him on or give him the wrong idea.

"That would be lovely, and Megan too? I'm so glad we've become friends." That, she thought, should do the trick, and judging by the way Duane's smile dimmed and then became even brighter like a lightbulb flickering, he had taken her point. Friends only.

"Sure, sounds great. Well, I'd better be off before I waste precious tanning time," he said, and walked off with a slightly effeminate sway that had Keeley suppressing a giggle as she made her own way out into the sunshine. The warmth on her skin brought back all the good feelings of the class, including optimism about her success here. Picking up some more classes and becoming known to the regulars at the leisure center would be a great way of finding customers for the café, not least because her emphasis on a healthy lifestyle would by default appeal to those who regularly attended classes.

There was also no denying that the morning had given her plenty to mull over in light of recent events. Ben's warning to stay out of the investigation had both frightened and annoyed her, and she had taken his comments to heart, but it had only briefly dampened her curiosity. As Ben had pointed out, the café should be her main concern, but it was precisely because it was her main concern that she wanted the murderer caught. If, as Ben suggested, the attack was in some way related to a personal grudge against her, then couldn't he see that she was naturally invested in the outcome of the murder investigation? For the first time, she acknowledged her anger toward whoever had done this: murdered a man, set fire to not just business premises but also her family business, and then possibly carried on by taunting her with that letter. She had every right to ask questions, she thought in annoyance. Particularly when Ben himself wasn't giving her any answers.

There was also the matter of the information about Raquel giving Terry money. That was vital information, and she really should have shared it, assuming, of course, that the police didn't already know. But she had held it back, partly out of spite because Ben seemed to have more than a professional interest in Raquel. For all she knew, Ben might even attempt to cover up for the owner of the diner, although that didn't feel right to her; she got the impression Ben was fundamentally honest, even brutally so, where his job was concerned.

Then there was the mayor's strange reaction to the mention of Terry Smith, and Ted Glover's hostility toward her. Not to mention the reaction of his wife. If he truly was a violent man, then bopping Terry Smith over the head with something wouldn't be so out of character. These were only impressions, however, feelings that may well be wrong, and no doubt Ben would just think she was being fanciful. The information about Raquel, though—that was different. Hadn't Ben said most crimes were money related, in the end?

Money related. That brought her back to her theory that Terry may have been blackmailing Raquel. Given the unsavory opinions she had heard about the deceased, the idea of him blackmailing the diner's owner over some grubby little secret seemed in keeping with his character. She wondered if she should mention her theory to Ben, then thought that the possibility of blackmail had most likely already occurred to him. But he might not know about Raquel, and the money she had given Terry. Whatever her feelings toward Ben and Raquel or the possibility that indeed there was a *Ben and Raquel,* it was information she had a duty to share. She rummaged in her bag for her phone and tried to call Ben, but there was no answer. When his deep voice came on, asking her to leave a message, she found herself tongue-tied, cutting off the call rather than speaking. She would ring him later.

Instead, she went home and took her moussaka from the fridge, ready to take round to her landlady's. Annie had been kind to her, and she wanted an opinion on her cooking. After Ben's visit, she had finally resumed her cooking, but neither her heart nor stomach was in it, and so the moussaka remained uneaten.

Annie lived farther up the hill than she had realized, and by the time she knocked her door, her hamstrings and calves were aching. The other woman's plump, friendly face was a welcome sight. She sat down gratefully in Annie's small kitchen while her landlady cooed delightedly over the moussaka and poured Keeley a cup of freshly brewed tea. Although she usually went for herbal, today she thought a cup of strong English breakfast with its kick of caffeine was just what she needed. She looked around the room, noticing a large, framed picture of a man who must be Annie's late husband hanging above the mantelpiece. He looked oddly familiar, but then, so did many of the residents in Belfrey. Strange, how she had grown up around these people yet they still felt like strangers on her return.

"This smells divine," Annie said as she dished up them each a plate of moussaka after quickly warming it up. It did smell good, Keeley had to admit, as the aroma drifted through the kitchenette. Annie's house was a small stone bungalow with just three rooms. Picturesque but tiny.

"Didn't you ever want to stay on at Rose Cottage?" Keeley wondered. Annie shook her head sadly.

"Not after my husband's death. We lived there not long after we married, you see, before we moved to one of the bigger houses near the Water Gardens. Then afterwards, well, it was the memories, you know. Plus it's a steady income and too big for a woman on her own."

"I'm a woman on my own," Keeley pointed out. Annie gave her a merry wink that made Keeley laugh, then blush as her landlady said, "But perhaps not for too long? You're a young woman; who knows but you could end up with a young man taking up some of the space."

"I doubt it," Keeley muttered. It had been a while since she had had a relationship with any man. She had thrown herself into work in New York, and although she had dated a little, she had used the excuse of being too busy to ever get into anything serious.

"First love, was it?" Annie asked, her face creased with sympathy. Keeley looked at her, startled.

"The way you said that, I'm guessing there's a bit of heartbreak there?" Annie patted her hand across the table. "Men can be fickle, especially when they're young."

Keeley looked away. That first heartbreak was something she would rather not think about now; it made her feel young and gullible. Although in a way, she supposed it had made her who she was now, having gone traveling initially as a way to escape the pain. She said as much to Annie, and the woman nodded.

"God works in mysterious ways," she said, the well-worn saying sounding somehow more profound the way she voiced it.

"My mother always said we make our own future."

"That too."

They dug into Keeley's moussaka in comfortable silence, Keeley feeling at peace in the little house. Rose Cottage had much the same atmosphere, which must emanate from Annie herself. Or at least it had until her own arrival. She debated whether to tell her landlady about the poison pen letter, but didn't want to worry her. She hoped that her theory that the author of the letter and the murderer were the same person wasn't accurate. A mean-spirited local resident she could handle; a murderer was a whole different proposition. Instead she told Annie about her run-in with the Glovers, and the way Ted's wife had flinched when talking about her husband's temper. Annie pursed her lips together, looking disapproving.

"I've often wondered about that man. He was a thug, you know, in his youth. Don't expect he's changed much now either. God only knows what poor Diana puts up with behind closed doors. I wouldn't take his comments to heart, dear, you were most likely the first person he saw that was an easy target for his temper."

Keeley smiled, though she didn't find Annie's words all that comforting. She didn't want to be seen as an "easy target," not after all the years of learning to be more confident and at peace with herself, taking her destiny—not to mention her body—in her own hands. She had thought Lardypants Carpenter dead and buried. Keeley pushed her moussaka away in a wave of self-pity, then looked up to see Annie, eyeing her astutely.

"Not been the easiest homecoming for you, has it, duck?"

"I just thought it would be more . . . seamless. But then, I don't suppose anyone expects a murder. It's almost like a bad omen."

The sun dipped behind a cloud as she spoke, causing the stone walls to seem suddenly closer and darker. Keeley shook her head angrily at her own fanciful images. She was seeing shadows everywhere.

"Well, it's not the usual run of things, I admit, but you shouldn't let it overshadow your plans. Have you thought of taking part in the food festival? That might help you establish yourself as part of the local community, and get some promotion for your café. Why, you'll be opening just a few days later, won't you?"

That was, Keeley thought, such a good idea, she wondered why it didn't occur to her the day before, when it had first been mentioned. But no, she knew why. The Belfrey Food Festival showcased traditional foods from the region, and although she had been gone ten years, she couldn't imagine it would have evolved to cover vegetarian and yoga-inspired foods in the meantime.

"Nonsense," Annie said briskly, "there were all sorts of things there last year, including a massive Polish stall and even a workshop for making your own sushi. Granted, it's still mostly pies and cheeses, but serve up good hearty food like this here—" she motioned to her now empty plate of moussaka, "—and you can't go far wrong."

Keeley looked out the window, mulling over the idea. The sun was shining again, and she saw the tail of a rabbit flicker for a second in the undergrowth. Rabbits were lucky, weren't they? It could work, she thought, especially if she used some local produce in her recipes. Why hadn't she thought of that before? Even the Glovers couldn't complain if she offered to use their eggs and dairy in her food. It could even be a regular thing. It wouldn't be cost-effective to use only produce she could buy from local farmers, but she could perhaps offer "specials" or breakfast omelets made with local organic milk and eggs that she could collect herself in the morning. In that way, the café could become a vital part of local trade. Musing over the possibilities, Keeley could feel herself getting excited, and she got up and gave Annie an impulsive hug, causing the older woman to turn pink in pleased embarrassment. She said her good-byes and hurried down the hill to Rose Cottage, fizzing with the excitement of new ideas.

Half an hour later, she had a notebook full of new recipes,

including some specifically for the food festival, such as a spicy root curry and a twist on the traditional summer fruit pudding—and, of course, the moussaka—and had finalized the spring–summer menus to go to the printer. On Monday, in just three days' time, the kitchen contractors and decorators would arrive. The revamp of the premises would also go a long way, she couldn't help thinking, to exorcising the shade of Terry Smith.

After a light tea, she settled down on the sofa to read a book, but found her eyelids drooping before she had made much headway on the first chapter. Keeley dozed off with the evening sun warm on her face and the sound of birds singing outside.

They were silent when she woke with a start. A different sound had woken her, but one that she couldn't quite place in her sleep-fuddled state. It had grown cold now and was creeping toward darkness, and her neck ached where it had been resting at a funny angle on the settee. Keeley sat up and stretched, her ears straining to locate the strange noise that had woken her, but there was no noise save the distant drone of a car at the bottom of the hill. She wondered if it had been the church bells, which rang out around six o'clock for evening prayers and, being only a few roads away, could be easily heard by everyone on Bakers Hill. But a glance at the clock showed it was well past that; nearly half past seven, in fact. She had been asleep for nearly four hours.

Wondering if it was something outside, she opened the back door and surveyed the back garden, but heard nothing. She chided herself for being so nervous as she padded back through the house, but nevertheless, the sense of something ominous remained with her. As she opened the porch door with a view to checking out the front, a part of her knew exactly what she would find even as her mind registered the clattering sound that had awoken her as having been that of the letterbox.

The white envelope looked innocently up at her. There was no name on the front this time, but then it scarcely needed one. *Please,* Keeley prayed even as she knew it was futile, *be a leaflet or something.* But as she picked it up, a single white sheet of paper slid easily into her hand, the single line of black letters staring out at her accusingly.

BITCH. STOP SNOOPING, OR YOU'LL END UP JUST LIKE HIM.

Keeley raised a hand to her mouth, her fingers trembling. The warning, coming as it did after Ben's admonition of her the night before, rang in her ears as though the letters themselves could speak.

A wave of reckless anger came over her then, and she unbolted the front door and stepped out, the paper clutched in her hand. She looked up and down the road, but saw no one.

"Why don't you come and say it to my face!" There was no reply other than the hoot of an owl, echoing back at her. Suddenly realizing she was very alone, she retreated into the cottage, slamming and locking the door behind her, then lowered herself onto the sofa slowly, staring at the paper in her hand. She felt very acutely that this was no mean joke; whoever was doing this hated her with a passion so tangible, it seemed to seep from the paper and between her fingers.

Regardless of how she felt about him, or that he would likely say "I told you so," Keeley knew what she needed to do, whether she wanted to or not. She reached for her phone and dialed Ben's number with quivering fingers.

UIJAYI—OCEAN BREATH

Also known as "the breath of victory." Enhances mental clarity and focus, and can fortify courage. Is also often used in conjunction with a flowing yoga practice.

Method

- Close the mouth and breathe through the nostrils. Inhale and exhale fully.
- On your next inhale, constrict the throat slightly. (Imagine you are trying to close it.) The inhalation should make a hissing sound coming from the back of your throat.
- Exhale normally through the nostrils.
- Repeat.
- Continue.

If you're not sure you are creating the noise correctly, think Darth Vader, and try to emulate the sound he makes on your inhalation.

Chapter Ten

Whether Ben privately thought *I told you so* or not, he didn't say so to Keeley, but was at the cottage within the half hour, and after looking at the letter, his face betrayed nothing but concern.

"Did you not see or hear anyone, or anything at all?"

"I was asleep. I think it was the letterbox that woke me up."

Ben dashed out then, leaving her looking after him rather bemused, until she heard his voice across the road and realized he was questioning her neighbors. He came back twenty minutes later, looking grim.

"What is it?"

"Nothing. Nobody saw anything. Old Mr. Crocker across the way heard a car coming up and down the hill, but didn't look out the window."

"I heard a car," Keeley said, remembering that distant drone, "but I don't know if it was too far away. I mean, it sounded like it was in the next street. If the letterbox woke me up, surely I would have heard a car pulling off."

"You would think. But sleep can play tricks on your perception."

He sat down next to Keeley, who hadn't moved the entire time he was asking questions and still had the letter clutched in her hands. Taking it off her with a pair of tweezers, Ben placed it into a Baggie that lay on the arm of the sofa. He put it with the message facing down and out of sight—deliberately, Keeley thought.

"Have you been asking any more questions today?" He sounded weary rather than accusing. Keeley shook her head with vehemence, her hair flying round her shoulders.

"No. Honest." She gave him a brief account of her day, particularly any conversations with Belfrey residents, though she found herself omitting the part where Duane had attempted to ask her out for dinner.

"Okay. I'm sorry to keep repeating myself, Keeley, but are you absolutely sure you can't think of anyone in Belfrey who would have reason to target you like this?"

"No, no one. Well . . ." She hesitated, wondering whether now was the time to share her information about Raquel. Ben gave her a curt nod, urging her to go on. "Raquel doesn't like me very much. She's been almost threatening, ever since I first bumped into her."

Ben didn't look surprised; neither did he jump to the other girl's defense, as Keeley had expected. "I'll talk to her tomorrow. It doesn't seem like her style, to be honest, but I know she can be very catty."

That's the understatement of the century, Keeley thought. "I'm guessing it was her that complained about my snooping," she said, the carefully blank expression that came over Ben's face confirming it even though he didn't answer. She took a deep breath, deciding now was the time to share both her information and fears regarding Raquel, whether Ben liked it or not. "I was asking her questions because I thought she might know something. You see—" she went on, ready to relay Tom's information, but was silenced by Ben's lifting a hand to her, the way one would hush a small child. Keeley bristled immediately, but fell silent nonetheless.

"You thought she killed Terry? I'm sorry to disappoint you, Little Miss Sleuth, but Raquel has a very good alibi for that night."

Keeley felt herself go red with annoyance at his gibe and with other, more secret irks. *How good an alibi? Because she was with you?* She tried to banish the thought from her mind even as it lodged itself there. It was nothing to her who Ben spent his time with; she shouldn't care. They didn't even *like* each other. Except she did care.

"I see." She put her head down, avoiding his eyes. "I know you two are friends."

"We are?" The sound of genuine surprise in his voice made her look up, and her spirits lifted when she saw an expression of distaste cross his face. "I wouldn't say so. But not liking someone doesn't mean I can go around accusing them of things they haven't done. As I said, her alibi checks out."

Keeley was barely listening to anything except that crucial phrase. *He doesn't like her,* she thought, the words fizzing in her stomach. Ben looked confused, and she realized she was smiling widely at him. She straightened her face, and as she did so, caught up with the rest of his words. If Raquel had an alibi, he must at some point have questioned her. Even so, he might not know about the money. If Raquel had some sordid secret, she would hardly want to share it with Ben. Annoyed at Ben's dismissal of her, she decided to keep the information to herself, at least until she had more proof than Tom's account.

"I still think she's behind the letters. She threatened me, said I would be sorry if I crossed her."

"Really?" Ben raised his eyebrows. "I'll question her in the morning. You definitely haven't been talking to anyone else?"

"Not about the murder, but Daniel Glover and his brother were quite hostile toward me yesterday." She relayed the conversation. Then added, as an afterthought:

"There's Maggie from my first night at the Inn and her friend Norma too. Not that they've been nasty to me or anything—they just seem, I don't know, the type." She fell quiet, fearing Ben would think her last comment inane, but instead he nodded as though he knew exactly what she meant. Either that or he was just humoring her. It was hard to know what were his real thoughts and what belonged to what she was coming to think of as his "detective face." She had thought she caught a glimpse of the real Ben at lunch the other day, until Raquel turned up. Now she looked at him from under her eyelashes, taking in the clean, masculine lines of his face, as well as the shadows under his eyes and the slight furrow in his brow.

"It must be difficult, being responsible for this case," she said, feeling a wave of compassion for him. His face seemed to soften and he leaned back into the cushions of the settee.

"I'm not strictly wholly responsible—the person officially in charge would be the detective chief inspector, but of course, they're busy with bigger things. A rural murder like this, they bring the big guns in only if it looks as though it's getting complex. Or if the investigating officer on the case isn't making any headway. That would be me. If I can solve this thing, I could even make detective sergeant. If not, well—" he spread his hands out on his lap, palms up, "—I'll look a typical country policeman who doesn't know his arse from his elbow."

Keeley swallowed a chuckle at the expression, instead giving him a sympathetic nod.

"It's a lot of pressure." She wasn't the only one this was affecting, although she doubted Ben Taylor sat alone in his house at night jumping at every noise.

"It's not what's important, though. What's important is catching this guy. And keeping you safe. Keeping everyone in Belfrey safe, I mean." He flushed a little, as though making an admission he would rather he had kept to himself, but any frisson of warmth she might have felt at his concern for her was swallowed by his reiterating, once again, that she was in danger.

"That's why you have to stop this silly snooping," Ben went on, and Keeley, who had been leaning companionably in toward him, sat straight up, affronted. His use of the same word that had stared up at her from the latest letter rankled.

"Well, maybe I would, if you told me anything," she snapped. "First you treated me like a suspect, now like a silly child. It was *my* café, you know, that nearly got burned to the ground, and it's *me* who is getting threatened. What am I supposed to do, sit here like a scared victim?" Keeley nearly shouted the last words, surprising herself with her own anger, an anger she hadn't fully allowed herself to express. She looked at Ben, expecting him to roar back, but instead saw a look of startled admiration cross his face; then he simply sat and regarded her until she snapped again. "What?" And then cringed at the petulant tone in her voice.

"You might be right. You have a right to know about the investigations to a point, but I can't share classified information with you, Keeley."

"Classified information," she snorted. "Don't sound so pompous." At the chastened expression on his face, she laughed, her anger dissolving. Ben looked mollified.

"I seem to keep getting off on the wrong foot with you, don't I? I don't mean to."

He looked so contrite, Keeley almost felt sorry for him.

"I'm trying to remain professional, but it's hard." He looked at her so intently, Keeley felt her heart skip.

"What do you mean?" she asked, holding her breath, which she let out in a deflated sigh as he went on.

"The trouble with working in a location like this is you know everybody, so everything is more close to home."

"I see. Haven't you thought of transferring to Derby City?" The idea made her stomach twist, unsure whether she would prefer him out of her hair or here, continuing to stir up unwanted feelings. She must be a glutton for punishment.

"Lots of times. My superiors have even suggested it, but this is home, I suppose. And lately, it's been anything but boring." He gave her a smile that was like the sun coming out, it was so sudden and broad. She looked at those full lips and strong white teeth and felt a murmur of heat in her stomach.

"Look," he said, serious again, "if I let you in on a few details of the case, will you at least agree to stop questioning potential suspects? I'm only thinking of your safety. What happened to your friend coming to stay?"

Keeley shook her head. She had spoken to Carly a few days ago, only to hear her friend was planning a holiday very soon with her "amazing" new boyfriend. Not wanting to burst her bubble, Keeley hadn't mentioned her troubles.

"How about your mother?" Keeley's reaction to that suggestion must have shown plainly on her face, judging by Ben's snort of amusement. "Okay, not your mother. Perhaps I'll arrange for one of the constables to keep vigil outside your house for a few nights. It might scare off your anonymous letter writer."

"Isn't that a little extreme?" Not to the mention the fact that local gossips would have a field day with that juicy bit of information. She wouldn't be going into the inn for a while; that was for sure.

"Not if the person responsible for Smith's death is indeed your mysterious letter writer. Although, I will question Raquel. I'd prefer it if I was wrong on that count."

So would I. Keeley wrapped her cardigan tighter around herself, feeling a sudden chill that wasn't all to do with the night air coming through the open window.

"You said you would let me in on some details?" she prompted, hoping he wouldn't change his mind. He hesitated, looking deep in thought, no doubt sifting through the facts to select those he was prepared to share with her.

"We're working on the assumption there was a business or financial aspect to Terry's death. Which may link in to the arson, though it isn't clear why."

"The only person who would benefit financially from the arson is my mother," Keeley pointed out, before remembering that Darla had indeed been complaining about Ben questioning her.

"It's just a theory."

"Could it be something to do with his betting shop? I mean,

that's all money based." Perhaps now was the time to share her blackmailing theory.

"We've looked at that, but nothing immediately obvious jumps out. Although—" He stopped abruptly. Keeley nodded at him to go on, then said when he still hesitated, "I'm not going to repeat anything." Although being warned off by a poison pen rankled, it was also starting to scare her more than any injured pride was worth. Also, although she would be dragged by wild horses before admitting it, earning even a modicum of Ben's trust gave her a fuzzy feeling of pleasure.

"There were a few strange deposits in his bank account—his personal, rather than business account. That's really all I can say, unless you're going to tell me you knew something about it?"

Keeley shook her head, even as she mused over this new information in her mind. Raquel obviously wasn't the only person Terry Smith had been targeting.

"It's blackmail, isn't it?" she said, trying to sound as though the idea had only just dawned on her. "He was blackmailing someone. Annie said he was the type to go snooping through people's dirty laundry."

Ben nodded. "Good at this, aren't you? It's a strong possibility. I should have a warrant to trace the accounts that the money is coming in from by next week."

"So you are making some headway."

"A little, but it could turn out to be something or nothing. I've questioned everyone in this bloody town, and just can't seem to get a handle on this case." He shook his head in frustration. Keeley was surprised, not having realized his questioning had been so thorough. "I've even spoken to Norma and Maggie," he admitted with a wry grin, "in the hope they might be aware of some juicy secrets worth blackmailing someone for, but all I got was a rather lurid account of Old Mr. Crocker's affair with the lady who runs the launderette."

Keeley laughed at that. "Good for him. I would imagine if those two knew anything, it would be all round the town, in any case."

"Most likely. If it is blackmail, and that's what prompted the murder, then somebody had a secret worth killing for. Something they didn't want anyone to find out."

Keeley thought about that. What secret could be bad enough to kill for?

"There's something I need to tell you," she said quietly. When Ben looked at her with alarm, she went on hurriedly, "Not about me. The reason I was questioning Raquel, why I thought she might have something to do with it."

Ben relaxed back into the cushions and raised an eyebrow at her. "Go on."

"Someone told me they had seen Raquel handing money to Terry from the till. The idea of blackmail did cross my mind then," she admitted.

Ben looked amused. "Giving out money is generally what people do with tills," he said. Keeley blushed.

"Yes, but this was a wad of money, apparently."

Now he looked more interested, if still a little skeptical.

"And who told you this? Are they, in your opinion, a reliable source?"

Keeley thought about Tom and his vacant expression, the smell of marijuana that clung to him, and his comments about naked yoga.

"Possibly not, no," she admitted. "But it would be a bit of a coincidence if it wasn't true." What was it with his insistence on defending Raquel? she thought with annoyance. "I mean, if it looks like she's responsible for the letters, and if she was being blackmailed by Terry, that seems pretty suspicious." Keeley had a thought. "You said he was hit with a blunt object? There must be lots of things that could do the trick in the diner."

Ben's mouth twitched. "You think she carried the coffee urn round to the café and clobbered him over the head with it?" When Keeley crossed her arms and glared at him, he held up his hands in a gesture of appeasement. "Okay, okay, I'm only teasing."

"Pretty bad taste," Keeley said huffily, "and you did say you didn't find the murder weapon."

"I said no such thing."

"You implied it."

"Maybe. But as I said, Raquel does have an alibi. But in light of the recent message, I will double-check it. And you have to promise me not to mention this to her until I do."

Keeley nodded with some reluctance, knowing she would have liked nothing better than to reveal to Raquel that she knew she was being blackmailed—if that was indeed the case.

"Scout's honor."

Ben laughed. "I was in the Scouts, you know. It was good preparation for the police force, in a way."

Keeley remembered Ben as he had been at school. He had belonged to all the clubs that the popular kids belonged to. Football, athletics, and the youth forum. She could well imagine him as a Scout. He had never seemed to have much time for girls, something that had given some slim comfort to a besotted Keeley. She hadn't been the only one to moon over Ben Taylor to no avail.

"I was never really the outdoorsy type," she said, remembering all the times she had been picked last for the hockey and netball teams, or been forced to run races on Sports Day that she had inevitably come last in. Plump and uncoordinated, her body had been a mystery to her, whereas Ben had displayed the same unconscious, masculine grace that was so evident in him now, even at an age when most boys were gangly and awkward.

"I remember you were always in your books. Cooked up a storm in Home Ec, though."

Keeley blinked at him, surprised. "You remember that? I never thought you took much notice of me, to be honest." She winced, wondering if her comment sounded as needy to him as it had felt to her, but Ben looked surprised himself. In fact, his cheeks were a little red.

"I did. It was third year we shared Home Ec class. I had the biggest crush on you."

"You had what?" Keeley blurted, shocked. When Ben looked offended, even hurt, she hastened to add, "I honestly had no idea." He must just be humoring her, she thought, trying to be nice.

"Well, I was a bit shy with girls back then. I made up for it in college," he said cheerfully, not noticing Keeley wince, then wince again as she remembered Raquel's comment at Mario's. She was beginning to think about the woman far too much. In fact, she couldn't help almost hoping she was behind it all, if only to get her away from Ben. Then she immediately felt awful for thinking such uncharitable thoughts.

"There's no significant someone in your life now?" she said, more to turn the conversation away from his college conquests than anything else, though as soon as she asked the question, she knew how much she wanted to know the answer. Part of her was still reeling from his revelation. He had had a crush on her? By the time they had reached third year and Home Ec class, her own crush had abated somewhat and he became just another popular boy to avoid, in case he too took up the sporadic teasing of her.

"No. I came out of a serious relationship about ten months ago. She got fed up with me working so much. You?"

"It's been a couple of years," Keeley admitted. "I've been busy with work too, I suppose. I was engaged once, after college," she said before even realizing she was about to. It wasn't something she liked talking about. Unfortunately, Ben looked very interested.

"Really? What happened?" When Keeley looked down, he touched her arm. It was the briefest of touches, yet felt searing through her cardigan. "Sorry, that was nosy. I get too used to asking people questions all day long."

"It's okay," she said. "He cheated on me." Embarrassed, she felt the sting of tears in her eyes and blinked rapidly to cover them, looking away. *I'm over it, what's wrong with me?* She admonished herself fiercely. To her surprise, Ben nodded in sympathy.

"That happened to me too, about five years ago. I suppose I should have expected it, it was a long-distance thing. Hurts like hell, doesn't it?"

"It does. But it was a long time ago now." Ben's confession had chased away her tears at least. It seemed ludicrous, that a woman would cheat on Ben, but logically, she knew she wasn't the only one to go through it, and even that it was no fault of her own. But knowing something intellectually and feeling it as an innate truth were very different modes of perception. Keeley had spent many an evening meditating on forgiveness after a particularly intense and purifying yoga sequence, but it seemed she was still more affected by it than she had thought. Or there was something about Ben's presence that seemed to bring her emotions much closer to the surface, leaving her feeling raw, as if her skin had been turned inside out.

Raw wasn't good. Raw meant getting hurt again.

Keeley stood up and looked pointedly at the clock.

"I'd better get ready for bed. It's been a long day."

Ben looked disappointed; then that blank, professional expression came over his face and he stood up as well, picking up the plastic Baggie containing the letter. Keeley looked at it. Talking to Ben, she had almost forgotten all about it.

"Don't worry," Ben said, noticing the direction of her gaze. "I'm going to get a patrol car doing the rounds this end of town, and keeping a close eye around Bakers Hill, in particular. Try to get some sleep, but make sure your phone is on and within reach. If you need anything, just call."

He was all professional concern again, and as Keeley opened the door to let him out, she opened her mouth to thank him, then closed it again in surprise as he bent down and kissed her swiftly on the cheek.

"Take care," he said in a tone that was almost tender, and then he was gone.

As Keeley bolted the door behind him, she noticed her hands were shaking a little, and didn't think she could put it entirely down to fear. One thing she was certain of, that her thoughts that night wouldn't be solely focused on Terry Smith or Raquel or even her plans for her business. No, they would be dominated by something else entirely. Something that gave her a tumbling feeling of both disbelief and pleasure low in her tummy.

Ben Taylor had had a crush on her.

Chapter Eleven

The next day, Keeley plucked up the courage to attend the morning's church service after an invitation from Annie after breakfast, and was grateful to see no one she recognized, especially Maggie or her friend Norma. There were only friendly faces, and the vicar's wife seemed very interested in the possibility of Keeley holding an evening yoga class at the church hall. Although she had never been a regular churchgoer, she had always attended Easter and Christmas services with her dad, and the familiar smells of wood polish and incense evoked a pang of nostalgia. Although she didn't take in all of the vicar's sermon, his lilting tones soothed her and she emerged into the sunshine feeling comforted.

"I told you you'd soon be fitting in fine," Annie said as they walked back up the hall. It was another nice spring day, the birds making a riot of sound, the hills stretching away into the distance, and Keeley felt a moment's gratitude that she lived here.

"I saw a police car driving up and down the hill last night." Annie gave her a tactful look out of the corner of her eyes. Keeley sighed, and decided it was time to let her landlady know what was happening at the cottage. Annie's eyes went wide as Keeley told her about the letters.

"How awful. Good Lord, but there are some horrible people in this world."

As they reached Rose Cottage, Annie peered up at the porch roof thoughtfully.

"Do you know, I could install CCTV here and round the back. That would deter whoever is behind it, I should think."

"That's a great idea," Keeley said, wondering why she hadn't thought of it herself. "But you shouldn't have to worry about that."

"Nonsense," Annie said in her kind but brisk manner, "I'll look into it this week. I've been meaning to get it alarmed for a while." They said good-bye and Keeley went into the cottage feeling a little more secure, though she still locked the door behind her.

That night, after waking up from a fitful sleep for the third time, Keeley made herself a cup of chamomile and sat in her bedroom window. She saw a patrol car come up the hill, its lights sweeping the road in front of it, and felt her breath quicken for a second before she remembered it wouldn't be Ben. He drove an unmarked car, being a detective rather than a uniformed constable. She gulped at her tea, swallowing down her disappointment.

Monday morning, however, she woke with a smile. Today work would finally begin on the café, and the place would be transformed over the next few days into her vision for it.

Armed with a large bag containing two tins of paint, brushes, and rollers, Keeley caught a cab to the High Street and got there a good half hour before the kitchen installers were due to arrive, letting herself through the front door and looking around. Although bare, it still had much the same layout as when it had been the butcher's, and this would be the last time she would see it like this. In spite of her adult aversion to meat, the memory of her father standing behind the counter with his white butcher's apron made her smile wistfully.

A sudden noise came from the direction of the kitchen and made her jump, nearly dropping her bag. She heard voices, then a sound like a bell ringing. Not quite in the kitchen, but very close. In fact, it sounded as if it were coming from her own backyard. Going through to the back, she saw the outline of a group of people through the windows. They began to talk at once in a strange monotone that made the hairs on the back of her neck stand on end. What on earth were they doing? Then she realized they were chanting. She had heard chanting before, some of the more meditative styles of yoga used it as a technique to calm the mind, but it had never sounded quite like this. Keeley unlocked the back door, unsure whether she should be angry, bemused, or scared. Or perhaps all three.

Five faces turned to her, mouths open mid-chant. She recognized one of them.

"Megan? What are you doing in my yard?" Keeley looked at her new friend, incredulous. Megan and her companions were dressed in long white robes, standing in a small circle. One of them carried a bell, which explained the ringing, and another was waving around a censer on a chain, from which emitted a foul-smelling smoke.

Megan smiled at her, her expression sheepish.

"I didn't think you would be here yet. Keeley, these are my

friends from my light-worker circle. This is Merdyn—" she indicated a portly man with long, matted hair, "—and this is Lilith Redfeather." A small woman with rather helmetlike gray hair gave her a little wave. Keeley held a hand up to stop Megan before she could introduce her other two friends, a woman with short pink hair and a young man with glasses and an earnest expression.

"I'm delighted to meet you. But Megan, what are you doing?" A gust of smoke blew into Keeley's face, and she coughed as she batted it away with an angry swipe of her hand. She was sure she saw curtains twitching in one of the windows from the houses that overlooked her yard. Wonderful.

"We were just doing a little banishing ritual. Of any lingering dark energies from the *murder*." She said the last word in a voice that, although hushed, somehow managed to sound incredibly loud. Her friends each gave a small shudder in unison. "I knew you were getting the café remodeled, and I thought it would give you an auspicious start. It's better done at the site of the murder, of course, but I wanted it to be a surprise. Of course, now that you're here, maybe we could go in?" Megan looked hopeful, but Keeley shook her head firmly.

"No, absolutely not. I don't want you doing this in my backyard either. How did you get in?"

Megan looked crestfallen, but also guilty. The man with the glasses piped up; "I just reached over and undid the bolt."

Keeley glared at him. "You weren't aware that a bolt usually means you're not permitted to come in?" She felt inexplicably furious at Megan, whether she had meant well or not. Her property had been invaded quite enough, and she couldn't quite believe her new friend could be so thoughtless. The man looked down, and his friends looked at each other, obviously uncomfortable.

"Perhaps we should go, Megs?" Pink Hair said, giving Keeley a nasty look. Indeed, Megan looked as though she were about to cry. Keeley sighed, relenting, and waved her into the kitchen, shutting the door firmly behind her before the others got any ideas.

"I'm sorry, Keeley," Megan sniffed, "I was just trying to help."

"Okay, I know. I'm sorry I was so angry. But, Megan, I've just been broken into, the place set on fire and a man killed." She stopped herself from automatically looking up at the ceiling. "The last thing I want is strange people coming into my backyard."

Megan's eyes widened. "Oh, Keeley, I just didn't think. I really am sorry. We just thought it would do the place, and you, good."

She looked so earnest, Keeley didn't have the heart to stay angry at her.

"Well, maybe when all the work's done, you can come and say a prayer or something? Just you. And no smelly stuff."

"It's only sage," Megan said a little huffily, then threw her arms around Keeley and squeezed her before stepping back and looking around. Her eyes went straight to the ceiling as if looking through it. Seeing not white plaster but the room above. Where it had all happened.

"The site of a murder can leave an awful negative imprint, you know. If you change your mind, I'm sure the group will only be too happy to help you cleanse the place."

"It'll be fine," Keeley assured her. She let her out the back door, giving her another hug, one that she instigated this time. Megan might be a little off the wall, but she was only trying to help, in her own inimitable way. Keeley hadn't made so many friends here that she could afford to lose them. Nevertheless, she bolted her back gate firmly after her white-robed companions. Then found herself leaning against it, shaking with silent laughter as the ludicrousness of it all hit her.

A masculine voice calling "Ms. Carpenter" at the front of the shop brought her attention back to the physical, rather than auric, transformation of the shop into her café. The kitchen contractors were here. Keeley greeted them with a warm smile, relieved to see only tool kits in their hands, not bells and censers.

After Keeley had shown them in and they got to work banging and hammering, Keeley retreated upstairs with her tins of paint. Although she was paying for the café itself to be decorated professionally, she had decided to give upstairs a fresh lick of paint herself. She wanted to be involved in the whole process, and any attempts on her part to cut costs would no doubt appease her mother. The little flat felt lighter than it had done now she had cleaned and aired it, and if any "imprints" of the murder remained, then Keeley was sure they were the product of her own mind rather than any supernatural residue. Although she agreed with Megan insofar as that bad atmospheres could indeed linger in a place, she felt the best way to create a better atmosphere would be to create happier memories there, rather than waft around some smoke. A coat of fresh paint would work wonders too. She threw herself into the task with gusto, relieved to feel that her plans for the Yoga Café were finally coming to fruition and she had work to do, a blessed relief from sitting in the cottage and jumping every time the wind rattled the letterbox.

Or thinking about Ben. His revelation had left her with a feeling she couldn't quite name. Pleasure, certainly, but also a tinge of regret that their apparently mutual interest in each other had never been made manifest. As she moved the roller up and down in continuous rhythm, she allowed herself to wonder how different her life would have been if Ben had been her first boyfriend.

And came up with the conclusion that any liaison would likely have consisted of little more than a kiss behind the proverbial bike sheds. She smiled wryly to herself at the thought of a teenage Raquel's reaction to a plump Keeley walking hand in hand through the school corridors with the best-looking boy in their school year. She would probably have tried to scratch her eyes out.

As she knelt down to put a fresh coat of paint on the roller, something sparkly caught her eye. Keeley frowned as she saw what looked like a gold coin wedged in a gap between the baseboard and the wall. After setting the roller down carefully, she prized it loose, only to realize it wasn't a coin at all, but a button. She stared at it glittering in the palm of her hand, a recent memory nagging at her consciousness. She had seen these buttons before. Then a thought struck her, bringing with it a throb of excitement. Could this have been left here from the night of the murder? Wedged into the skirting as it had been, it was possible the police would have missed it; they were searching for murder weapons, not buttons. Keeley stood up slowly, still staring at the button, her mind whirling through possibilities. It looked new, as though it hadn't been here very long, so it could well have come from the clothes of Terry Smith.

Or the murderer himself. Perhaps they had struggled? Keeley tried to imagine what item of clothing it could have come from. A blazer, jacket, or cardigan, most likely. It didn't look like the sort of thing Raquel would wear, she mused.

Keeley was so intrigued that when she heard Raquel's voice calling her name up the stairs, it took a minute to register that the voice wasn't just a product of her imagination. Then she heard the deeper voice of one of the workmen directing her upstairs and the insistent clip of Raquel's stilettos approaching.

"In here," Keeley called, slipping the button into the back pocket of her jeans. She drew her shoulders back and took a deep, fortifying breath, steeling herself against whatever vitriol Raquel was about to subject her to. Ben must have spoken to her by now. Keeley prayed that Raquel hadn't managed to sweet-talk herself out of it. Not that Ben seemed a soft touch by any means, but she still wasn't convinced there wasn't some kind of relationship between them, and if anyone could sweet-talk a man, it was Raquel Philips.

Raquel entered the room with a thunderous look on her immaculately made-up face, stopping a few feet away from Keeley, directly opposite her like a gunslinger at a noon showdown. Keeley resisted the urge to pick her roller back up.

"Is something wrong?"

Raquel moved her mouth in what was definitely a snarl.

"Yes, there is. What exactly were you thinking, sending Ben round to accuse me of some kind of smear campaign?"

So he had spoken to her, then. Quite harshly, judging by Raquel's reaction. Keeley swallowed and lifted her chin, looking the other woman directly in the eyes, determined not to be intimidated in the face of her anger. And she was angry—shaking, in fact, her curves quivering under her ultra-tight linen dress.

"I received some letters," Keeley said in a neutral tone, "that we thought might have come from you."

"We?" Raquel sneered. "A member of the police force now, are you? And why on earth would they come from me? You think I've got nothing better to do than harass you, Keeley Carpenter? Well, you're wrong. You came questioning me, remember?"

Keeley nodded. "That's why I thought of you. You were complaining to Ben that I was snooping."

"Because you were!" Raquel shouted, taking a step toward Keeley. Keeley felt her breath catch in her throat, though she stood her ground. She glanced at the door that led to the stairs, relieved to see Raquel had left it wide open. The banging noises from downstairs had ceased, and Keeley guessed the workmen were listening in the hopes of catching a juicy bit of gossip. Embarrassing, but at least Raquel couldn't try to hit her round the head with anything. She noticed how strong the other girl's arms looked, how stocky her shoulders. Terry Smith had, by all accounts, been a weedy little man.

"I was just asking a few questions," Keeley protested.

"About Terry. As if I had anything to do with it. And I suppose now the whole of Belfrey will know, won't they? Who told you?"

Keeley felt confused, aware that the subject had been changed but not sure to which topic.

"Told me what?"

Raquel took another step toward her, her face growing redder by the minute.

"Don't play dumb with me. You were always like that at school, with your big cow eyes, all innocent. But I know better. You told Ben about the money I was giving Terry, so who told you?"

Clarity dawning, Keeley shook her head.

"It wasn't anyone. Just something I, er, guessed."

"So you're psychic now, are you? Like your silly friend with the dreadlocks that was dancing around the backyard earlier." Raquel laughed, a cold and bitter sound with not a trace of humor in it. Keeley closed her eyes briefly, remembering the twitching curtain. Of course, the back of the diner would overlook her own backyard. Great.

"If you've got nothing to do with it, I don't see what you're so worried about," Keeley pointed out. Whatever Raquel had been paying Terry for, it was clearly something she wanted kept very quiet. Although she wasn't about to risk asking the irate woman in front of her directly, she couldn't help wondering just what her secret was. A married lover? Some kind of scandal related to the diner?

"I don't want the whole town knowing!" Raquel all but screamed. "How that horrible little man found out, I'll never know. I paid good money to make sure they looked as natural as possible."

Keeley frowned in confusion, then understood what Raquel was referring to as the woman gestured toward her own torso.

"You've had breast surgery," Keeley said, trying not to stare at the offending area, "and that's what you were paying Terry to keep quiet about?" *The woman's mad,* she thought.

At Keeley's words, Raquel gave a little moan and seemed to sag like a burst balloon. "You didn't even know, did you?"

Keeley shook her head.

"I knew about the money, but not why. Is it really such a concern to you?" The idea that she had been paying Terry Smith good money to keep quiet about a bit of cosmetic surgery seemed beyond vanity. Keeley had seen plenty of enhanced bodies during her time in London and America, and although in her experience, women didn't generally want to shout from the rooftops that they had had work done, she had never heard of anyone going to such lengths to hide it either. Although in a small town like Belfrey, any bit of gossip would no doubt become as overinflated as Raquel's breasts.

"Of course it is," Raquel snapped. "When I went away to uni, I had them done and never told anyone. I used the money Mum and Dad had given me to fund my studies."

"They don't know either," Keeley guessed. Not just vanity, then, but the very real possibility of having access to Daddy's money cut off. Mr. Philips was a rich man, owning properties and businesses all over Amber Valley. Keeley often thought that one of the reasons Darla hadn't liked Mrs. Philips was pure and simple jealousy. That and the unfortunate sharing of their first name. A few times, Keeley remembered her mother introducing herself, only to follow it up with, "No, not *that* Darla," with a touch of what sounded like regret in her voice, no doubt due to envy of her namesake's richer husband and more glamorous daughter.

The glamorous daughter who was now glaring at Keeley, her anger banking its fires again.

"No, and you're not going to tell them, do you hear me?"

"Of course not." Keeley felt offended. "I told Ben about the money only because, well, it looked suspicious." She wasn't entirely convinced the other girl wasn't behind the letters either.

"Suspicious!" Raquel hissed. "Says you, turning up the day after he was killed, and in your shop. You're probably making it up about the letters to get some attention. I suppose it's the only way you can." Raquel looked her up and down with a deliberately disdainful look. Keeley felt her own temper flare white-hot, remembering each and every one of Raquel's put-downs and malicious gibes over their formative years.

"How dare you!"

At that, Raquel stepped forward, closing the remaining gap between them, and pointed at Keeley.

"I had nothing to do with it, do you hear me? But if you tell anyone about this, I'll kill *you*, Keeley Carpenter."

With that, Raquel spun on her heel and stormed out, her stilettos striking the stairs with even more force than they had coming up. After a pause, during which Keeley stared at the door after her, the workmen resumed their hammering and banging. She hoped they weren't local, or the truth about Raquel's impressive physique would be all round the town by teatime.

Keeley raised a hand to her head, let out a slow breath, and bent down to pick up her roller and resume her painting, trying to make sense of that strange interlude. The whole day was turning out to be the one of the most bizarre she had ever experienced, and that was saying something, given the events of the past two weeks.

Even so, alibi or no alibi, Keeley was far from convinced that Raquel should be ruled out as a suspect. Her threats certainly didn't feel idle.

A few hours later, her shoulders and arms in need of a good stretch after a morning's painting, Keeley once again braved the Tavern for a bite to eat. Although there were plenty of other, nicer places to eat along the High Street, she felt drawn to the Tavern, knowing her father used to drink there.

Thankfully, Jack was alone this time, apart from Bambi, who waved his tail and gave an enthusiastic woof when he saw Keeley walk in. Tom wasn't in his usual spot, the bar being attended by an older woman with meaty forearms who leaned over the counter, looking bored. The Glovers were nowhere to be seen, for which she gave a loud sigh of relief. Jack nodded at her, and remembering Diana Glover's words about Jack giving Ted a talking-to for being rude to Keeley, she gave him a warm smile.

"Do you want a drink, Jack?"

He looked pleased. "Aye, I'll have a whisky and Coke, duck."

Keeley ordered their drinks from the sullen-looking barmaid and went to sit with Jack, scratching Bambi under the chin. The dog lolled his huge head to one side and looked at her through half-closed eyes with an expression of bliss. If only humans were so easily pleased.

"Everything going all right with the shop, then?"

"The café, yes." Keeley couldn't help correcting him, now that her vision for the place was finally coming together. "The work should be done on it by early next week; I've got the kitchen fitters in today."

Jack gave her a sage nod and took a slow drag on his pipe. It was hard to judge what Jack thought about anything, Keeley mused. Unless he chose to make his views plain, he was somewhat inscrutable. She got the impression that a lot more went on behind that closed countenance than people perhaps gave him credit for.

"It must be strange for you to see it being done up, after you worked there so long." It often slipped her mind that Jack had taken on the butcher's business for a while after her father's death.

Jack just shrugged, obviously not in a nostalgic mood.

"Things change." He took a long swig of his whisky. Keeley surveyed the menu and decided on the vegetable lasagna—the only vegetarian dish they offered. It had to be better than the sandwiches.

As she went back to the bar to place her order, the door to the

Tavern swung open, letting some much-needed light and air into the dingy interior, and the mayor came in, a smile on his face that grew a little fixed as his eyes lingered on Keeley. Then he beamed and waved at her, as if only just remembering who she was. To her surprise, he pulled up a chair to sit with her and Jack, and the old man greeted him amiably. Keeley went back over and sat down, and Bambi looked at Gerald and gave a little growl low in his throat before edging closer to Keeley and putting his great head in her lap, looking at the mayor as if to warn him away. Keeley gave him a rub behind the ears, confused.

"The mayor here isn't a fan of dogs," Jack said, "and Bambi picks up on it, you see. Dogs don't like it when they sense nerves."

She wasn't the only one to think there was a nervous edge to the mayor, then, who was now dragging his seat farther round the table, putting more distance between himself and the dog.

"All ready for the food festival?" Jack asked. Keeley leaned forward, remembering Annie's advice. She had meant to find out today about booking a stall, but what with Megan's chanting and Raquel's confessions, it had completely slipped her mind.

The mayor was nodding, a touch of pride in his voice as he spoke. "Oh yes, most definitely. It will be up the High Street as usual, and as we've got extra stalls, there will be some in the community center also. We've got some extras too—workshops for the kiddies, that sort of thing."

"Mr. Mayor?" Keeley cut in, feeling a little silly at her use of his role but feeling she should acknowledge it. "Is it you that's in charge of organization? Only I was wondering if it would be too late to get myself a stall."

"What a lovely idea!" Gerald exclaimed after a moment's hesitation. "It's a little late to apply, but I do believe there are one or two spaces. It's organized by the local farmers and the church ladies mostly, but I'm sure I can pull a few strings to get you a spot. I'll do it this afternoon, in fact. And do call me Gerald."

"Thank you." It was a start, Keeley thought, to making the Yoga Café an integral part of the High Street. The people of Belfrey may take a while to accept outsiders, but she also knew that once you were "in," you were "in." She wondered if it wouldn't be too late to have a template of the shop sign made, just as a cardboard display for the stall. She would have to hope all her new utensils and pots and pans arrived on time too. Paper plates and cups would do for eating off, and they could always go into the recycling bin to save waste.

"What do you think, Jack?" she asked, turning to the older man, who was still puffing away silently on his pipe. "A vegetarian stall at the food festival."

Jack gave one of his trademark shrugs.

"Hardly my sort of thing, lass. Some folks might like it, I suppose."

Keeley felt deflated, but soldiered on. "I was speaking to Diana Glover on Saturday, she came to my yoga class. I was thinking I could have some eggs and milk off her to use in my dishes. It might appease Ted, anyway."

Jack didn't answer, just puffed away on his pipe, looking deep in thought. Gerald, on the other hand, seemed to think it was a great idea, nodding at Keeley so hard, his extra chins wobbled.

"Yes, that's a fantastic idea. Community spirit, that's what the food festival is all about."

"We could do with some of that," Jack said, "after Terry going and getting himself killed."

An odd choice of phrase, Keeley thought, as if Terry Smith

had had a foolish accident, or was somehow implicit in his own murder.

"Well, let's not talk about that unpleasantness," Gerald said quickly with a sidelong glance at Keeley. "I'm sure Miss Carpenter here has had quite enough."

In a flash, Keeley recalled exactly where she had seen the gold button before. She had thought Gerald's manner, and his reaction to the murder, odd the first time she had met him, in Megan's shop.

When he had been wearing a cardigan with flashy gold buttons, exactly like the one she had found lodged in the wall above her café. Had one of them been missing? She tried to recall, her heart beating a tattoo in her chest, while she kept her face neutral, not wanting the mayor to sense there was anything amiss. Instead she gave Gerald a happy smile as though she were grateful for his apparent concern.

"I heard you were going on holiday not long after the Festival," Jack said, changing the subject.

"Yes, to Australia to visit my brother and his wife for a few weeks. A holiday is long overdue, I'm afraid. I only hope Belfrey can tick along without me!" He gave an overloud laugh that neither Keeley nor Jack returned. Jack was tapping his pipe on the table, gazing at it intently.

"It's blocked," he announced to no one in particular, then said, still glaring at his pipe, "That will cost you a pretty penny won't it, Gerald?"

Gerald looked less happy. Almost flustered, in fact.

"Very reasonable rates, actually. Very reasonable." Gerald drank his pint in one long swallow and stood, smiling at both Keeley and Jack without looking directly at either of them.

"I must be off. See you soon, the two of you. Keeley, I'll let you know about the stall, splendid idea." And he was gone. Keeley looked at Jack, who was puffing on his now unblocked pipe. The button felt as though it were burning a hole in her back pocket.

"That was a bit strange, don't you think?"

"What's that, lass?"

"The way he rushed off then. As soon as you mentioned his holiday."

Jack sat back in his chair, eyeing Keeley as though he were weighing her up. Bambi gave her a palm a little lick, a seal of approval, Keeley thought, as Jack then leaned over the table and spoke in a quiet tone.

"He was in here a few weeks ago, had a bit too much to drink and was all but crying into his pint. A sorry sight, lass. Said he was in financial difficulties. Then he clammed up and rushed off. Just like then, in fact."

Keeley mulled that over, along with her surprise that a usually stoic Jack had repeated that bit of information to her.

"He must be doing better now, then, if he's off to Australia. Or maybe you made him feel guilty about spending the money." *Or maybe,* Keeley's newly awakened inner sleuth reared her head, *he's not planning on coming back.*

Maybe he had a secret too. One more serious than a bit of cosmetic surgery. One that he had been paying to keep quiet—hence the financial difficulty. Pieces of information came together in Keeley's mind like a kaleidoscope, an image that would come into focus if she could just find the right way of looking at it. A little spark of excitement flared inside her, her curiosity sharpened. Gerald had cornered Terry and killed him in the flat—but why there? A thought struck her, one that would explain why her café had come into play at all. Perhaps Gerald had been planning some kind of secret liaison there, and Terry had followed him? Of course, that raised the possibility of another person who knew the truth about what had happened that night.

The author of the poison pen letters?

Keeley felt her mouth go dry with a mixture of excitement and fear. She felt sure she was on to something.

Debating whether she should attempt to question Gerald, she reflected that as she had already incurred the possibly murderous wrath of Raquel, she didn't need to go making an enemy of the mayor as well.

Plus, she had promised Ben.

Nevertheless, the little button nagged at her all the way home, and later that night when she took it out of her pocket and placed it on the dresser next to her bed, it seemed to wink at her in the lamplight, as though daring her to find out its secrets.

Chapter Twelve

Keeley didn't see Ben until the following night. After a long day of painting, not to mention her confrontation with Raquel, Keeley felt physically and mentally drained and slept like a baby for the first time in a long time, oblivious to any patrolling cars keeping a watchful eye. She had woken up feeling refreshed, threw herself into a rejuvenating yoga flow, and caught the bus to the café, where she spent another productive day. The upstairs apartment was nearly finished, the kitchen had been installed, and the decorators had begun downstairs. Watching her mental picture of her business emerge before her eyes made her feel almost maternal, as though she were watching the dream she had been incubating finally being birthed. She put all thoughts about Gerald and his mysterious money worries to one side and had thankfully had no more visits from Raquel. All in all, it had been a good day, and late evening found her curled up on the sofa in front of her favorite cookery program.

The sharp rap on the door made her look up, at first startled, then with annoyance as she realized it was indeed the knocker she had heard and not the rattle of the letterbox delivering another ominous missive.

When she opened the door and saw Ben, she wished she had stopped to check her hair or apply a little gloss. Dressed as he was in casual blue jeans and a long-sleeved tee, his hair slightly rumpled and with a five o'clock shadow, she couldn't deny how delicious he looked.

"Hey," she said, feeling suddenly shy.

"Hey, yourself." He looked awkward for a second before regaining his usual composure. "I just thought I would stop by in person tonight, to check on you. I know you were a bit shook up the other night."

"I'm fine. Everything's been quiet ever since."

"Good, I'm glad."

They stood in silence for a moment, Keeley wondering whether she should invite him in, or if it would seem inappropriate now he was obviously off duty, before they both went to speak at once. Giving a little laugh, Ben waved his hand to indicate she should go first.

"I was just going to say that Raquel came to see me. She didn't look too happy."

"She wasn't too happy with me when I questioned her either," Ben said with a grin. "She called me some very rude names, in fact."

"So you don't think it's her, then?"

"I wouldn't rule her out on the letters, no. I'm sure you

won't be surprised to hear that no fingerprints came back. But hopefully, if it was her, then being caught out will be enough to warn her off."

Or hate me even more, Keeley thought.

"Did she tell you why she was giving Terry money?"

Ben nodded, and as they caught each other's eyes, they laughed simultaneously.

"I can't believe she thinks no one knows. I would have thought it was obvious." Ben said.

"Well, I didn't realize, and I'm a girl," Keeley pointed out. Ben looked thoughtful, and not wanting him to be considering Raquel's breasts any more than he had to, she heard herself add, "Do you want to come in? I was just putting the kettle on." She winced at the white lie. Ben gave her a wide smile and stepped inside, shutting the door after him. Acutely aware of his close proximity in the small porch, Keeley felt her body temperature rack up a notch or two and hurried into kitchen. She expected Ben to sit down in the lounge, but instead he followed her through, looking round with approval at her cottage. It was a traditional kitchen, with stone floors and big windows that let in a great deal of light, wooden beams overhead and another open hearth with a small log burner.

"That will come in handy in the winter," Ben said. "They get cold, these old cottages. Very beautiful. Those flowers need watering," he added. Indeed, the glorious bouquet Annie had left her was looking rather wilted. She added a little water into the heavy vase before getting on with making the tea, but reflected they would most likely be dead in a day or two.

"I'll have to replace them. Annie gave me them when I moved in, and the vase. She's been very kind."

"Yes," Ben smiled. "She's a nice woman. I always got on very well with Donald too. She was absolutely distraught when he died, poor woman."

"What happened?"

"Had a sudden stroke. Completely unexpected, he was as fit as a fiddle. A bit like your—" He stopped abruptly, his eyes widening as he realized what he was about to say.

"It's okay." Keeley gave a small shrug in spite of the wave of sadness that washed over her, "One nice thing about being back is hearing people talk about him."

"Doesn't your mother ever talk about him? I suppose we all handle grief differently."

Keeley shook her head cynically. "I don't think my mother has enough emotional depth for grief." *In fact,* Keeley thought, *I don't think I've seen her cry once.*

She carried the cups through and sat on the rug in front of the sofa, feeling as if she shouldn't sit too close to Ben. She had spent the last two days with his words chiming in her head, filling her with a strange, fluttery sort of hope, but now that he was here, she was beginning to feel like that shy schoolgirl again. Ben took his cup from her and sat down, not on the farthest side of the sofa as she expected him to, but the one nearest to her, so that she was effectively sitting at his feet. That wasn't right either, but she would look a little strange if she now got back up and sat next to him, so instead she scooted a little nearer the hearth on the pretext of placing her cup there. Another awkward silence descended.

"I saw Gerald in the Tavern today," she said, searching for something to say. She was about to tell him of her plans for the food festival, when Ben put his cup down and looked at her, his face serious.

"I hope you haven't been asking questions again?"

"No, of course not. I said I wouldn't, didn't I?" She had been going to tell him about Jack's comment regarding the mayor's finances, along with her discovery of the button, but seeing that grim look on Ben's face decided Keeley against it. He would never believe she hadn't deliberately tried to uncover the information, and until she could definitely connect the button to the mayor, she had little concrete evidence to go on. Instead she told him briefly about the stall, and then lapsed again into quiet. What she really wanted to know was the details of this "crush," she thought, but was far too embarrassed to bring it up and make it obvious his words had made an impression.

In the end, it was Ben who both broke the silence and brought up that very subject.

"About what I said the other night—I hope I didn't offend you?"

Keeley felt her heart rate increase, beating a tattoo in her chest. She shook her head. "When you mocked my attempt at sleuthing?" she asked with a laugh, although she knew exactly what he was referring to and felt her mouth go dry.

"No, the bit about my crush on you at school."

Keeley felt her cheeks catch fire and turned her face slightly, her hair falling forward in an attempt to cover it.

"Of course not. I was quite flattered, really."

"It's just that you seemed to want to end the conversation all of a sudden."

Keeley thought back to that moment.

"Not because of you. We were talking about past relationships, and it's a bit of a sore subject, I suppose."

"Because of the guy who cheated on you?"

Keeley nodded, her face flaming again. Although she was coming to appreciate Ben's directness, apart from when he was accusing her of something, it could be a little disconcerting, to say the least.

"It was a long time ago," she said, aiming for nonchalance.

"Still hurts, though, right?" When Keeley didn't answer, he added, "Tell me to be quiet if you want, I don't want you to think I'm interrogating you. You're just so, I don't know, intriguing. Elusive."

Ben thought she was intriguing? Keeley pushed down the little jump of excitement in her belly.

"I was so gullible, really," she began, feeling now that she wanted to talk, wanted to share something of herself with him. "I was eighteen, had never really had a proper boyfriend, and he came along and said all the right things. He was older than me, very handsome, and we were engaged within a year. I thought I had the fairy tale—even my mother was pleased." And had made no secret of the fact that she was thoroughly disappointed in her daughter when she had failed to keep such a prize catch, she thought to herself with a touch of long-buried bitterness.

"Then he cheated on you." Ben made it a statement, not a question. He shook his head, looking almost angry. "What an idiot."

"I think he probably always was," Keeley admitted, feeling the sting of betrayal even after so long, "and I just didn't want to see it. I was so grateful he even wanted to be with me." Ben tutted in annoyance at her statement, but didn't say anything. Keeley sighed, wincing as she thought back to how weak and insecure she had been.

"It toughened me up," she said, not sure if her attempt at a positive spin was for Ben's sake or her own, "and if we had stayed together and got married, I would probably be desperately unhappy right now. It always annoyed him that I wouldn't eat meat as well. Made eating out a little more difficult."

"It wasn't because of him you got into the whole vegetarian thing?" Ben sounded genuinely interested, leaning forward on the edge of the seat so that the gap she had deliberately placed between them was traversed. Any physical awareness of his presence, however, was diminished by the memories that assailed her. One in particular that still, every so often when the nights were particularly long and lonely, haunted her dreams.

"No," she said in a small voice, so that Ben had to lean even farther forward to hear her. "Not exactly. I met him at the gym, and found yoga through a friend of his, so I suppose I should thank him—Brett, his name was—for that, at least. But I stopped eating meat after my father died. It didn't become a conscious nutritional choice until later on."

"Oh?" Ben gave a hesitant nod, as if wanting her to go on but not wanting her to say more than she wished. Keeley shifted uncomfortably.

"My father had a small abattoir out the back of our house on the High Street," she began, closing her eyes against the visual images that took shape before them, "as there wasn't much room outside the shop, you know. Sometimes the local farmers would bring animals, to, you know . . ."

"That couldn't have been nice to grow up with."

"Well, it was just normal, really. And he took pride in being very humane in his methods. Anyway, when he had his heart attack, he was in there, preparing a pig carcass."

Ben grimaced. "Did your mother really need to tell you that?"

Keeley shook her head, her mother being, for once, blameless. "She didn't need to. It was me that found him."

Ben sucked his breath in sharply. Keeley went on, her voice sounding far away even to her own ears, as though it were someone else who was relaying events. Describing how she had seen her father lying on the floor, his face waxy and unreal looking, as though it were a puppet made to look like her father. How the pig carcass lay next to him on the floor. How she had looked from one to the other, her brain struggling to process what was happening.

Then she had screamed.

"I haven't touched meat since. About a year after he died, I came out of my shell a bit, started college, got into my fitness, and, of course, met Brett."

"You were vulnerable," Ben said, sounding as though he spoke through gritted teeth, "and he took advantage of that."

"I let him, I suppose. But if I hadn't met him then, I might not have ended up doing what I'm doing, and this is definitely the right path for me. I started studying nutrition when I realized I was never going to eat meat again and couldn't survive on cheese sandwiches for the rest of my life." She smiled, but Ben looked at her seriously.

"It must mean a lot to you, then, that this café is a success here."

Keeley frowned. She hadn't consciously connected the two, but perhaps Ben was right. After all, she could have carried on her teaching practice and even opened a café anywhere, using any profits from the sale of the shop. In taking it over, coming back to Belfrey, maybe what she was really attempting to do was lay the ghosts of her father's death to rest.

Instead, she seemed to have created a few more. She thought of Terry Smith, whose body would have been left to burn if the killer hadn't been interrupted, again like so much meat. Apparently without even anyone to mourn his passing.

Ben reached for her hand, which was swallowed by the size of his palm. His fingers brushed hers, and she stared at their joined hands, thinking with a strange detachment how strong and brown his forearms were, how rough his palms. Worker's hands, rather than a detective's.

There was a strange hush in the room, as if even the night air held its breath, and Ben was looking at her so intently, Keeley found herself holding hers too.

Whatever he had wanted to say was forgotten as a sound like the crunching of gravel came through the open window and broke the silence. A sound like someone was outside. Ben dropped her hand and jumped up, cursing, and went to the window, then to the front door when he obviously saw nothing. He came back in, shaking his head, while Keeley sat frozen in the same spot, unsure what had just passed between them but feeling that something had, something new.

"Probably a cat or something. Even I'm jumping at shadows now. I hope you're locking all your windows and doors at night?"

Keeley nodded. Ben sat back down, but angled a little away from her now, making no attempt to retake her hand. Her palm seemed to burn where he had touched it. Feeling suddenly self-conscious, she sat on it.

"I'm sorry," he said, not meeting her eyes. "I didn't mean to bring up so painful a subject."

"It felt good to talk about it," Keeley said honestly. Although what she knew of Ben wouldn't prompt her to describe him as someone who would make a likely confidant, she had indeed felt strangely comfortable sharing such an intimate memory with him. It must make him a good detective, she thought, if it was an effect he routinely had on people.

"Would you like another drink?" She stood up, and Ben stood up with her, putting them close enough that she had to tip her head back a little to look up at him.

"No. Not another drink, no," he said obliquely. Keeley frowned, trying to decipher his response, when he stepped forward and made it easy for her.

He kissed her.

It wasn't a soft kiss either. No gentle brushing of his lips against hers, no hesitancy in his touch. He pulled her against him, lifting her up onto his toes, and kissed her with enough force, it stole her breath. *I should stop this,* she thought, then realized she was kissing him back with just as much urgency, and that her hips were pushing forward into his body, her back arching against his hands, as though her body had a will and an intention all of its own, and that intention was an exact opposite to the one her thoughts had just expressed.

Ben buried a hand in her hair, giving a slight tug on the nape of her neck that resulted in a low moan from deep in her throat, a spontaneous sound that would have embarrassed her had she had any coherent thoughts left. Her body felt on fire in his arms, a pool of liquid heat gathering low in her belly. Her own hands were coiled around his neck, pulling him to her as fiercely as he gripped her.

It was Ben who broke the kiss first, though he didn't let go of his hold on her but stared into her eyes. His own burned with such an obvious desire, it scared and excited her all at the same time.

"I have wanted to do that since I walked into the Tavern and saw you last week," he murmured, his voice low, and dropped his gaze back to her lips. This time, their mouths met more slowly, more sensuously, exploring the feel and taste each of other. The change in pace, however, did nothing to slow down her heartbeat, or the waves of desire that crashed into her. Every nerve ending on her body felt alive, and Keeley was suddenly aware of exactly how long it had been since a man held her like this. Scratch that—a man had *never* held her like this. She had to stop and get ahold of herself, she knew, before she pulled him down onto the rug and threw caution to the wind, but her body seemed to be oblivious to any sense of reason. Judging by the way Ben held on to her arm, one hand now clutching at her buttocks, drawing her into him, he was thinking—or rather not thinking—in much the same way.

The loud knock at the door made Keeley jump, jolting her back to reality and out of Ben's arms. She stared at the door, disoriented, and made no attempt to cut in when Ben, his composure regained while she still stood gaping, went into the porch and opened the front door authoritatively.

"Is Keeley there?" asked a hesitant and evidently curious female voice. Megan. Keeley hurried to the door, breathing a sigh of relief until she saw Duane standing next to her, a bunch of flowers in his hand. Ben and Duane were staring at each other, a not-so-subtle display of machismo that Keeley found alarming rather than flattering. It was, of course, Duane who dropped his eyes first, but there was the hint of a smirk in his eyes as he turned to Keeley and held out the flowers.

"For you, beautiful lady," he said in a voice so dripping with charm, she could spread it on toast. The corner of Ben's mouth curled just slightly with a hint of contempt, then his face became carefully blank, his expression betraying nothing as he turned to look at Keeley.

"I'll be going, then, Ms. Carpenter. Be sure to lock up securely. If you're alone tonight." He said the last in a flat, neutral tone, but there was a definite hint of something in his eyes. Disappointment, perhaps. He left, leaving Keeley staring after him, her mouth feeling swollen from their kiss, wanting to call him back but reluctant to do so in front of her visitors, who were both staring at her curiously, and in Duane's case with a definite touch of jealousy. Keeley ushered them in, flustered.

As soon as they were inside, Keeley thanked Duane for the bouquet, but Megan interrupted her with a loud tut directed at her cousin.

"The flowers are from me, Keeley; I gave them to Duane to hold when I knocked the door. I wanted to say sorry for yesterday, I understood only after thinking about it afterward how much of an imposition it was."

"It's fine, honestly," Keeley said, trying not to glare at Duane for having deliberately misled Ben as she took the flowers from him and went into the kitchen. She may as well replace the wilted bunch with these fresh ones, she thought, and began emptying out Annie's vase. Megan followed her in, Duane staying in the lounge.

"Why was DC Taylor here?" Megan asked, her brow furrowing. "Have they found out who it was yet? The High Street is getting very jumpy about it all, you know. The Derby City paper covered the murder yesterday, and with it coming up to the food festival, I think the worry is that fewer people will come."

"I would have thought there would be more, out of curiosity," Keeley said as she arranged the flowers and sat the vase back onto the window ledge. Although she had neatly sidestepped Megan's inquiry about Ben, she wasn't about to let it go that easily.

"I hope he doesn't still think you had something to do with it?"

Keeley felt her face go hot as she thought of herself and Ben kissing by the fire.

"No, I really don't think he does," she said in as noncommittal a tone as she could manage. Which wasn't so convincing as she might have liked, judging by the way Megan's frown eased and a sudden understanding showed in her eyes.

"Ah, you like him," she said, her voice low. "So that's why Duane acted so weird about the flowers."

Keeley smiled. For all her talk about auras and psychic impressions, it seemed Megan's grasp of good old-fashioned body language and male pride wasn't quite so far reaching. Then she thought about Megan's statement. Did she like Ben Taylor? "Like" seemed a woefully inadequate word for the unrest he stirred in her. She had had various different reactions to the man since arriving in Belfrey, some of them far from positive, but they were all powerful. As she followed Megan into the lounge after they had both cooed appropriately over the flowers, Keeley looked at Duane standing near the fire, looking awkward, right in the spot where she and Ben had been kissing, and wondered how she could ever have even contemplated dating the gym instructor. "Like" was about as strong as her opinion of Duane was ever likely to be.

The three of them made small talk, with Megan intermittently repeating her apology and Keeley hastening each time to once again forgive her, but her attention was elsewhere. Her mouth still felt warm and tender from the touch of Ben's, so much so, it seemed to her that Megan and Duane must be blind not to see it. Part of her was disappointed their impromptu visit had interrupted their clinch, but a larger part of her was glad. Because she'd never been the type to jump into bed with a man at whim, the strength of her reaction to Ben and the knowledge that she had been a breath away from losing all sensibility made her nervous. Yet also, strangely reckless. She found she wanted to see him again, very badly and as quickly as possible, for reasons that had nothing to do with recent murder cases or arson attempts or even anonymous letters. Keeley wasn't sure that Ben the detective was someone she could ever be comfortable around, but Ben the man, that was turning out to be a very different prospect.

She saw Megan looking at her with a strange expression on her face.

"Is it a bad time, Keeley? I should have called first."

Keeley flushed. "No, of course not, it's just been a funny few days, that's all."

"Right," Megan looked uncertain, and Keeley hoped she wasn't going to start apologizing again. "Well, perhaps we had better get off." She glanced at Duane, who unusually for him had said very little. Now he looked at Keeley hopefully.

"I might pop in the Baker's Inn for a drink, after I've dropped Meg home. Do you want to join me?"

He looked so keen that Keeley felt like she was kicking a puppy as she said a polite no.

"I need to be at the café early, the decorators are coming. But I'll see you Sunday at the center perhaps?"

Duane nodded, giving her his trademark dazzling smile, though it seemed a little forced. He barely looked at her as she showed them out, although Megan gave her another incense-scented hug and waved warmly as they went down the hill.

Hopefully Duane would get the message this time; although his persistence was flattering, it was also a little embarrassing for them both. She guessed Duane wasn't used to being turned down by any woman, and hoped he wasn't the type to turn sulky. He was, after all, sort of a friend, and she was having enough trouble making them in Belfrey as it was.

What was Ben? The thought nagged at her as she went round locking up, double-checking everything just to be absolutely sure she could feel safe in her bed that night. Not that she was expecting to get much sleep. Not with the memory of Ben's mouth on hers, of his hands on her hair, and other parts of her. What was Ben? She couldn't call him a "friend." Less than a day ago, she would have placed him in a much lesser category, physical attraction notwithstanding. Now, in the space of an hour, he had become something else, something more, which was she was almost afraid to put a name to.

DIRGA—THREE-PART BREATH

This *pranayama* is nourishing, calming, and relaxing. It will bring the blood pressure down, making it perfect for grounding oneself after an unexpected romantic moment.

Method

- Close your eyes and consciously relax the face and body.
- Take a few deep, slow breaths through the nose.
- As you inhale, let your belly fill up with air like a balloon. As you exhale, let it return to normal.
- Continue these "belly breaths" for five inhalations and exhalations.
- Inhale deeply, drawing breath into the belly; then pause.
- Inhale a little more, feeling the breath fill your rib cage.
- Inhale a little more, feeling the breath fill your chest and heart, up to your throat.
- Exhale part of the breath, emptying your chest.
- Exhale part of the breath, emptying your rib cage.
- Exhale the rest of the breath, emptying your belly.
- Continue for ten breaths.

You can perform this breath while lying on your back for extra relaxation. Try it before bed to aid restful sleep.

Chapter Thirteen

The next morning, Keeley was still asking herself the same question, even as she let in the decorators, made various phone calls to the wholesalers and the sign installers and furniture company, who seemed to be in some confusion over the new delivery date. Usually on the patient side—or at least she tried to be—Keeley felt agitated and angsty. More so as the morning wore on and there was no word from Ben.

She replayed the kiss in her mind over and over, and the strangely intimate conversation that had somehow prompted it. As though by letting him into that hidden part of her psyche, she had issued him an invitation. On some level, she felt that was exactly what she had done. An invitation to exactly what, that was the part she hoped Ben hadn't misinterpreted. She wasn't a roll-by-the-fireside type of girl, but kissing him in that way, only to be interrupted by a flower-wielding Duane, well, it didn't look good.

She wondered if Ben hadn't called because of that, assuming Keeley was involved with the fitness instructor in spite of her earlier dismissal of him. That little face-off in her doorway had reminded her of the male-dominance displays she'd seen on wildlife programs, pheromones and testosterone heavy in the air.

Or he could just be busy with work. Or not really that interested, the kiss having been a spur-of-the-moment impulse he later regretted. The suspense, Keeley thought, was just as sweaty-palm-inducing as any involvement in local murder cases.

After nearly dropping the hammer on her foot while hanging pictures in the studio apartment above the flat, missing her little toe by a hairsbreadth, Keeley gave in. It was around lunchtime; he had to take a break from work at some point. She would call him.

Ben answered on the third ring. He had her number, she knew, because other times she had called, he answered saying her name, but this morning there was a pause when he answered, a slight clearing of the throat, and then a neutral "DC Taylor." Keeley felt her insides flip at the sound of his voice.

"Ben?" Her voice came out high-pitched, more of a squeal than the sultry purr she had been aiming for. Ben was immediately concerned.

"Keeley, what is it? Have you got another letter?"

"No," Keeley made a conscious effort to talk more calmly, "everything's fine."

"Okay." He sounded relieved; then there was a uncomfortable pause as Keeley desperately sought for something to say. She should have rehearsed this first, she thought, but whatever she had been expecting from Ben, it wasn't this utter normality. As if nothing had happened. She felt her tummy sink and leaned against the wall with one hand. There was an expectant silence on the other end of the line.

"I was calling about last night," she said. There was a pause, a small inhalation of breath, but when he spoke, his voice was neutral. Worse than that. It was distant.

"What about last night?"

Keeley closed her eyes in distress. He was being deliberately obtuse, and there could be only one reason for that: he regretted the kiss. Almost hoping it was because of Duane, she steeled herself and went on.

"Duane came round with Megan, you know. She brought those flowers for me."

"Is this going somewhere?" Ben sounded annoyed. "Because I really do have a lot to do today." Disappointment hit Keeley like a ton of bricks, coupled with a tinge of humiliation. Closing her eyes against the onslaught of feelings, she said in a tight voice, "Of course. I'm sorry."

"Okay." Ben put the phone down without even the courtesy of a good-bye. Keeley crouched down on the floor, feeling nauseated even as she tried to tell herself not to be so silly. That it was just a kiss. That it clearly meant nothing to him, and so it should mean less than nothing to her.

Pulling herself together, she got up and finished hanging her pictures. The upstairs apartment looked just as she wanted it, fresh and inviting, but she found it hard to muster up any enthusiasm after Ben's dismissal. She tried not to read too much into his manner, but the taste of rejection was bitter in her mouth. When the phone rang, her heart jumped in her chest, only to sink again when the call display showed it was merely her landlady.

"I saw Renee, that's the minister's wife, this morning, and she asked me to let you know they've got a stall for you next week at the food festival." Annie's warm voice, sounding pleased with herself, vibrated through the speaker. Keeley forced a smile, even though the older woman couldn't see her.

"That's brilliant, Annie. Thank you."

"Not at all. Let me know if you need any help preparing anything. Oh, and you need to fill out some sort of vendor license for the day. Renee said she would drop a form off, but if you're on the High Street, Mr. Buxby should have some too, if he's around."

"I will. Thank you." Her attempt to inject some cheeriness into her tone obviously fell flat, as her landlady asked her, after a pause, "Are you all right, dear? You sound a little upset."

Keeley hastened to reassure her, blaming the fact she was up to her ears with getting the café straight, and rang off before her friend could question her further. In truth, she could do with someone to talk to about Ben, another female, but it didn't seem appropriate to discuss last night with the older widow. There was Megan, but Keeley was sure she would try to brew her up a love potion or similar. With a pang, she realized how much she missed her old friends and resolved to phone Carly when she got home.

Slipping her phone back into her pocket, she felt it jingle against the gold button, which she had picked up that morning, and thought again about Annie's comments. Mr. Buxby was, of course, Gerald. Who had apparently been having financial problems until recently, and now was not. Because Terry Smith had been killed and he couldn't blackmail him anymore? Because he had been the one to make sure of that? Leaving a vital clue behind in the process? What with thinking about Ben's kiss, she had all but forgotten about the button and that she had meant to tell him about Jack's little bit of gossip, until he had frowned on her for asking questions.

Which she hadn't done, of course. Jack had volunteered that bit of information quite freely, and the impression she had of Jack was that if he had done so, then he thought it was significant. And Jack, she was sure, was nobody's fool. As for not asking questions—well, she was certainly in no mood for Ben Taylor to tell her what to do. She shrugged her coat on and set off for Gerald's house before she could change her mind.

As she walked there, however, she wondered if she wasn't being too impulsive. Her attempts to uncover the murderer before, when she had thought it might be Raquel, had resulted in little but trouble and alerting the murderer to her interest. She would be wiser, not to mention safer, to be a bit more discreet this time. Her steps slowed as she neared Crystals and Candles. Perhaps she should just go in for a cup of chamomile with Megan and have a well-needed moan about Ben.

Crystals and Candles displayed a large CLOSED FOR LUNCH sign on the door. Keeley peered through the windows but saw no sign of Megan. She stood for a moment, torn between continuing to Gerald's house or returning to the café. She had the pretext of picking up the license form, but she doubted the mayor really wanted to be bothered with paperwork. In fact, she wasn't sure just exactly what a mayor did, having only a vague idea that it involved ceremonial jewelry and historic buildings. She decided to knock the door, ask for the form, casually mention Terry Smith, and see if he had the same nervous reaction that she had noticed before. That was all.

The mayor's residence was a large, white brick house with

well-tended gardens, yet not so grand as she had expected. She rang the doorbell, hearing it echo inside the building. It seemed to be a long time before anyone answered, and she was about to turn away when the door creaked open a few centimeters. It wasn't Gerald but a small, thin woman with iron-colored hair in a high bun and steely eyes. She stared at Keeley, waiting for her to announce herself.

"Hello, I was wondering if Gerald was in."

"You mean Mr. Buxby." The woman's voice dripped with disapproval. This must be Edna, Keeley thought, the housekeeper with the terrible headaches.

"Yes. Sorry. Mr. Buxby. It's Keeley Carpenter, about the food festival. Annie, Mrs. Rowland that is, said he might have some sort of license form I need to fill out?"

The woman tutted, but held the door open for her to come in. Keeley stepped into a large hall with gleaming white walls and floors. Edna might not be much of a conversationalist, but she was clearly a good housekeeper. She went into a room, presumably to fetch Gerald.

A few framed photographs lined the walls, mainly of the mayor at various functions, and Keeley went over to look at them. Looking for a face she knew, or even, she admitted to herself, for Terry Smith. She also scanned the mayor's clothing.

"Keeley!" Gerald appeared in the doorway Edna had gone through. "Come in."

Keeley went into a small drawing room, trying to ignore Edna's glare as she walked past her and left the room, shutting the door behind her with some force. Keeley raised her eyebrows at Gerald.

"Don't mind Edna. She's been with me for years, she's terribly protective."

Keeley thought that was an odd comment. Why on earth should he need protecting from her? She gave Gerald a polite smile, noticing the plain, wooden buttons on the olive green waistcoat he was wearing and wondering what had happened to the cardigan.

"You wanted the forms for the festival? I've got some here." Gerald went to a small desk and began leafing through some papers while Keeley looked around the room. More photographs lined the walls. She cleared her throat, wondering where to begin.

"I expect you get to know everyone in town, being mayor," she began. "It must be very interesting."

"Yes, it is," he agreed after a moment's pause, as though he suspected she was probing for something. He produced the right form with a flourish, handing it out to her with one of those insincere, wide smiles. He must have been taking lessons from Duane, she thought.

"Did you know the man who was killed? Terry?" As she took the paper from him, their eyes locked, and there was no mistaking the flash of fear in his eyes. He let go of the forms as though he had been burned.

"Not very well, no. Why do you ask?" His tone was bordering on aggressive now, the smile gone, and for the first time, Keeley asked herself just what she thought she was doing, confronting possible criminals on her own.

"It was just a thought," she said softly, tucking the forms into her bag and turning, ready to leave. Gerald's next words stopped her in her tracks.

"Ben Taylor been tittle-tattling, has he?"

"Excuse me?" What did Ben have to do with this? Gerald gave her a rather nasty sneer.

"The whole town knows about his little evening visits to Rose Cottage, my dear. You've hardly been discreet."

"How dare you!" Keeley felt outraged. "Ben has been keeping an eye out for me, that's all."

"Because you were number one suspect, weren't you? Was it you that put him on to questioning me, then, to take the heat off yourself?" The mayor had lost his anger now and seemed almost imploring. Keeley felt confused, then realized that Ben was, of course, one step ahead of her. For whatever reason, he thought the mayor was up to something too, and had been round to question him. So much for letting her in on the details of the investigation.

"If you're being questioned by the police," Keeley pointed out in a low voice, "then I'm not the only suspect, am I?" She thought again about the button and realized this was the time to play her hand.

"What were you doing in my flat the night of the murder, Mr. Buxby?"

Gerald's face showed what appeared to be genuine surprise.

"That's preposterous," he said, his cheeks reddening. "I was nowhere near the place. I was at a function, in fact, a very public one. As I told Detective Constable Taylor. I have witnesses who can vouch for my presence."

Keeley faltered at that. Still, the fact of the button remained. But she could hardly ask to go searching through his wardrobe. Instead, she reached into her pocket and pulled it out, handing it out to him.

"Is this yours? From one of your cardigans, perhaps?" She watched him carefully, hoping the abruptness of her question would trip him up.

Gerald bent and peered at the gold button, his brows creasing together. Then he straightened and shook his head.

"This is what you have to go on? Those buttons are two-a-penny; the old haberdashery on the High Street used to sell them. Why, I can think of at least five of my acquaintances who have the very same ones. Would you like me to give you a list?" Sarcasm dripped from his voice; then he stalked over to the door and wrenched it open, calling for the housekeeper. She appeared with the same sour expression on her face when she looked at Keeley, which immediately softened when she turned her attention to the mayor.

"Edna, you do my laundry. Do any of my cardigans or other attire have buttons missing?"

Edna raised her chin proudly.

"Certainly not. I wash everything by hand and take the utmost care."

Keeley put the button back into her pocket, feeling now decidedly foolish. Gerald held the door open wider and looked at Keeley as he addressed the housekeeper.

"Ms. Carpenter was just leaving. If you could show her out, Edna."

Keeley walked out with as much dignity as she could muster.

The housekeeper didn't look at her as she let her out, only gave a clipped command: "You watch my floors, girl, I've just mopped."

Keeley breathed a sigh of both relief and bewilderment as she walked down the path, away from the oppressive atmosphere of the house. She still felt there was definitely something going on with the mayor, even if she had been wrong about the button it-self. She badly wanted to ask Ben what had prompted him to question the mayor, but it seemed Ben had no desire to talk to her whatsoever.

A fierce grip on her arm made her spin round, startled, to see Edna standing on the path, her eyes burning with hatred.

"You leave him alone, you hear me? He's a good man. Any mistakes he's made—well, it was a long time ago, you should let him be."

Keeley was interested in spite of the woman's ferocity. Edna opened her mouth, then closed it again, cutting off whatever she may have been about to reveal. Instead she stared at Keeley for a moment, then gave her a nasty smile that reminded her unnervingly of Raquel.

"Carpenter, you said? George Carpenter's girl?"

Keeley nodded, wondering where the old woman was going with the change of subject.

"You've got some cheek, then, coming round here, trying to dig up dirt on poor Gerald."

"What do you mean?"

"I mean, you should clear out the skeletons in your own closet before you go rummaging through other people's, girl." The woman clucked her tongue in disapproval, a malicious gleam in her eye. "Everybody talks about your father as if he didn't have any secrets. A terrible thing, infidelity," she said, and then turned on her heel and stalked into the house, slamming the front door behind her before Keeley could formulate her next question.

Infidelity? Whose? For a moment, she thought Edna was talking about Gerald, and her thoughts skittered as she tried to make sense of the woman's remarks, before a terrible conclusion took shape: Edna was talking about her family. Her father, to be specific.

Her father had been unfaithful? Keeley shook her head, dismissing the thought as soon as it came and taking a step back up the path, intending to bang on the door and demand that the woman explain the meaning behind her words. Her father had been the consummate family man, had adored both Keeley and her mother, even if to Keeley's mind, Darla went out of her way to be hard to love. That thought stopped her in her tracks.

Could that be why her mother had been that way, why she had always seemed so bitter? Because her loving husband was not so loving as he seemed? It would be just like her mother to not say a word to anyone and soldier on in silence, letting it twist her up inside.

But if Edna knew, then someone had said a word to someone, at some time.

Keeley saw a curtain twitch at one of the front windows and turned away, realizing she was still standing frozen in the middle of the path. She walked away as fast as she could without actually breaking into a jog, Edna's words whirring around in her head as she searched for a memory that might make sense of her words. If there had been such serious problems in her parents' marriage, then surely she would have known, or would have at least suspected. She wanted to come to the conclusion that the old woman was simply being nasty in retaliation for Keeley's provocation of her beloved boss, but there was something about the way she had uttered the words that rang true.

Edna, at least, believed in what she was saying. Which meant the story had come from somewhere.

Keeley picked up her pace as she turned back onto the High

Street and headed toward the Tavern. It seemed she would be asking questions after all, but not about Terry Smith's murder. Not anymore.

Jack was in his usual spot, though he was alone today without Bambi, and he frowned as Keeley walked over and sat down without her usual smile and greeting.

"I need to ask you something, Jack," she asked in a low voice, not wanting to be overheard. The old man drew his eyebrows together, causing even more lines than usual to snake their way across his forehead.

"Go on."

"My father," she said, and then stopped, hardly able to believe she was about to ask him this and wondering if she should just leave well alone. He was dead, and her parents' marital problems were their own business, at least now that Keeley was a grown woman and more than capable of looking after herself. But part of her needed to know, and with more urgency than she wanted to ask Gerald about his financial affairs or even uncover who had been leaving corpses in her café.

"What about him?" Jack's expression looked guarded, and Keeley had a horrible feeling that Jack knew the gist of what she was about to ask him.

"Do you know if he ever cheated on my mother?"

Jack blinked slowly and reached for his pipe, but not before Keeley saw the flash of knowledge in his eyes. He knew something.

"Now, why would you ask me something like that?"

"That's not answering my question, Jack."

He gave a shrug.

"Seems a funny sort of question to be asking, lass, that's all. Someone said something they shouldn't, have they?"

With that, Keeley knew there was some truth to Edna's words. She felt tears sting her eyes as she understood just how much she had wanted it to be a lie. Her father had always seemed to her the very model of goodness, of decency.

"It was Edna," Keeley said, and then gave Jack a shortened version of the whole sorry affair, trying to minimize her attempts to uncover the mayor's secrets. By Jack's skeptical look, he knew exactly what Keeley had been doing at Gerald's. She felt foolish. She had gone round there, thinking she knew something, that she was clever, driven by some kind of stupid spite at Ben, who had been one step ahead of her anyway. Keeley shook her head at her own stupidity. All of a sudden, it didn't matter that the murder was, as she had herself argued, very much her business, in that she had been swept up in events against her will. If trying to discover the perpetrator had been her attempt to try to exert some control over a scary situation, then she had failed dismally. All she had succeeded in doing was opening a can of worms that would have been better left to rot.

Jack was looking at her keenly, his old eyes sharp, but when he spoke, there was a sympathy in his voice that nearly had Keeley crying in earnest.

"It's not my place to say anything, lass. It wasn't that nasty old baggage's either. You need to ask those involved."

"You know something," she stated.

"Only rumors, and they're never good to know. Like I said, it's best coming from the horse's mouth."

Keeley sighed in exasperation. She could hardly ask her father, could she? Then she understood what he meant, because her father might be in no position to clarify anything, but her mother was. The thought of asking Darla something like that made Keeley cringe. Her mother wasn't the sharing type.

"I understand," she said to Jack, although she felt like she would never really understand anything again. "I have to go." She left without saying another word, her vision blurred through the tears that still threatened to spill. Over at the café, she let the decorators out in near silence, looking around at the admittedly wonderful job they were doing with a feeling of miserable detachment, and then she locked up. She still had a list of things to do, but they could wait until tomorrow. Everything could wait.

There was a lone taxi outside the Tavern, and Keeley got in it, unable to face walking or even the bus, in case she saw anyone she knew and was obliged to make small talk. Back at the cottage, she put on the kettle and ran a bath, comforting rituals that didn't offer any comfort.

Lying back in the hot water, she asked herself just why Edna's words had affected her so badly, and could only conclude that it was the final straw. Murders, anonymous letters, and hostile townsfolk were bad enough, yet a combination of curiosity and hope for her career had kept her going. The sense that she was doing something both with the legacy of her father's shop and to uncover the person who had threatened it. This, now, was the last straw. It had all finally become too much, and the true magnitude of events seemed to weigh on her all at once, a physical weight on her chest. She should get out of the bath, she thought, stretch her suddenly lethargic body and try some heart-opening poses. Yet she just couldn't be bothered. Her limbs felt leaden.

She thought back to her conversation with Ben, when she had

poured her heart out to him about her father's death, and about Brett. Brett, who had cheated on her, as her father had apparently done to her mother. It just felt all wrong. Like everything she thought she knew and believed in had been spun around and turned upside down, leaving the very ground beneath her feet shifting. She couldn't imagine her father capable of such a thing, though God knows her mother was probably enough to drive any man to seek comfort elsewhere, but to lie and cheat on his family seemed antithetical to what she remembered of George Carpenter.

Maybe it was just a fling, some village garden party that got out of hand. Brett had used that very excuse: "It was just sex." As if that made it all okay. As if it wasn't the act itself that constituted the cheating, as if it counted only when it was more than just the physical. In any case, Keeley had never believed there was such a thing as "just" sex. There was always a deeper reason, a motivation, even if it was one that was very far from love. Whether need, or loneliness, or the urge for reassurance, or even pure and simple ego flattery, sex was never "just" sex. She thought about Ben then, or more specifically about her and Ben, and was glad she hadn't given him the chance to think of her as "just" anything.

Finally, as the water started to turn uncomfortably lukewarm and her fingers to groove and crease, she got out, wrapped herself in one of the fluffy white towels Annie had provided, went upstairs, and lay on the bed. She felt exhausted.

Her phone, lying on top of her clothes where she had taken them off, rang loudly. She let it ring, but when it began again, she sat up with a sigh and leaned over to check the caller display. Her tummy gave a funny sort of flip as she saw the name. Ben.

She reached out to take it, then thought better of it. Probably he was going to chew her out for talking to Gerald and once again act as if the kiss had never happened. In truth, last night felt like a decade ago.

She fell back onto the bed and let his call ring through. Whatever it was that DC Ben Taylor had to say to her, right now she didn't want to hear it.

Chapter Fourteen

Keeley smiled at the man as she opened the café door, wishing she could muster up some more enthusiasm. Other than the actual opening day itself, this was the moment she had been waiting for most—a mundane thing to some, maybe, but full of significance to her.

This was the day her sign went up. When the café announced itself to the world, or to Belfrey at least. When the "old butcher's shop" finally became "Keeley's café." Or to be more exact, the Yoga Café. It was a moment she had been excited about, until Edna's revelations three days ago put a gray fog over everything. One that she just couldn't seem to shift. Even her yoga practice, which she had relied on for so long to keep her body balanced and her mind clear, didn't seem to help for more than an hour or so, and then the fog descended again. She had spent the last few days just going through the motions, watching the café take shape with the dispassionate eye of an observer, as if it were happening to someone else.

Keeley had half expected another letter by now, and when none arrived, had felt a vague disappointment, for at least a touch of fear was better than feeling nothing. For it wasn't that she felt sad, or angry, or even simply shocked; she just felt numb. If the murderer confronted her now, Keeley didn't think she would bat an eyelid. Somehow whoever had killed Terry Smith didn't seem to matter anymore.

As the man unwrapped her sign, however, a flicker of pride sparked. It looked great, and they had captured her design perfectly, the letters fluid and graceful, the renditions of silhouettes performing poses for the Y and C were beautifully done, and the peppers on either side looked good enough to eat. She looked around at the interior of the café itself. She had yet to arrange the furniture, the wall hangings, and to add the details that would make the interior come alive, such as fruit baskets on each table, the napkins she had had printed with the logo and cake baskets for the counter, but the framework was there. The fresh lemon walls and pale laminate floor made the space open and inviting, and the new white counter looked professional and tempting. She should have been itching to get behind there to serve her first customers. Not to mention the newly installed kitchen, complete with new appliances and implements that the cook in Keeley should have been in raptures about.

Of course, that had been slightly marred by the fact that she had also had an alarm system installed, in case of any more break-ins. Or arson attempts. If that had been an attempt to derail Keeley's plans as opposed to covering up a body, then she wasn't taking any chances. She just wished she could summon back her initial passion for the place.

"You're not happy," Carly had observed during a phone call the night before. "Why don't you just come back to London? You can open up your business anywhere. Everyone in London loves yoga." She was right, of course. Although there would be more competition, there were also more customers. But if she decided to shut up shop before she had even opened, her mother would have to sell, and was highly unlikely to fund another start-up. Besides, she admitted to herself now that it hadn't been purely for financial or business reasons that she had come back to Belfrey. She had come back out of some nostalgic longing for "home" and to feel she was somehow following in her father's footsteps, albeit with a meat-free alternative.

And look at how that backfired, she thought to herself despondently. She should have listened to Ben in the first place and left well alone. Now she felt like she was walking around with that dreadful weight of knowledge on her chest, wondering if her entire childhood had been a lie. She had had to drag herself out of bed and into the shower that morning, and had pulled a brush through her hair and left without even bothering to check the result of her administrations. No doubt Darla would tell her to stop being so melodramatic and in this case be right, but Keeley was in a funk that seemed all-encompassing.

Darla. She had spoken to her mother also on the phone last night, with the intention of asking about Edna's accusations, but the words had caught in her throat. As hard as it was to picture her mother as the wronged woman, nursing a secret hurt all these years, Keeley still didn't want to upset her.

Or maybe she just didn't want to know. She wished she had never been to talk to Gerald, had never spoken to the malicious cleaning lady, or, failing that, that there was some way to give herself selective amnesia, to take back the words. Maybe then she would be standing watching her sign being installed with the joy she should be feeling.

"Ooh, that looks lovely!" exclaimed a woman walking past with a pushchair, smiling at Keeley. The man walking with her squinted up at the sign and shrugged. "There's too many cafés here as it is. What do we need another one for?"

What indeed? Keeley watched them walking up the hill. Maybe Carly was right; maybe she should just go back to London.

She was still ruminating when she arrived at the center the next morning to teach her class. It was even more full than it had been the week before, a few of the women having brought friends along. Maggie was there again, as was Diana, looking even more twitchy and nervous than before. Keeley realized she had expected the woman not to come after the way she had shied away last week, and felt pleased that she had after all. She faced the class and took a deep breath as she prepared for the preliminary stretches.

As she took the women through the sequence of postures she had carefully choreographed for their different fitness levels and abilities, she felt the shift in her own body, the lethargy lifting as she moved her body in time with her breath. For all that her practice hadn't seemed to help over the past few days, something about the very act of practicing with and, more important, for others caused something in her to respond, some little spark to ignite. By the time they reached back bends, she felt, if not exactly happy, then at least more alive, more aware.

As the class came to an end, she smiled round at the women,

grateful for their presence, which had nourished her in ways she knew they wouldn't understand. In yogic philosophy, it was called *seva,* the act of doing something for others that in turn made one feel better about oneself. Altruism, basically. Although she couldn't feel too noble, given the prices that the ridiculous insurance premiums at the center forced her to charge.

But pricey session or not, the rows of faces looking back at her looked nothing short of serene. Even Maggie's seemed to have lost its predatory gleam—temporarily, at least.

"Namaste," Keeley said to them, the traditional way of opening and closing a class. It was Sanskrit word that meant roughly "I honor the Spirit in you." A sentiment Keeley found particularly profound, acknowledging the common thread that united everyone, regardless of age, gender, or background. Or meat-eating preferences, she thought, suppressing an unexpected urge to giggle.

"That was great," Diana sighed.

"Yes," agreed a silver-haired woman next to her. "Are you going to be taking on any more classes here? Through the week?"

"She's going to be opening her own studio," another woman said knowledgeably. Keeley blinked in surprise, gratified that they had taken such an interest in her plans.

"It's not quite a studio," she said, "but I was planning on holding a few evening classes above the café."

"Was?" Trust Maggie not to miss a thing.

"I am considering moving back to London," Keeley admitted. The women looked taken aback, even disappointed. Diana looked almost stricken.

"Really?" One of the younger women, Sasha or Sonia or something, pouted in disappointment. "I thought your café was opening at the end of this week? I was quite looking forward to coming along." The two women next to her nodded. "Yeah, we thought it was a great idea." There were nods throughout the room, even from Maggie. Keeley felt touched.

"Well, I haven't made a decision yet. Maybe I'll see how things go." She should at least open, she thought, after all the work she had put into it. She said good-bye to her class as they trooped out, feeling almost maternal toward her students, which was bizarre, as at least two thirds of them were older than her.

"I'll see you on Tuesday, then," Maggie called.

"Tuesday?" Opening day was Thursday.

"For the food festival."

Keeley had all but forgotten about it, she realized in panic. She had given herself less than forty-eight hours to prepare her dishes for the stall. Trying to hide her consternation, she said good-bye to Maggie and rummaged in her gym bag for her phone. Hopefully she could recruit Annie to help. She had a vat of her spicy root curry to make, a dish she hadn't even tried out yet, veggie burgers and sausages, a large dish of her moussaka, and various sides. She would have to do some of the cooking in the café, as her little oven at the cottage wouldn't be able to cope with it all in time.

Shaking her head at her own carelessness, the name on her caller display, showing a call she had missed half an hour before, took a few minutes to register. Ben had phoned her again. She hesitated, then pushed the redial button, raising the phone to her ear with fumbling fingers, finding herself both relieved and disappointed when it went straight through to his answer machine. As she hoisted her gym bag onto her shoulder and left the center with a wave at the bubble gum–chewing receptionist, a little chink of hope slipped through the armor she had built around her conflicting feelings for Ben Taylor. A hope that allowed her to wonder if he regretted his abruptness to her the day following the kiss. If after all, it had meant something to him too.

When she reached the High Street and the bus stop, she was in the act of redialing his number when she spotted something across the street that stopped her. Ben's car, parked outside the Tavern. He sat in the front seat, talking to someone with their heads close together. Keeley stepped forward just enough to confirm what she thought she was seeing, then ducked back out of sight behind the bus shelter. Ben had been in his car with Raquel, leaning so close together their heads were almost touching. Keeley felt a wave of humiliation wash over her. They had looked close. Very close. As though she was a lot more than a possible suspect. So much for his claims not to even like the woman.

When she heard the bus pull up, Keeley got on it quickly, keeping her head down in case they saw her. The last thing she needed to see was Raquel's smug face as she cozied up with "Benny."

As she sat at the back of the bus, mercifully alone, Keeley waited for the heavy despondency that had only lifted with her class to settle back over her, tinged this time with the stab of jealousy. It didn't descend. Rather she felt a restless sort of anger, and a desire to do something about the situation. Her café was days away from opening, and she had the Festival to prepare for. Her thoughts of going back to London, of slinking away with the proverbial tail between her legs, had all but evaporated. Damn Ben Taylor, and Raquel. And whoever was apparently trying to scare her away from Belfrey. She had put too much into this to give up now.

There was one thing she did need to do, though, before she could move on, and that was talk to her mother and find out exactly what Edna had meant. No matter how painful the knowledge might be, she needed to know what was lurking in the past before she could fully focus on the future.

As soon as she entered the cottage, she walked over to the house telephone, took a deep breath, sat down, and dialed her mother.

Darla answered on the second ring. "Hello?" She sounded, as usual, impatient.

"Mum, I need to talk to you."

"Oh, what's happened now?" she snapped in a tone that clearly implied her real meaning was *What have you done now?*

"Do you remember a woman called Edna? She's now Gerald Buxby's housekeeper."

"Is she?" Her mother actually sounded interested. "She wormed her way in there, then. She always had a bit of a thing for him."

"Never mind that. How well did she know you and Dad?"

Her mother went quiet.

"Not particularly well, really. Where is this going, Keeley?"

"She said that Dad had an affair. Or affairs. That he was unfaithful. Is it true?"

Keeley heard Darla's sharp intake of breath and realized she was holding hers as well. She closed her eyes. *Please say it's not true,* she prayed.

"It's not true," her mother said firmly. Keeley let her breath out in a long, slow exhale, then promptly sucked it back in at Darla's next words.

"It was me she was talking about, Keeley. I had the affair, not your father. I'm sorry."

Chapter Fifteen

She didn't sound sorry at all. More irritated that Keeley had dared ask.

"You? But when? With who?" Relief made her less angry with her mother than she might have been. She should have known that if either of her parents would do such a thing, it would be the chronically dissatisfied Darla.

"Never mind who. It was a very, very long time ago. Why on earth that woman brought it up now, I have no idea. I hope you haven't been going round upsetting people?"

"Mum, this isn't about me. There shouldn't have been anything to tell." The anger started to trickle in as she thought of her father, who had tried so hard to make both her and her mother happy, and felt desperately sorry for him. "I take it Dad knew?"

"Of course he knew."

"Well, half of Belfrey certainly seems to."

Darla went quiet at that. If anything would bother her mother, it was the idea that people were talking about her in less-than-favorable terms.

There was a long silence. Then hesitantly, in a small voice Keeley couldn't remember her mother ever using before, Darla started to speak.

"It was a very long time ago, Keeley—before you were even born, in fact. We hadn't been married for very long, and I had moved to Belfrey to be with your father. I found it very hard. I missed my friends in London, and I never really fit in in Belfrey."

Keeley felt a flash of sympathy for her mother then; she knew what *that* was like, but she swallowed it down.

"Why move here, then?" she asked bluntly. "Why not get Dad to move up to you?"

"He had the shop. And I wanted to move, at first. I thought it would be worth it, to be with him. I loved your father very much."

Keeley, who had been leaning against the arm of the sofa, sat down in surprise.

"You never show it," she blurted out. "I've never even seen you cry."

"What good would that do?" Darla said in something like her normal voice. "Crying isn't going to bring him back, now, is it? Besides, I had to be there for you."

"There for me," Keeley echoed, thinking she had never heard such a ridiculous phrase in her life. Not once could she remember a cuddle or soft word from her mother, particularly after Dad had died.

But then, that just wasn't Darla's way. Rather she had bullied Keeley out of her stupor of grief until Keeley had gotten up and moved on with her life purely so she could get away from her. It had never occurred to her that the constant nagging might have been the only way Darla knew how to show her concern. And she had paid for her to go to college, and to study classes that Darla had frankly described as a waste of time. Had let her have free rein with her father's shop when she could have just sold it. For the first time, Keeley wondered if she had more reason to be grateful to her mother than she had ever realized.

"You were telling me about the affair," she said, unwilling to start examining her tangled relationship with Darla right now.

Her mother gave a heavy sigh. "I was young, Keeley, and lonely, and gullible." *Like me with Brett,* Keeley thought, though it was admittedly very different circumstances. Her mother continued. "It didn't go on for very long—the guilt was too much. I told him in the end, and, well, it was awful." Keeley was sure she heard Darla's words catch in her throat, as though suppressing a sob, but told herself she must be imagining things. Hadn't her mother just admitted she never cried? But there was no denying the tremor in her voice as she went on.

"He threw me out. That's the only time I ever saw your father really angry. He threw me out, and I went back to London."

"You actually broke up?" Keeley found herself fascinated by this story of her parents' marriage, of events that had occurred before she even existed. Tried to imagine her mother young and vulnerable, and failed.

"Yes, for some time. I wrote to him, called him, even got my friends to call him, but he wouldn't speak to me. I was on the verge of giving up when he turned up at my parents' house one day, a bunch of flowers in one hand. 'Darla Carpenter,' he said, 'you had better be getting your bottom back home this minute.' I threw myself at him so hard, I nearly knocked him over. By the time we got back to Belfrey, I was pregnant with you. Although we didn't know that for a while."

Keeley felt stunned. Whatever she had been expecting to discover from the dreaded conversation, it wasn't this. Trust her mother to manage to frame her infidelity in some kind of positive light.

"Well, that's lovely," she said, trying not to sound sarcastic but not entirely succeeding, "but what about when you came back? Why does everyone know?"

"Everyone meaning who?" Darla said, her tone sharp.

"Edna, obviously, so I suppose Gerald. I asked Jack Tibbons, and he wouldn't tell me anything, but he knew."

"Keeley Carpenter," her mother said in that voice that had always cowed her as a child, "I'd thank you not to go around Belfrey asking about my past indiscretions. They would know because they were your father's friends, I suppose. Really, it should be forgotten about now. But then, Edna never liked me."

Keeley had a sudden, horrible thought. "Did Terry Smith know?"

"The man who died?" Darla sounded puzzled. "I shouldn't have thought so. Why?"

There was something nagging at the back of her consciousness, something her mind just couldn't get a grasp on, but for some reason, her mother's revelation felt significant.

"Apparently," Keeley said, trying to sound as if she had come by the information quite by chance, as though it were common knowledge, "the police believe Terry was killed because he was blackmailing people. Discovering their secrets and extorting money out of them not to reveal whatever they were hiding."

"That's got nothing to do with me. Goodness, it was nearly thirty years ago, Keeley. And as you've discovered, it's hardly a secret."

But what about the other person? she thought to herself. Had they too been married, with a family?

"Who was it?"

Her mother gave a light laugh, a noise Keeley recognized. It meant she was going to ignore whatever you had just said to her, because she had no intention of responding.

"No one important. No one you know."

"No one from Belfrey?"

"No," her mother said, a note of finality in her voice. Keeley felt that Darla was still hiding something, or at least telling her as little as possible, but she also knew her mother wasn't going to be drawn out any further. She dropped it, at least for now. There were other questions she wanted to ask about her parents' history, but she had gotten as much as she was going to out of Darla for one day. It was the most honest conversation she could ever remember having with her mother.

Darla took the lull in conversation as an opportunity to change the subject, asking Keeley instead about the café and opening day. After making it clear she held Keeley fully responsible for ensuring it turned a profit within the first year, she rung off, leaving Keeley staring at the telephone, wondering what had just happened. So she did what she often did when struggling to process events or emotions.

She cooked.

With the food festival fast approaching, it was a necessity in any case, and so she threw herself into washing and chopping vegetables and fruits. Tomorrow she would give herself the best part of the day to make up her recipes and ensure everything was perfect. Being as it was a festival stall, she wouldn't be able to make too many main dishes for practical reasons and so had decided to go with one main dish as a showcase and a basic recipe for veggie burgers that she could then serve with fresh bread rolls and her favorite rainbow salad from her proposed salad bar for the Yoga Café. It had occurred to her that desserts were always a crowd pleaser, and so she had decided to make up a summer fruit ice cream that could be kept in her cool box for the day and would hopefully attract the children; and for her main dish, she was going with a spicy root curry. It was a bit of a gamble, as she hadn't used the exact recipe before, but Keeley thought it a better option than the moussaka, as curry was a dish that tended to taste better the day after, when the spices had had chance to fully develop and were at their most flavorsome. For a while, as she immersed herself in her work, her recent worries receded. She was aware she should be angry at her mother, but for reasons she wasn't quite ready to fully explore, her overwhelming feeling was one of relief.

Cooking, she mused and had often thought before, was in many ways a type of practice of yoga. The central point of yoga, as her teachers had taught her and she tried to impart to her own students, was not just to relieve a backache or get thinner thighs—as nice as that thought was—but to experience a union of body and mind. A sensation of being in the moment, or being in flow, that one sometimes heard athletes or artists talk about. For Keeley, cooking often had the same effect. At the ashram in India, cooking was considered an act of *seva* as much as teaching or offering help and kindness, and as Keeley washed and chopped, she tried to imagine people eating and enjoying her food, without worrying about whether or not the café turned a profit or she would ever feel accepted back in Belfrey. Or the killer would ever be caught. Or if Ben Taylor would ever kiss her again.

After she had finished for the night, she made herself a comforting carrot and coriander soup, taking the time to say grace over it before she tucked in, and went to bed feeling rather more serene. Talking to Darla had, she felt, restored some kind of balance, albeit a tenuous one.

She started the next day with a vigorous yoga practice and then walked up to the Glovers' farm, trying not to hope that Ted Glover would be nowhere to be seen. A sign advertised fresh free-range eggs and milk, and Keeley smiled to herself at the expression "free-range," guessing that Diana had written the sign. The Glovers indeed ran a free-range farm, which chimed with Keeley's attitude toward ethical eating, but they had done so for decades, out of tradition, before ever "free-range" was part of the public consciousness, and given Ted's obvious hatred for "hippie types," the use of the term seemed incongruous.

As she had hoped, Ted was somewhere out on the farm proper, and only Diana was present up at the farmhouse. She was delighted by Keeley's idea to use fresh produce in her recipes, and when Keeley told her she intended to use their milk for the ice cream for the food festival, Diana beamed with pride.

"It might cheer Ted up a bit, at least," she said in a bright voice, though a shadow that Keeley pretended not to see passed over her face at the mention of her husband's name.

She then popped into Annie's to enlist her help for the next day, then went back to Rose Cottage to get on with her preparation. The afternoon flew by, and it was well into the evening before she was finished, and then she had the cleaning up of her own chaotic kitchen to do. Finally, she stepped back and surveyed her handiwork with a satisfied sigh.

If ever a girl deserved a glass of wine, she decided, it was now.

Reaching the Baker's Inn, Keeley nearly changed her mind about going in, then squared her shoulders and stepped inside. As usual, every head in the bar turned, but this time, there were a few friendly nods and Keeley walked to the bar with a little more confidence. The barman served her with a distinct lack of interest, and she took her glass of wine over to a table in the corner, feeling almost disappointed when no one attempted to talk to her or question her. She almost wished Duane were there.

Instead, when the door swung open and a man walked in, it was exactly whom she didn't want to see. As Ben walked to the bar, Keeley rummaged in her handbag, letting her hair fall over her face in an attempt to hide herself. At least, she noticed as she peeped through the layers of her fringe, he was alone.

"Keeley." He said her name in a matter-of-fact tone as he pulled a chair out opposite her and sat down. Keeley pushed her hair back from her face and sat up, trying to look surprised to see him, as if she hadn't been deliberately trying to escape his notice. "I've been trying to call you."

"I've been busy," she said, not looking at him.

"I'm sorry." She did look at him then, surprised at his words.

"This is the second time you've apologized to me this week," she said, her voice deliberately light, although even she could hear the sharp edges. Ben seemed chagrined, a look that seemed at odds with his usual composure.

"I was abrupt with you the other day, on the phone. I didn't mean to be. Things are just . . . complicated."

Keeley didn't respond, just held his gaze, wondering how much of that complication had to do with a certain glamorous mutual acquaintance. She thought of him and Raquel in his car, leaning into each other, and felt a stab of anger.

"What's complicated?"

"You're not going to make this easy for me, are you?" When she didn't answer, Ben sighed and leaned back in his chair, gazing around the room.

"It would help if I knew what 'this' was," she said, and then blurted out, unable to hold it back any longer, "Is this about Raquel?"

"Raquel?" Ben looked surprised, but also, she thought, there was a trace of guilt in his expression.

"I saw you in the car with her," she said, and immediately cursed herself silently for even bringing it up. For a moment, Ben looked nonplussed; then his expression cleared. He shifted in his seat as he spoke so he was leaning toward her, glancing around to make sure they weren't being overheard.

"You think there's something going on," he stated. He sounded amused, and Keeley glared at him.

"Isn't there? You seem so certain she has nothing to do with either the murders or the letters, yet she has repeatedly threatened me. You spoke about her as though you don't particularly like her, then I see the two of you as thick as thieves."

Ben shook his head.

"You've got it all wrong." He looked around again, then got up, walked around the table, and slid into the double seat next to Keeley. The small confines of the space meant they were very close, their thighs pushed up against each other. She raised her eyebrows at him.

"Listen," he said quietly, an urgent tone to his voice, "I was talking to Raquel about her statement, because I, er, have to be careful what I put in the paperwork. I had to formally question her after those letters."

Keeley felt confused.

"What do you mean?" she whispered. "Is her alibi fake? You said there was no way she could have done it—the murder, anyway."

Ben's face said he felt conflicted, frowning so that a groove appeared between his dark brows as he seemed to struggle with how to or if he should answer her.

"There isn't. She was with someone that night, but that some-one needs to be kept out of any paperwork. And no," he said quickly, guessing at the thought that flitted across her mind, "it wasn't me."

"Then why would you cover up for her?" Keeley snapped at him, feeling self-conscious. Although no one had turned to look at them or even paused in their conversation, she had felt a dis-cernible interest in the air. The fact that they were huddled in the corner together only made them look more conspicuous. She re-membered Gerald's gibe concerning her and Ben and winced, then took a long sip of her wine.

"I'm not covering up for her," Ben snapped back, "the man in question is married. And also my superior."

Keeley paused mid-gulp, then set her glass down on the table with care.

"You mean, the guy who you said was pressuring you to solve the case?"

"The very same. As you can imagine, he was none too pleased when I questioned her about these letters you've been getting."

"Then why did you?"

Ben looked at her as though the answer were obvious. "Because you thought it might be her, and it was a logical assumption. I'm not going to skimp on my job just because the senior officer can't keep it in his pants."

Keeley stifled a laugh at his words, then thought about the implications of what he had just told her. No wonder he was angry when she had gone barging in the diner with her accusations; he had probably gotten a good talking-to, thanks to her. And no wonder he was getting so frustrated on this case if the only feasible suspect was his superior's secret girlfriend. His married superior. She thought again about her parents, and Brett. Was she the only person who seemed to think fidelity a trait worth having?

"So did you have to doctor her statement?" she asked quietly, not wanting to think of Ben doing such a thing. To her relief, he shook his head firmly.

"No. She was never formally questioned about the night of Terry Smith's death; you were the first person to float that idea. No, what she wanted was for me to leave mention of her surgery out of her statement concerning the letters. I said the best I could do was to not specify the body part."

Keeley couldn't help laughing out loud at that, and this time a few curious looks did turn their way. Ben smiled at her.

"Shall we get out of here? There are a few things I'd like to go over with you." Although both his voice and expression were perfectly neutral, something about the way he said those words made her insides tighten. Keeley allowed her gaze to travel from his eyes down to the sensual lines of his mouth and back up again. She wondered if half a glass of wine had made her bold.

"Are you going to try to kiss me again?"

Those lips curved in a surprised smile.

"If I do, are we likely to get interrupted again?" Meaning Duane. He had been jealous, she thought, much as she had been over Raquel. She didn't want to focus too much on what that might signify, the fact that they both had such proprietary feelings toward one another, so she finished the last of her wine and then stood up.

"I hope not."

They left the inn, her walking in front of him with his hand resting lightly on the small of her back, a gesture that felt both alien and yet familiar, as though it were perfectly natural for him to place his hands on her. As the cool evening air hit her, she felt quite giddy, and with the lightness came a wave of relief. About her father, about Ben and Raquel, and simply just for the fact that they were walking together, apparently at ease with each other, as if the tension between them had, if not dissolved, then at least changed.

If only the murderer could be caught, things would be looking up indeed.

"I heard you questioned Gerald Buxby," she said, wondering if he was still so keen to let her in on some of the details of the case. She had gotten the impression, when he told her about Raquel and the senior police officer, that it had been a relief for him to talk about it. No wonder he felt under pressure.

"Where did you hear that?" he said, instantly suspicious. She had obviously misjudged his level of openness. She decided to come clean, at least partly.

"Someone mentioned the mayor had been in some financial trouble."

"Someone," Ben said flatly, although to her relief, he didn't ask her who that "someone" was.

"Yes, and I went round to pick up the license form for the food festival, and he seemed very agitated. I asked him what was wrong, and he said you had been questioning him." Her explanation rang false even to her own ears. Ben stopped walking, his hand falling away from her back where it had still been resting, and he turned to face her.

"You were doing it again, weren't you?"

When Keeley didn't answer, trying her best to look as though she had no idea what he was talking about, Ben carried on walking, though at a markedly quicker pace.

"You're angry," she stated. He gave a little snort and carried on walking, so quick, she had to almost jog to keep up with him.

"Ben—" She reached out to touch his arm and was startled when he stopped and abruptly whirled around.

"You are so infuriating!" He was glaring at her now.

"I'm sorry, I just—" she began, but had no time to finish before Ben pulled her toward him and was kissing her again, crushing his mouth to hers. Keeley froze, startled and confused, then found her body and mouth responding to his of their own volition.

When he broke away, he looked calmer; almost resigned. He stroked her cheek with the back of his hand, then picked up a tendril of her hair and curled it around his fingers.

"You are the most stubborn, inquisitive woman I have ever met," he said, somehow managing to make the words sound like a compliment.

"Should I say thank you?" she teased. Ben shook his head at her; then he looped his arm through hers and they carried on walking, this time at a more manageable pace. Keeley touched her fingers to her lips, barely able to believe what had just happened. Or what it might mean. They walked to the bottom of Bakers Hill in silence; then Ben started to speak, as if the intimate interlude had never occurred.

"I suppose you were thinking that Gerald was a victim of Terry's blackmailing tactics, hence the money difficulties?"

"It seemed to make sense," she said tentatively, hoping he wasn't going to get angry with her again.

"Well, you were right. He left a paper trail, paid him straight out of his own bank account, so once I finally managed to get my hands on Terry's financial statements, it was all there in black-and-white."

Keeley felt a stirring of excitement. "So you think it was him?"

"No. Aside from the fact that he would have to be very silly indeed to murder a man when there was evidence to show what was going on, he was attending a public function over in Bakewell at the time of the murder. Very public, lots of witnesses."

Keeley felt deflated. Another dead end. Then she had a thought. "What about the housekeeper?"

"Edna?" Ben sounded bemused.

"It's possible," she said defensively, remembering the malice in the old woman's face when she had confronted her. "She seems very protective of him. My mother said she's had a thing for him for years."

"Did she?" Ben sounded as though he was considering the idea.

"Was that why Terry was blackmailing him? Some sort of affair?" It seemed to be the theme of the moment. Ben shook his head.

"No. I can't go into too much detail, but it was to do with misappropriation of public funds during his first year as mayor. Nothing terribly exciting, but Gerald takes his reputation very seriously. He has quite the gambling problem, apparently, hence his association with Terry Smith."

"How did that man find out these things about people?" Keeley wondered.

"Seems he had a knack for wheedling secrets out of people, especially over a few drinks. Raquel came across him while she was up in Manchester; he was up there betting on the dogs."

Keeley thought about that. It didn't seem right, that one apparently unlikable man should be able to possess people's secrets, but then if that man was the sort to chase up every throwaway comment, every suspicious look . . . She gave a little shudder. She had never known him, but the more she discovered about him, the harder it was to have much sympathy for the man, to remember that he was the victim, not the villain.

Of course, that meant anyone, in theory, could have killed him. Not some evil, ruthless murderer but a normal person driven to desperate measures. Somehow Keeley found that idea more disconcerting than the image of a depraved killer lurking in the shadows.

Once again, she had to ask herself, just where did she fit into all this? What was the link between her, the café or her father's shop, a blackmailer with no friends, and his killer? She leaned into Ben, as much for reassurance as to her immediate safety as out of attraction, although the fizz of pleasure that went through her when his arm tightened around her and his hand stroked her hip felt anything but safe. Still, he carried on talking about the murder as though it were quite natural for them to walk to-gether this way.

"It still seems we're on the right track with the killer being one of the blackmail victims," he said. Keeley felt he was including her in that "we" rather than just referring to the police force, and linked her hand through his. "Why's that?"

"He was depositing regular large amounts into his account. There's no other explanation for the money. So we can assume it was another victim of his, one paying in cash. Therefore not leav-ing a paper trail."

"The killer."

Ben nodded. They were nearly at Keeley's door now, and his pace slowed.

"It seems likely."

When they paused outside her door, it felt as if the very eve-ning was observing them, the shadows themselves watching to see their next move. Keeley was on the verge of asking him to come in, without even pretending it had anything to do with the case, when he leaned down and kissed her again.

This time he kissed her with tenderness rather than urgency, his lips slowly exploring her own, before stepping away, though he kept an arm loosely around her. Keeley wanted to invite him in then, very badly, but didn't want to seem too forward, or risk him saying no, or let down her own carefully guarded defenses, so she stood mute, until Ben made the decision for her.

"I should go, I suppose. We've both got an early start." He made no move to go. Keeley nodded. "You should," she agreed, not moving an inch herself. Finally they moved toward each other at the same moment and shared a lingering kiss, until Ben detached himself with obvious reluctance and began to make his way down the hill. Keeley watched him go until he merged with the shadows, then let herself in, locking up as usual and doing a last-minute check that everything was ready for the morning. She was as prepared as she would ever be, she decided.

Certainly more prepared than she had been for the sudden, sure knowledge that she was falling hard for DC Ben Taylor.

ANULOMA VILOMA—ALTERNATE-NOSTRIL BREATHING

Restores balance to the body and mind, calming the nervous system and relieving stress. Brings the breath into balance and is perfect before meditation or any event where you need to be calm and focused.

Method

- Sit up tall, in a firm-backed chair or cross-legged on the ground.
- Make Vishnu Mudra* with your right hand. To do this, bend your index and middle fingers down into your palm while keeping your thumb, ring, and little fingers straight.
- Inhale and exhale deeply.
- On your next inhalation, use your right thumb to close your right nostril, so that you inhale through the left nostril only.
- Lift your right thumb from your right nostril and use your right ring finger to close the left nostril. Exhale through the right nostril.
- Now inhale through the right nostril; then close it with your thumb.
- Lift your ring finger from the left nostril, and inhale through it.
- Repeat the entire sequence three to five times.

* Mudra is the name for certain hand postures used in yoga. Most people will be particularly familiar with Prayer Mudra, where the palms of the hands are placed together to pray in an age-old posture common to many religions, and with the traditional meditation mudra (known as Gyan Mudra) where the hands are upturned on the knees with the tips of the thumb and index fingers touching.

Chapter Sixteen

Prepared or not, Keeley couldn't shake the feeling that something was going to go horribly wrong as she drove down with Annie in her landlady's battered old Mini to the High Street, the backseat stacked with trays and pots of food, cutlery, and disposable plates. The feeling had persisted throughout her morning routine, and even a vigorous workout and a calming and balancing breathing exercise hadn't managed to shake it off. It was a bright morning, the sun warm on her face through the window, but dark clouds were gathered over the hills, just waiting to descend on the town.

The High Street was dotted with colorful stalls, and people were already milling about, an encouraging sign. She hoped she had been allocated a prominent stall, hopefully near the Yoga Café itself. She allowed herself a proud smile as she saw the sign hanging above, announcing its presence.

However, as she quickly discovered when she tracked down

one of the organizers, a stocky woman with a prominent mustache whom she had spoken to at church the week before, she was about as far away from the café as she could get.

"You're in the community center," the woman told her, waving a hand in its direction. The center was tucked away behind the back of the High Street, next to the police station and the library. Not exactly a prime location to get her wares noticed. It also meant she would have farther to go if she needed to run over to the café to get more supplies, as she had made extra of everything, reasoning she could keep things warm in the café's kitchen while she ran the stall.

"It's probably just because you're new," Annie said in an upbeat voice, though she gave Keeley a concerned look as she helped her carry things to and fro. Keeley wasn't so sure, wondering if Gerald himself had had something to do with this. The stall itself was small, just a wooden table with a grubby white tablecloth thrown over it, in the far corner of the community center. There were only two other stalls in there; one showcasing a sorry selection of homemade cakes and the other representing the soup kitchen for the homeless in Derby City. Keeley wondered if anyone was even likely to venture in here.

"I'm sure it will get busy this afternoon," stated Annie firmly, her unwavering optimism making Keeley smile. "I've got a few things to do, but I'll pop back soon and see if you need any help." Her landlady gave her shoulder a squeeze before she left.

The next hour or so ticked by inexorably slowly, leaving Keeley feeling more despondent with each minute that passed. All that preparation, and it looked as though most of her lovingly made dishes would be going to waste. She wondered if the woman from the soup kitchen would want some to take back with her.

Her head was drooping onto her chest and her eyes closing when she heard a familiar laugh and was jolted out of her near sleep to see Megan and a few friends—including Pink Hair from the space-clearing incident—coming in and making a beeline for her stall. Keeley smiled at her gratefully as they all asked for a tofu burger with her rainbow salad and a bowl of the spicy root curry.

"Delicious!" Megan exclaimed, finishing her bowl in a few mouthfuls and handing it back for a refill. In a quieter tone, she said, "I can't believe they've stuck you in here out of the way. The High Street is so busy."

Keeley gave a resigned shrug, having decided over the course of the morning that there was little point in worrying about something she could do nothing to change. Then she heard the clacking of stilettos and knew even before she saw her that Raquel was approaching.

Dressed in a trouser suit that must have cost as much as Keeley's entire wardrobe, she was hanging on the arm of the same man she had seen her with before at Mario's. Keeley wondered if this was Ben's superior, then decided not, seeing as that man was apparently anxious to keep their liaison secret. No doubt Raquel had the proverbial black book full of men willing to give her an arm to hang off when the occasion called for it. Keeley willed herself to smile as the couple approached, although the glare Raquel aimed at her could have lasered through glass.

"I wondered if you would be putting in an appearance. Not doing so well, I see." She took in Keeley's little display in one look, the disdain on her face as heavy as her makeup.

"It's still early." Keeley tried to sound as friendly as possible, though she kept her hands stiff at her sides, half-fearing they would reach to scratch the other woman's eyes out of their own accord. "Would you like to try something?"

"It's delicious," Pink Hair chimed in—and not just for effect, as she was on her third bowl of the spicy root curry. Raquel wrinkled her perfect nose, and Keeley wondered if she had had work done on that, too.

"No, thank you. I'm a little more fussy in my tastes, I'm afraid."

Keeley nearly bit her tongue trying not to reply, and felt gratified when Megan said incredulously, "Are you serious? Your place serves pie and chips, for God's sake. And they're not even homemade!"

Raquel looked shocked at the un-Megan-like outburst; then her lips curled in a sneer as she looked at Megan as though she were a rather amusing cockroach. Megan visibly shrank back under the force of Raquel's glare, looking upset. Pink Hair looked furious, chewing on her food rapidly. Raquel gave Keeley a triumphant glare and turned to her companion.

"Let's go, there's nothing worth seeing here."

Keeley inhaled sharply. "Raquel," she called. The woman paused and looked back over her shoulder. "I saw Ben last night. I thought you might like to know you were in the clear, seeing as you were otherwise engaged." As soon as she said the words, she regretted them, hoping they wouldn't get back to Ben, yet she couldn't help but feel a sliver of satisfaction as Raquel's face drained of color. Her eyes narrowed, and her parting shot came out as a snarl.

"You *rotten* bitch," she said, and stalked out, virtually dragging her harassed-looking escort with her.

"Nice girl," Pink Hair said dryly, swallowing the last of her curry.

"She's positively evil," Megan said, looking a little shaken. That was one of her intuitions Keeley felt inclined to agree with. But where did that leave them with the murder? So far, the only person she knew in Belfrey who seemed quite capable of committing evil acts was Raquel, and who better than a police chief to provide a watertight alibi?

"It's raining," Megan announced, even though the grubby blinds on the windows of the community center were drawn down. Keeley wondered if her ability to read auras had morphed into weather premonitions, then saw what Megan had noticed: a small group of people had just entered the room, one of them shaking raindrops off a red umbrella. Keeley stood up straighter, organizing her face into a welcoming smile as they came over.

"I'll pop back later," Megan said with a encouraging wink.

The rain proved to be a blessing as more and more people retreated to the warmth and dryness of the community center and decided a sampling of Keeley's food was just the thing after getting drenched.

An hour later, she was relieved when Annie returned, bringing a handful of the church ladies with her who were all very enthusiastic about Keeley's dishes. Before she knew it, there was a queue of people to serve, and Keeley was fielding questions left, right, and center about ingredients and the café itself, along with promises to attend the opening. Annie donned a spare apron and joined her in serving after a group of sticky-fingered children nearly capsized the stall, trying to get to the homemade ice cream. "I'm so sorry," their mother muttered, looking beyond weary. Keeley grinned at her. The day had taken an unexpected turn for the better, and she doubted even a reappearance from Raquel could upset her now.

"All right, lass?" A gruff voice caught her attention. Jack stood at the front of the queue with Bambi next to him, his great tongue lolling as he sniffed the aromas of food in the air.

"I'll have one of those burger things in a roll with some of that salad, and one on its own for Bambi here," Jack said. Knowing that a tofu burger was likely to be the most exotic thing Jack had eaten in a long time, Keeley felt touched at the old man's show of support.

Unfortunately, it was a step too far for Jack, who chewed his first mouthful with a painful slowness, looking anywhere but at Keeley as he tried to mask his distaste.

"Not quite my thing, lass," he said with regret, then looked down at Bambi, who had swallowed his down in one gulp and was pawing at Jack's leg hopefully. He gave an excited yelp when Jack gave the dog the remainder of his own, mumbling an apology to Keeley. She gave a shrug.

"At least Bambi approves." The dog wagged his tail, giving her a low woof before following Jack out.

The spicy root curry at least was going down well, particularly as the afternoon went on and the day grew colder and wetter. English weather was something she definitely hadn't pined for on her travels, and as the rain drew more people into the community center, Keeley found herself glad that she hadn't been given one of the bigger stalls outside. She was soon ladling out more paper bowls than she could cope with, and was glad when Annie came back to help.

"Have you got any more of this, dear? It's certainly proving popular."

Keeley nodded, glad she had erred on the side of making too much rather than too little, and untied her apron.

"I'll run over to the café, there's another tray of it."

It was indeed miserable outside, the sky gray and heavy and the rain running down the slope of the High Street, causing little rivulets and brooks in between the cobbles, which were slippery under her feet. Picturesque they might be, but there were times when there was nothing wrong with a bit of basic tarmac, she thought as she nearly slid across the street.

As she righted herself, she nearly slipped again when a young boy bumped into her, gave her a startled look, and then ran off downhill, his shoes slapping on wet stone. He had looked panicked, his eyes wide and frightened, and Keeley looked in the direction he had just come from, and saw Jack Tibbons's front door wide open. As she drew nearer, she could hear raised voices from inside and felt her stomach lurch. Something was very wrong.

"Jack?" she called through the doorway, then when she got no reply knocked the door loudly and stepped inside into a small hallway. She saw Jack in the lounge room, kneeling down on the floor, making a strange keening sound as though in terrible pain, while a woman stood next to him with her hand on his shoulder, making soothing sounds. His sister, Keeley recalled as the woman turned and saw her.

"Do you need any help? What's wrong with Jack?" she asked, but before the woman could answer, Jack turned and gave her a look of such hatred, she stepped back in shock. His face was twisted almost beyond recognition.

"It was you," he hissed at her, a wild look in his eyes. "That bloody hippie food of yours!"

Only then did Keeley see why he was crouched on the floor, noticing the twitching form in his arms. Bambi lay stiff and jerking in his master's arms, foam at his mouth, his eyes bloodshot and unseeing. Keeley's hand flew to her mouth as Jack's sister came over to her and guided her gently out of the room.

"It couldn't have been," Keeley heard herself saying, her eyes still fixed on Jack's hunched figure through the doorway, "Lots of people ate those burgers." The woman went to speak; then a man in a white coat came rushing through the doorway with the young boy who had nearly knocked her over close behind him. The vet, she realized as the man ignored them and went straight to Jack and the dog, crouching down beside them and reaching for Bambi, looking at his eyes and inside his mouth, his brow furrowed. The dog spasmed violently.

"What has he eaten?" the vet said, looking at the sister, as Jack was openly sobbing now, and any answer likely would be incomprehensible.

"One of this lass's burgers, he said." Although the woman's voice was carefully neutral, it sounded damning to Keeley, especially as the vet turned his cool eyes on her.

"It was just a veggie burger, there wasn't even any meat in it, everyone's been eating them," she said, aware she was gabbling and staring at the dog, tears burning her own eyes. The vet had taken a syringe from his white coat and was preparing to give him a shot. The boy pushed his way past Keeley and through to the back of the house, no doubt too upset to watch.

Bambi gave another jerk as the vet pushed the plunger on the needle, went stiff, and then flopped in Jack's arms, going very still.

"Can you bring him out, Jack?" the vet asked the old man in a calm voice. "Let's get him down the road to the surgery and we'll see what we can do for him."

Jack stood up, Bambi lying lifeless and limp in his arms. The boy appeared again, holding something in his hands.

"Bambi was in the yard," he said, holding up what looked like a choice hock of ham, "and he was chewing on this." He held it up.

"Who gave him this?" the vet said, looking at Jack and his sister. His sister had gone white.

"It's not mine."

"He's been poisoned," Jack said, his voice hollow with pain. "Some bastard has poisoned my dog." He followed the vet out, not even looking at Keeley, who leaned against the doorframe, her legs weak. The sight of him carrying the huge dog, cradling him in his arms like a baby with now silent tears flowing down his craggy features, made Keeley look away, unable to bear the anguish in his face.

Jack's sister turned to Keeley, her face white. The young boy was crying too now, hanging on to her arm.

"Will Bambi be all right, Nana?"

She patted him on the head and hushed him even as she turned unbelieving eyes to Keeley.

"Who could do such a thing?" she said, echoing Keeley's own thoughts. "My brother adores that animal. Who could be so cruel?"

Keeley couldn't answer her, at least not to give her a specific name, but she had a horrible feeling that the same person who could be cruel enough to poison a beloved pet was the same person who had been interrupted, by that very pet, burning the evidence of their deeds. Keeley looked at the hunk of meat, now dropped at the boy's feet. The woman followed her gaze.

"Wash your hands, Robbie, right now," she said in a shaky voice, then looked at Keeley. "I think I had better call the police."

Keeley nodded, and took Robbie into the drawing room while his grandmother did just that. Kate was there within ten minutes, having obviously been over the road at the station. She raised her eyebrows as she saw Keeley.

"You again?" she said, though her tone wasn't exactly unfriendly, more puzzled. "You seem to be at the center of everything that happens around here lately." At the policewoman's words, Jack's sister shot Keeley a curious look.

Kate asked her a few questions, then went out to the yard with Robbie and his grandmother. There was nothing else she could do, so Keeley made her way back to the stall. Annie would be wondering where she had gotten to.

Her landlady knew at once there was something wrong, for all Keeley's attempts to arrange her face.

"What is it?" she said, coming out from behind the stall and guiding her to the back of the room, away from interested onlookers, "You look as white as a sheet!"

"Jack—I was going to the café—" Horrified, Keeley heard her breath catch on a sob, and her vision went blurry. She turned her face away, fighting tears. Annie stared at her for a moment, then patted her arm briskly.

"Right. You compose yourself and I'll pack up. You've done a fair day's trade as it is."

Keeley gave her a grateful nod, watching as her landlady bustled around, a model of plump efficiency. Her limbs felt weightless, as though they would float away if not tethered to her body. She looked around for a chair and found a wooden stool by the window, sat down, and leaned forward, feeling a wave of nausea as though she had been poisoned herself. *You seem to be at the center of everything lately.* Kate's words scuttled round in her mind like blind mice, trying to find something solid to hold on to. It didn't make sense. Bambi's poisoning couldn't have anything to do with her, yet she couldn't shake her initial thought that it had only been Bambi raising the alarm that had saved her café. She had to stop skirting around the issue: this didn't just involve her—she was, at Kate had stated, at the very center of things.

The trouble with being in the middle of it all was that she couldn't see the woods for the trees, couldn't fathom any logical path from A to B. She felt as though there was something right under her nose, that she was missing, and now that *something* was affecting the people around her. Like a bad luck charm, she thought morbidly.

"She's over there," she heard Annie say, and looked up to see Ben approaching, a worried look on his face. In spite of herself, she found herself jumping up and quickly smoothing her hair, a sensory recollection of last night's embrace heating up her skin. At the same time, she felt an overwhelming desire to throw herself into his arms and sob on his shoulder, pride be damned. Instead she heard herself ask, "How is he?" not sure if she was referring to Jack or the dog or both. Ben shook his head, his face grim.

"Not sure yet. I think it much depends on whether he makes it through the night. Jack's taking it hard, as you would expect."

"He thought it was me," Keeley said, her voice bleak. When Ben looked quizzical, she added, "My food, I mean, making him sick. Until we realized it was poison." Her words sounded as though they were coming from very far away.

"I'll take you home," Ben said, his voice brooking no argument.

"I came with Annie, and I need to clear up," she protested. Annie looked over at the mention of her name.

"I can clear up here, and I'll sort the pots and things and bring them over. You go on now."

There didn't seem much point in arguing, and indeed, Keeley found she couldn't wait to retreat to the relative safety of the little cottage. She went with Ben, then remembered she had left appliances on in the café and went over to turn them off and lock up, Ben close behind her. She avoided looking up as she went past Jack's front door.

They drove back to the cottage in silence, though Ben kept shooting her little concerned looks. The spare dish of her curry sat in her lap, and Ben sniffed the air as he opened her car door and took it from her.

"Smells good. Maybe you could heat us up some?"

Keeley stared at him. How could he think about food right now? But her stomach betrayed her, giving a low grumble, and she recalled she had had nothing to eat since a muffin and orange juice first thing that morning.

"Good idea; come in, then." She reached for her keys, then noticed a small parcel sitting by the front door. Thinking her napkins and menus for the café had come to the cottage by mistake, she picked it up and put it under her arm. As they went in the door, she smelled a bad odor, like decaying food, and eyed the pot of curry Ben held in trepidation, hoping there wasn't something wrong with the second batch. Then as she began to untie the parcel in her arms, the smell grew stronger. With a creeping terror, she looked at the label on the parcel, which stated her name and address, but with no stamp or postmark. It had been hand delivered, and the small black type used for the lettering was all too familiar.

"What is it?" There was a urgent note to Ben's voice as he realized something was very wrong.

Keeley pulled at the strings, then at the neatly taped package. As she pulled it away, the odor was so strong, she gagged and her eyes watered, so that it took her a moment to understand what she held in her hands. Chunks of rotting flesh tumbled from the package as Keeley threw it away from her and ran into the bathroom, retching. Behind her, she heard Ben cursing in shock.

The rotten smell permeated the small cottage, even though by the time she had freshened up and emerged from the bathroom, Ben had taken everything outside. He was on the phone, ordering a constable to come at once, and when he saw Keeley, he ended the call and came to her, pulling her into his arms. Only then did Keeley notice she was trembling.

"Who is it? Are they . . . human?" A visible tremor went through her, and Ben clutched her tighter.

"No," he said quickly, in soothing tones that she suspected he used on victims and their families during the course of his work. He guided her over to the sofa and sat down with her, holding on to her still shaking hands. "It stinks too much for me to get a proper look and be sure, but I think it's just pieces of pork. Rotten meat."

Keeley felt sick.

"Why would someone send me that?" But then she knew, of course: it was to thoroughly upset her. A jab perhaps at the fact she was a vegetarian and had taken non–meat stuffs to the traditional food festival. It was such a horrid, disturbing thing to do that

Keeley felt her blood chill in her veins. Someone, for some reason, really hated her.

They sat in silence, Ben rubbing her hands, until a police car
pulled up outside and Kate got out. Ben had left the parcel of
rotting meat on the porch, and the wind must have been carrying
the smell downhill, as Kate grimaced as soon as she was out of the
car, then held a hand to her nose as she walked past the offending
flesh and into the cottage. Ben let go of Keeley's hands and stood
to greet the young WPC as though it were perfectly normal for
him to be comforting a female that way, but Keeley didn't miss
the way Kate's eyes flickered over the spot he had been sitting, or
the way her mouth pursed in obvious disapproval. Or more likely,
remembering the way the policewoman had simpered over Ben
the first time Keeley visited the station, with jealousy.

Kate asked her questions and inspected the exterior of the
cottage in a way that gave Keeley a distinct feeling of déjà vu.
Really, this was becoming a commonplace event, although her
tormentor had been rather more imaginative this time. Kate took
a statement, then helped Ben place the offending article in a
secure Baggie. She left without barely a glance at Keeley, though she
murmured to Ben on her way out, "He's stepping up his game,
isn't he?" to which Ben gave a curt nod, then looked at Keeley with
concern. They meant, she knew, the person who had sent her the
parcel.

Ben made her a hot drink and heated her up some of her own
curry, which she stared at listlessly, thinking that after today, food
was the last thing she wanted, taking only a mouthful when Ben
said "Eat," in tones that brooked no argument. Even through her
haze, she knew it was good, and the taste and aroma of the spices
helped inure her senses against any lingering rotten odors, soothing

her queasiness rather than adding to it. Ben ate his with un-abashed gusto, but then, she supposed he was used to seeing—and even smelling—unsavory things.

"This is damned good," Ben confirmed as he tucked in. After finishing, he took the bowls in to the kitchen, and she couldn't help a smile as she heard him running the tap to clean them. He obviously had no aversion to cleaning up after himself. She won-dered what his own house was like, thinking that although she knew him from childhood, knew his parents and his childhood home, she really knew very little about Ben the man, other than that he was a dedicated professional and an exceptionally good kisser.

When he came back in the room, she looked at his face and thought he looked weary. This case was a strain on him too, she reminded herself, and thought about Kate's parting words with a shudder.

"You said the murderer was stepping up his game?"

Ben drew his brows together and didn't answer her, but Keeley guessed at his train of thought. "You're still not sure it's the same person, are you?"

Ben leaned back and sighed, shaking his head. His earlier ret-icence to share details with her had largely gone, and although in some ways that pleased her, she feared that was as much to do with Ben and the local police being at a total dead end than a growing closeness between them.

"On the face of it," he said, "they could be separate events. Your poison pen, the murder, Jack's dog. It's like trying to put a jigsaw together when all the pieces of different puzzles are jumbled up and you're not sure what goes where. It *feels* like it's all related, and yet, where does the dog fit in to all this?"

Keeley remembered her initial reaction to the dog's poisoning, and suddenly it made perfect sense.

"It was Bambi's barking that prevented the fire getting any worse, and possibly destroying evidence of Terry's murder. I mean, if the body had been badly burned, you might not have known how he died, right?"

Ben frowned.

"You think Bambi was poisoned out of revenge for interrupting the arson attempt?" Ben didn't look as if he bought that theory, but as Keeley pointed out, what was the alternative?

"It's either that, or you've got some other psychopath running around Belfrey." Or Jack's somehow involved, she thought but didn't want to say. Remembering the old man's face when he had lifted his dog in his arms gave her a tangible ache in her chest. Following the death of his wife, the wolfhound was obviously his closest companion. To target the dog seemed somehow more shocking to Keeley than the murder of a man she had never met and would most probably, by all accounts, not have liked. She felt uncomfortable with that knowledge; all life was precious, and Terry's murder should be no less a tragedy than anyone else's. Yet Bambi's near brush with death had pained her far more.

Ben's thoughts were following a different track, it seemed, as he regarded Keeley with his head tilted to one side, looking as though he were puzzling something out.

"What is it?"

"I was just thinking it's interesting how, apart from Gerald, every person you've suggested as the culprit is a woman. To be honest, initially I was looking at a man for this. It takes a certain amount of strength to hit someone hard enough over the head to kill them. But I'm starting to wonder if you might be right."

"Oh?"

Ben gave a brisk nod. "Yes, it's a possibility. Assuming it's all the same person, it all smacks of a certain kind of pettiness, even though there should be nothing petty about murder. Vindictiveness, that's a better word."

Ignoring the slight to womankind, Keeley thought about his words. There was only one person she would automatically apply that word to. Rotten meat through her door. It had been just a few hours earlier that Raquel called her rotten, snarling the word at her. She didn't voice her suspicions, mainly because she didn't want Ben to think she was unhealthily fixated on the idea of Raquel as the culprit, but Keeley couldn't help feeling that if the shoe fit, then Raquel was most certainly wearing it. Even though she had to admit it all seemed somewhat over the top for the sake of covering up her cosmetic surgery. But then, Raquel had deeper secrets than that.

"What about your superior, the one Raquel's been seeing?" Keeley regretted the words as soon as she said them, and was surprised when Ben regarded her with a look of grudging respect.

"I've wondered that myself," he admitted, "but it doesn't fit with what I know of the man. And I'm not sure their affair is, how can I put it, serious enough to warrant murder, even with the threat of exposure."

"Then what about looking into her other men? I've seen her out with another man."

"Another avenue I've looked into. I did take your accusation against her seriously, you know."

Keeley felt chastened. Not least because Ben had clearly always been one step ahead of her.

"And you turned up nothing?"

"Nothing useful. Anyway, if she's seen out with someone, then it's hardly a secret. I'll be honest with you, Keeley, the whole thing is really starting to get to me. And I'm worried about you." He looked directly into her eyes, an expression in them that made her blush, though she wasn't sure why.

"About me," she parroted, feeling not so much scared as quietly thrilled at his admission. Hardly knowing what she was doing, she moved closer to him on the sofa, their gazes still locked. She was holding her breath, a fact she became aware of only when he reached to stroke her cheek and she exhaled with a soft sigh. "Ben," she began, only to be cut off when his lips brushed hers. She kissed him back, their mouths meeting in a rhythm that was already becoming familiar and, somehow, perfectly natural and correct, as if kissing Ben were something she should really be doing every day, as a matter of course. The thought made her kiss him back even harder, and he made a low, almost growl in the back of his throat and pulled her onto his lap. She gave a surprised laugh, then buried her fingers in his hair, tugging on it a little, feeling both wicked and wanton when he nipped at her lower lip in response.

Maybe it was the shocks she had had that day, or the tension that had been building between her and Ben in one way or another from her first day back in Belfrey, but all Keeley's restraint, her carefully guarded feelings, burst like a dam. In a fluid movement she stood up, watching Ben's look of disappointment change to surprise mixed with desire when she held out her hand to him.

"Shall we go upstairs?"

There was an awful moment when Ben just stared at her, when for a split second she thought that she had gone too far, that he would say no and she would die of embarrassment, but then he stood up and picked her up, right into his arms, and proceeded to carry her up the stairs. Keeley shrieked in delight at his actions, pointing out the way to the bedroom for him with any trace of embarrassment forgotten. As he laid her down, his touch becoming tender, all thoughts of mysterious murderers and poisons blurred into one and were then swiftly eclipsed by Ben's expert hands. For a few hours that evening, then later that night, then again in the early hours of the morning when she awoke to find him next to her and reached for him with a kind of wonder, all her fears were forgotten.

Chapter Seventeen

"Morning, beautiful."

Keeley woke with the sun on her face and Ben smiling down at her, and had to blink a few times to be sure she was truly awake and not having some kind of wish-fulfillment dream. No, she realized with a little thrill, it was all real, and he was there, in her bed, clad only in his underwear and a smile.

"Hey, there."

Keeley watched him from under her hair as he got up and strode across the room, completely unself-conscious in his near nakedness. Admiring the long lines of his thighs and tight curves of his butt, she pouted with disappointment when he pulled on his jeans.

"I've got to get to work soon," he said, misreading her pout, "but I've got time for some breakfast, if you like? If vegetarians eat breakfast?"

Keeley laughed. "Of course. How about I make us some-thing?" She couldn't remember the last time she had had a man to cook for in the morning, and being able to make the offer gave her a funny little thrill. *Oh dear,* she thought, *one night with him, and I've turned into a '50s housewife.*

Ben looked uncertain. "Don't take this the wrong way, but I like a hearty breakfast, not nuts and seeds and things."

Keeley glared at him, thoughts of picket fences and marital bliss momentarily forgotten.

"I do eat proper food, you know. You liked my curry last night."

Ben looked mollified. "I did, it was lovely. Okay, I'm in your hands."

Keeley sent him down the corner shop for eggs and milk, hav-ing used up everything she bought from Diana Glover, and set about chopping mushrooms, onions, and tomatoes for an omelet. With some French bread toast and fresh orange juice, that should send Ben on his way with a full stomach. By the time he came back, she was singing softly to herself. Ben came up behind her, dropping a kiss on the back of her neck that sent a shiver of plea-sure down her spine.

"You sound happy," he whispered into her ear. Keeley put down her knife and turned to look at him, their faces just inches apart.

"I am," she said, her voice serious. She was—in fact, she felt happier than she had since coming to Belfrey. She leaned up and kissed him, and lost a few minutes in his arms, until Ben disen-tangled himself with a frustrated sigh.

"If we carry on like that, I'll never get to work."

"And you'll never get your breakfast. Sit," she commanded,

waving him toward the kitchen table. Ben did as he was told, never taking his eyes off her.

"So am I," he said. Keeley frowned, not understanding his meaning.

"Happy. About us."

"Oh." Keeley felt herself blush, then grinned as she understood what his words implied. *Us.*

They ate in comfortable silence, every so often stopping to grin at each other over the table. Keeley didn't want him to go, for the day to begin, bringing with it the knowledge that they had yet to unravel the mystery. Ben broke the spell first.

"I had a call from Kate while I was walking down to the shop."

Keeley waited for him to go on, praying there was no more bad news.

"Bambi made it through the night. He's still very poorly, but it looks as though he'll hang in there."

Keeley breathed out a sigh of relief, along with a little pang of guilt that she had been so wrapped up in Ben that the events of the day before had slipped to the back of her mind.

"It's been confirmed that the meat was poisoned. Not that there was much doubt, but we needed to be sure it wasn't something else that caused the seizures. Apparently he was barking at people in the street just a little while before, which Jack says was most unlike him."

Keeley nodded, thinking about Bambi's seemingly gentle nature.

"Perhaps it was the crowds. The High Street was very busy yesterday."

"Maybe. Either way, that meat was definitely left there for him to find. It was laced with an anti-inflammatory painkiller often used to treat arthritis."

Keeley felt surprised, realizing she had been expecting him to say something like arsenic or cyanide, not something so mundane.

"That could have killed him?"

"According to Rogers, the vet, a lot of everyday medications can be absolutely fatal to dogs, even in small doses."

"That gives you something to go on, then, doesn't it?" A killer with arthritis, who knows about dogs. It sounded less than sinister even to her own ears. Maybe she was wrong about Bambi's poisoning, and it had nothing to do with the actual murderer, just a neighbor who didn't like dogs.

"Not really. It was an over-the-counter medicine, so it's not as though it would have to been obtained with a prescription. And Rogers regularly gives talks and things on animal care and suchlike. It's not necessarily an indication of specialist knowledge."

"Plus there's always Google," Keeley pointed out. She imagined it would be possible to find out anything on the Internet these days. All that potentially dangerous knowledge, available at the click of a button. Ben reached over the table for her hand.

"Whoever is doing all this, I'll figure it out, Keeley. It's personal now. I suppose," he said, looking away from her, "it's why I was so reluctant to get involved with you at first. I didn't want it to compromise the case. If there's one thing my dad has always drummed into me, it was to never bring work home with you. I guess that's one rule I've decided not to keep."

Keeley sat back in her chair, taken aback by his little speech. She felt a rush of feeling for him that went far beyond desire.

"You thought about it before? Us getting involved?"

A flush rose on Ben's cheeks, though it was gone so fast, Keeley wasn't sure if she had imagined it.

"As soon as I walked into the Tavern and saw you, and you spat your drink all over me, I knew you were the One."

He laughed, and Keeley with him, and there were a few more lingering embraces before Ben managed to leave after arranging to pick her up and take her to dinner that evening. But once he had gone, Keeley couldn't help her mind turning to darker things. Ben's declaration that the case had now become personal to him as well drove home to her that, one way or the other, this wasn't likely to end smoothly. Whoever was behind all this was clearly gunning for Keeley herself, for whatever reason, and now with her and Ben developing a relationship, and the opening of the Yoga Café just days away, Keeley understood just how much she now had to lose.

She was reminded of that again later that day as she put the finishing touches to the café itself. She had distributed flyers and leaflets around the local shops, on her guard for any hostility that may possibly mask something more, but it seemed that on the whole, the locals were warming to the idea of the Yoga Café. She was congratulated on her food at the festival the day before, and interest was also growing in her class at the center. She met Megan for lunch, opting to take sandwiches into her friend's shop rather than going to the Tavern as usual, not wanting to see Jack and Bambi's usual place empty. She was bursting to tell her about Ben, but unsure if Megan might think she had somehow been unfair to Duane.

It seemed she had no need to worry, as Megan had something to tell her.

"Apparently Duane's started seeing someone, though he's being very cagey about who it is. You don't mind, do you?"

"Of course not," Keeley assured her, trying not to make it so obvious that she was, in fact, delighted. "I've got a date with Ben this evening." For some reason, she wasn't ready to confide in Megan about the previous night. Not that she thought the other woman would be at all judgmental, but it was something still new enough that she wanted to keep it to herself.

"Police officer Ben? Like I needed a crystal ball to see that coming. Lucky you."

"Thanks." Keeley felt a warm glow creep through her. Which was halted somewhat by Megan's next words.

"It will put that cow at the diner's nose out of joint, and serve her right for being so mean to you. Everyone in Belfrey knows she's been after Ben for years."

"Time for her to back off, then," Keeley said firmly, before changing the subject. She told her what Ben had said about Bambi. Megan nodded thoughtfully.

"When he brings the dog home, I'll pop round with some herbal remedies for him." Seeing Keeley's dubious expression, she said with a touch of defensiveness, "Dogs react very well to natural medicine. And they're sensitive creatures, you know. He may well be emotionally affected by his ordeal."

Keeley remembered something else Ben had told her that morning.

"They thought he might have been ill, at first, having some kind of fit. Apparently he was barking at people on the High Street."

"I was there," Megan said with a slow nod as she recalled the previous afternoon. "I had not long left you, and I was looking at one of the stalls and I saw Mrs. Rowland. I had just gone over to talk to her when Jack went past with the dog, and he was making a right noise. Scared myself and Mrs. Rowland something terrible."

"Perhaps he had already eaten some of the poisoned meat and it was starting to take effect," Keeley mused.

Lunch over, Keeley gave the café one last clean and polish before setting off back home. She was looking forward to her first proper "date" with Ben, even if they had gotten the order of things rather back to front, and was having the predictable panic regarding what she should wear.

She had settled on a polka-dot sleeveless dress that was snug on the top, then flared from her waist to her knees. It was one her mother had bought her, that she had never worn, maybe for that precise reason, but it fit like a dream and made her feel just the right combination of flirty and feminine. She wrestled her hair into something resembling a chic updo, and even opened a new red lipstick she had bought in New York but never had occasion to wear. As she applied it in the mirror, she resolved that she was not going to utter one word that night about murder or arson or poisonings or smelly packages. She would just be a young woman, out on a date with her new boyfriend. Considering they had already spent the night together—and what a night—she felt justified using the word.

The doorbell went, and she nearly smudged her lipstick. Glancing at the clock, she saw he was early. Her heart skipped in her chest as she went to let him in, smoothing her hair one last time.

Her face fell when she opened the door not to Ben but to Annie.

"I just thought I would see how you were, dear, after that awful thing with Mr. Tibbons's dog yesterday."

Keeley smiled at her, trying not to look disappointed.

"That's very kind of you. I'm just on my way out, actually." She fidgeted in the doorway, wondering if Annie would be terribly offended if she didn't let her in. But Annie was taking in her outfit and makeup with a knowing smile.

"I see. Would that be with a certain young police officer?"

Keeley couldn't stop herself from grinning. "Yes, it so happens it would."

"Well, I'm delighted for you, dear, it's about time you had a bit of luck. And I daresay you'll be much better for him than the Philips girl he was dating before. Never have liked her much." Annie sniffed in disapproval, not noticing Keeley's look of confusion.

"Do you mean Raquel? I don't think they were ever dating."

"Oh, they definitely were," Annie said with a nod, "though it was a while ago now." Her landlady's expression grew troubled. "I haven't said anything out of turn, have I?"

Keeley shook her head, though her heart felt like a lead weight in her chest. She made her excuses and retreated back into the cottage, shutting the door and leaning her back against its solid frame as though it could lend her strength. Ben had dated Raquel? Although she had thought as much, especially after the way the girl had cozied up to him that day at Mario's, but after Ben's insistence that he didn't even like her, and his obvious disapproval of her relationship with the senior officer, she had decided any relationship between them was purely wishful thinking on Raquel's part. Now she wasn't so sure. From what Annie said, Ben had been a willing participant.

She should have asked Annie how she knew, she thought, because although she didn't think her landlady was one to listen to idle gossip, her sources might not have been totally accurate. If the information had come through Norma or Maggie, for example. In just a few weeks, she had already seen how the Belfrey rumor mill could operate. There had been insinuations about her and Ben before anything had even happened, after all.

But no matter how hard she tried to convince herself that Annie was mistaken, she couldn't stop remembering Raquel's sitting on "Benny's" lap at the Italian restaurant, or the memory of them in Ben's car, their heads close together. She only had Ben's word for it that there was nothing more to it, that Raquel was in fact involved with another officer. What if, she thought with a stab of jealousy that physically pained her, causing her to clutch at her stomach, he had in fact been covering up for her all along?

The door went again, and this time Keeley knew it would be Ben, but now her heart was skipping with dread rather than excited anticipation.

She opened the door and let him in without a word, ignoring the puzzled look on his face. In light-colored chinos and a pale blue shirt, he looked almost unbearably handsome, and she prayed Annie was wrong. Or that she could just forget about it. Ben's past relationships had nothing to do with her at all, really. But even as she thought it, she knew it wasn't something she could just let go. He would have lied to her, at least by omission, and she had had more than enough of secrets and lies to last her a lifetime.

"Keeley, what is it?" he said with an urgent note to his voice. "Has there been another letter, or worse?"

"No," she said quickly, "nothing like that. But I do need to ask you something."

"Go on."

At once, Keeley felt foolish, wishing she hadn't said anything at all, but it was too late now. She looked directly at him, trying not to notice how piercing his eyes were, or think about the way they had gazed into hers the night before while he had made love to her.

"Have you dated Raquel?"

Ben looked taken aback. Whatever he had thought Keeley wanted to ask, this clearly wasn't it.

"What? Keeley, what is this about? I explained to you what I was discussing with Raquel before. Why would you ask me this now?"

He looked angry, but he also, she noticed, hadn't directly answered her question.

"Because it's apparently common knowledge," she said, and her voice came out much snappier and more petulant than she had intended.

Ben raised an eyebrow at her.

"Is it, now?" He sounded cold now, his face taking on that closed expression she was familiar with from her return to Belfrey. The very temperature in the room seemed to have dropped a few degrees.

"Well, is it true?" She held her breath for his answer, wincing when it came even though it was by now expected.

"Yes, I did date her. Very briefly. Exactly how is this relevant to anything?"

Keeley's mouth fell open at that piece of barefaced cheek.

"How is it relevant?" Her voice was raised now, and she was too angry to care whether she was being irrational or not. "How is it not relevant? She's got to be the chief suspect, at least for the letters, and she's gone out of her way to be vile to me, and you didn't think this was worth mentioning before you took me to bed?"

A look of hurt crossed Ben's features, to be swiftly replaced with a mask of disdain.

"What I think," he said slowly, his words cutting her like knives, "is that you are being completely ridiculous."

Keeley turned away, unable to look at him, not wanting him to see how much he had upset her. "You should go. This was a bad idea." She deliberately made her tone as cutting as his own. She heard a sharp intake of breath from Ben, felt rather than heard him step toward her, but then he whirled around and was gone, slamming the door after him.

Keeley crumpled. She sagged against the wall, hot tears pooling in the corners of her eyes. How could she have been so stupid? She was torn between running outside and calling for him to come back and going upstairs and burning the sheets they had slept on. Made love on. It had been so long since she allowed a man so close, and not just in the physical sense, and she had been wrong. He had lied to her.

A niggling little voice told her she was overreacting, but it was overridden by a fresh wave of anger. Rather than racing upstairs to take her frustrations out on the bed linen, she went into the kitchen and started brewing a pot of herbal tea. The flowers in Annie's vase needed watering. She got on with the mundane tasks, trying to deepen her shallow breath, trying to pretend her hands weren't trembling, but all the while, her senses were on hyper-alert, desperate for Ben to come back through the door and tell her he was sorry, and it was all right, and she hadn't just ruined every-thing with her irrational jealousy.

If it was irrational. Something told Keeley that Ben was no Brett; he would never intentionally deceive her, and yet, she couldn't allow herself to be certain.

Even so, when the door went she ran to it, suppressing a howl of frustration when once again it wasn't Ben but Annie Rowland.

"Are you all right, dear? I saw young Ben tear off down the hill at some speed, and I thought, that will be because of me and my big mouth."

"It's not your fault," Keeley said, opening the door to let her landlady in, though she did half wish that Annie had never said anything. She had always thought of the woman as the epitome of genteel discreetness.

"I take it you had a quarrel, then?"

Keeley nodded, feeling tears sting her eyes again.

"Well, I'm sure you will sort it out, although honestly, I don't think he's quite the young man for you, really."

Keeley felt puzzled. Did Annie know more about Ben? She held a chair out for her landlady in the kitchen and poured them both a cup of tea from the pot. Annie sipped at hers daintily.

"What makes you say that?" Keeley said. Her phone, which she had left on the kitchen counter, buzzed with a message, and she nearly tripped over herself to get to it, expecting it to be Ben. It was Megan, wishing her good luck on her date. Keeley groaned and sank back into her chair.

"He just seems such a serious young man—he would be mar-ried to his job, I would imagine. And I don't think he'll be long for Belfrey."

"Neither will I, at this rate," mumbled Keeley; then she waved her hand as if to refute her words when Annie gave her a concerned look. "No, ignore me, I'm just feeling sorry for myself. I'm not going anywhere, in fact, I'm really looking forward to the opening."

Annie didn't smile at her or give any encouragement as she might have expected her to do. Instead she gave Keeley an inscrutable expression that seemed to be hiding a touch of anger. About what? Keeley wondered.

"Honestly, dear, don't take this the wrong way, but I'm surprised you're going ahead with it, given everything that's happened. It sends out the wrong message, don't you think?"

Keeley felt puzzled, and more than a little hurt. Annie had always seemed so supportive, and now even she was turning on her.

"Oh dear, I've said too much." The usual look of concern was back on the woman's face, and Keeley thought she had just imagined that flash of anger she had seen in them.

"I'll be going," her landlady said regretfully, picking up her bag and swinging it over her shoulder. "I do hope I haven't upset you?"

"No, of course not," Keeley said, the words automatic, but she was looking at Annie's skirt. Her landlady's jumper had ridden up as she lifted her bag, revealing what should have been a set of two gold buttons at the side. One was missing. The one that remained, however, was a dead ringer for the one upstairs on Keeley's dresser.

Chapter Eighteen

Her heart hammering, trying to keep her expression carefully neutral, Keeley smiled at her landlady.

"You don't need to go," she told her, trying to look anywhere but at her waistband, "you haven't upset me. To be honest, you're probably right."

The relief on Annie's face was palpable as she sat back down, and for a moment, Keeley told herself not to be so stupid. She was chasing shadows now, seeing murderers in the friendliest of faces. Yet something worried at her, some half memory that wanted to make itself known but that she couldn't quite seem to grasp at. If she was right, she should probably be running screaming for the door, but instead she wanted to speak to Annie further, if only to rule the hitherto kindly woman out. After all, Gerald had said the buttons were commonplace, and lots of people lost buttons, all the time.

"Really? Oh, I am glad. I worry about you, you know, with all this dreadfulness that's been going on. Poor Jack and his dog, and of course, Terry getting killed like that. Awful, isn't it really. One minute here, and the next, bashed around the head and that's it, gone. Such a waste."

Keeley stared at Annie, a creeping sense of dread pervading her limbs as she digested the woman's words. Bashed around the head . . . As far as she knew, the exact method of Terry's death wasn't common knowledge. It hadn't been in the papers. Keeley knew only because Ben had told her, that first day, that Terry was hit with a large, blunt object. Keeley swallowed, trying to smile as though nothing were wrong, but her features felt frozen on her face. Annie stared back, and Keeley saw the knowledge dawn in her eyes that she had said something wrong, something out of place.

Keeley wrenched her gaze away from the woman and conjured up a bright smile, hoping it was enough. That Annie hadn't seen the dawning realization on Keeley's own face.

She reached for her phone, her hands clammy, murmuring that she should really text Megan back, then sat back in alarm when Annie reached for her phone and slid it out of Keeley's grasp, then picked it up and placed it in her own handbag.

"What are you doing?" Keeley aimed for a tone of interested bemusement, to keep up the façade, but her voice came out as no more than a terrified squeak. They sat for a few moments in silence, every nerve ending on Keeley's body bristling as she tried to judge the distance between herself and the doors, her stomach roiling when she realized Annie blocked her exits. She stood up and reached for the teacups, and Annie sprang to her feet, almost diametrically opposite her now. Challenging her, her eyes as cold and still as a snake's. It was as though she had been wearing a mask earlier; there was nothing of the kindhearted landlady in the figure now standing before her.

"Give me my phone, Annie, please," Keeley said firmly, though she could feel her thighs trembling. Annie tipped her head to one side as if considering her request; then her voice, now so unfamiliar, rapped out, "No. I think not."

Keeley looked her landlady straight in her eyes. She should probably scream now, she thought, but instead a different sound came out of her mouth.

"Why?"

For a moment, she thought Annie wouldn't answer; then a desperately sad look came over the older woman's face.

"I didn't really have a choice, you see. I did it for Donald."

"Your husband?" When Annie nodded, Keeley went on, "I'm sure you had your reasons, Annie; we're all capable of different things. I'm sure if you explain to Ben—"

Annie's chin snapped up, her eyes flaring with rage, any remorse forgotten. The woman's kindly old lady mask had well and truly come off; the angry sneer she now directed at Keeley would have terrified the hardest of men.

"To Ben? To your fancy man? You're nothing but a little tart, Keeley Carpenter, just like your mother before you."

Her mother? Ignoring the insult to herself, Keeley shook her head, puzzled. "What does my mother have to do with any of this?"

"Everything," Annie said. "It was all her fault, even in the beginning. Seducing my Donald, as if she didn't have a husband of her own."

Keeley felt as though an iron fist had planted itself in her gut.

Donald Rowland? That had been the man her mother had an affair with? And Annie had known all this time? Things began to drop into place in her mind, fitting together with a horrible understanding.

"That's why you wanted to burn down the shop. You must have heard my mother was reopening it and thought she was coming back. But I don't understand," Keeley frowned, aware she was still missing a very big piece of the puzzle, "why it should bother you after all this time? My mother's affair was years ago, why didn't you take it up with her then?" Before, the idea of the gentle Mrs. Rowland facing down Darla would have been laughable, but seeing this version of Annie, Keeley thought her mother might have had something to worry about.

"Because," Annie said with impatience, as though Keeley were dim-witted for not understanding. "I didn't know then. It was only after Donald died, and I was moving our things from the town house, that I found the letters." Annie's face twisted with grief and other, darker things. "Your dear Darla this, my darling Donald that. He had been in love with her, can you imagine? Even wanted to leave me for her." There was the hint of a sob in Annie's voice, and in spite of herself, Keeley felt sorry for her. She knew what it felt like to be cheated on and lied to. So this was what her mother's infidelity had wrought.

"Annie, I'm sorry," she said, surprised to find that for that at least, she genuinely did feel for the woman in front of her. "What my mother did to you was awful. But surely, it's in the past? She can't hurt you anymore." *And her husband's dead too,* she thought.

Annie gave her a look of disdain, then laughed, a hard brittle sound that was so unlike her usual quiet chuckle, it filled Keeley with dread.

"It isn't your mother I'm concerned about, you silly girl," Annie said, shaking her head at Keeley's apparent stupidity. "It's *you*."

Keeley felt her stomach turn over, certain that whatever Annie was about to reveal, it would certainly be something she didn't want to know.

"You tried to burn down the shop to get at me," she said in a flat voice. Annie nodded, looking triumphant.

"Clever girl. Well, not to get at you as such, that would be petty, but to stop you coming here, or at least make you go home. But no, you had to be a stubborn thing, didn't you? That's just like *her* as well."

"But why?" With the inevitability of one watching a train wreck, Keeley knew she had to find out. Had to hear this out until the end.

"Because you're his. Donald's. His and your mother's dirty little secret." Annie's face held a hatred so raw and deep that even if her revelation hadn't caused Keeley to collapse on her chair, legs shaking, that would have. "She spoke about you in the letters, about the 'little love child.' Sickening."

Keeley shook her head fiercely, to block out Annie's words even as they made an awful kind of sense. Annie, who had adored her husband, who couldn't have children of her own; it wasn't hard to imagine how she could hate Keeley enough to want to derail her plans. To keep her away from Belfrey.

"You sent me the letters. And the meat." Keeley felt sick as she remembered the smell and feel of those pieces of rotting meat, and her initial assumption that they were the parts of a human. Annie, however, smiled as though proud of her own creativity.

"Yes. That was a stroke of luck, really. I hoped the letters would be enough to scare you away, but instead you started going round asking questions; just couldn't leave well enough alone, could you? I knew I needed something else. Then I was about to visit you one night and heard you talking to Ben." Annie smirked. "Your so sad little tale about finding your father, and it putting you off meat for life. So I went home and cut up a good joint of ham I had and let it sit in the sun for a few days."

Keeley glared at her. "That's just evil."

Annie just shrugged, unperturbed.

"I tried to do more, just little things, to get you to go. Spread a few rumors about you being implicated in the murder, had a word in Ted Glover's ear, dropped hints about Ben visiting you, and even told Renee you had asked for the stall in the center because you didn't want to mix with all the meat-eaters. Of course, that backfired when it started to rain, but the weather's one thing no one can control, I suppose." Her tone was almost conversational now, even though each new revelation cut Keeley like a butcher's knife.

"But you were so nice to me," Keeley protested. "You were supportive, and gave me advice, and I'm renting out your cottage, for God's sake!"

Annie gave her a look of annoyance, then a melodramatic sigh that made Keeley want to punch her. Hard.

"Yes, and I absolutely hated it. I had to let you think I was your friend, didn't I, dear, so that you didn't suspect. When you made inquiries about the cottage, well, I thought someone up there was having a good old laugh at my expense, I can tell you. Then I thought that if I turned you down, you would only rent somewhere else, or even buy, and then I'd never get rid of you. So I thought to myself, at least with you here, I could keep an eye on you. I wasn't sure if you knew or not, you see."

Keeley shook her head as the full implications of Annie's words sank in. Her father wasn't really her father? Generous, kind George Carpenter, whom she had looked up to and tried to emulate her entire life, wasn't really her flesh and blood at all. She wondered if he had known, had realized he had been raising a little cuckoo in the nest. A wave of desolation washed over her.

Annie was still talking, either not noticing or not caring about the impact of her words on Keeley. She suspected the latter.

"I couldn't let it get out, could I? Donald was a well-respected man. He was just weak, easily tempted, and once that trollop got her claws in, well, what do you expect? He was only a man." Annie gave a sad smile, as if masculinity were a valid justification for all sorts of wrongdoing.

"So Terry Smith was blackmailing you," Keeley said flatly. That was the crux of the matter, the reason her café had become a crime scene. Annie jerked her chin in confirmation.

"Yes. Nasty, horrible little man. He used to do odd jobs for people, you see, as well as the betting, no doubt so he could go through people's things. I asked him to help me clear the attic after Donald's death, and he must have seen the letters before I did." Annie paused, her expression far away, and Keeley risked a glance around her toward the back door, thinking she might just make it. But was the back door locked, and where was the key? Her mind, already burdened with more than it could bear, drew a complete blank.

"He didn't say anything right away," Annie went on. "He bided his time. Then a few months ago, one of his regulars at the betting shop, a young man who works at the letting agents, let it be known that Darla was leasing the shop over to you. That's when he came to me and started asking for money. He knew I wouldn't want everyone to know, to look down on me. That I couldn't give my Donald a child, but that bitch could." Annie's face twisted again with such pure fury, Keeley felt genuinely scared. For the first time, she understood that she might in fact be in mortal danger. Not wanting to risk making a run for it, she looked around for something she could use as a weapon, at the same time trying to keep Annie talking.

"So you killed him."

"Well, that wasn't my original intention. In a way, it was an accident."

"Oh?" In spite of her fear, Keeley couldn't help but be interested in what had happened on that night.

"I couldn't find a way of stopping you coming here, with your silly little café, dragging it all up again. I thought if I got rid of your business, well, there would be nothing to bring you back here, or that it might scare you off. But Terry saw me going to the shop, even though I checked and thought the street was deserted. Horrible snoop." She gave her assessment of Terry with a pursed mouth and look of disapproval, as though a spot of evening loitering were far more amoral than attempting to burn down someone's property, in an attempt to hide a dead man's transgressions.

"He followed me," Annie went on, "sneering at me in that way of his. Offered to help me, as long as I paid him, of course. I knew I had no choice, and he was already leeching more money from me than I could afford. All of our savings were going."

"So you killed him." Keeley resisted the temptation to shake her head in disgust, not wanting to antagonize the woman. If Annie would just move out of the way, she might be able to make a dash for the door. Her eyes alighted on the vase of flowers on the windowsill, wondering if she could reach it. It was heavy, she knew, and would make a suitable defensive weapon. Annie's eyes followed her own and Keeley tensed, ready for some kind of attack, but Annie had misread her intentions. Her landlady gave a sly smile.

"Yes, that's right. I lured him upstairs, so we could talk without being seen, not really knowing what to do. I had vague ideas of pushing him out of the window, I suppose. Then I saw the vase the last tenant had left. Pretty, isn't it? I asked Terry to go downstairs and fetch the gasoline—he thought it better to start upstairs, you see—and hit him with it. He didn't die, not straightaway. He struggled, grabbed at me. I had to hit him a few times." She recounted the killing in an almost singsong voice, and Keeley saw, very clearly, that Annie was nothing short of severely mentally disturbed. If not an outright psychopath. How could she have been living in such close proximity to such madness, even evil, and never have noticed? Had even seen the woman as a friend, a mother figure? Keeley felt sick, right down to her toes.

"I didn't know what to do with the vase. I had to get rid of it, but I didn't want it found. It was so funny, seeing you coo over it and the flowers when you moved in." She gave a little giggle, and Keeley felt her nausea replaced with a wave of white-hot fury. She stood up, her limbs shaking, her breath catching in her throat.

"And Bambi? Was that you too?" When Annie didn't answer, only responded with a sly smirk, Keeley remembered what it was that had niggled at her before. Something Megan had said. "It was you he was barking at, wasn't it? Just like he barked that night. He remembered you."

"Yes," Annie looked annoyed. "I never did like that dog. Great smelly thing. As soon as I knew it was barking at me, I knew it was only a matter of time before it happened again and Jack put two and two together. I was lucky that yesterday the High Street was crowded enough that no one would have realized just what he was barking at. So I bought a piece of meat from the one of the stalls—everybody was buying that delicious ham on the bone—and mixed up some of the painkillers the doctor gives me. I get a touch of arthritis in my left shoulder at times, you see, but it's not bothered me for a while now. So luckily, there was plenty left."

In spite of Annie's continuing speech, given in that awful lilting tone of voice as though they were discussing mundane matters, the atmosphere had perceptibly changed. The woman had visibly tensed, her eyes tracking Keeley's every glance ad flinch. Waiting for her to make a move. Her soft, plump frame had become a solid barrier to Keeley's escape, and she had no doubt that the woman would attack her if she tried to leave. But she wasn't going to stand there and wait for Annie to decide that she too needed dealing with.

Keeley made a feint to the left, then darted to the right and dashed for the back door, relying on the fact that though Annie may be a great deal stronger than she looked, Keeley was both younger and faster.

Not, however, fast enough to get through a locked door. Cursing, Keeley scrabbled for the key that hung from the nearby hook on the wall, and her fingers had just closed around the metal when her head was yanked viciously backwards. Annie had grabbed her hair with such force that Keeley felt a sickening wrench in her neck. She tried to twist away, which only increased the pull on her scalp, then aimed an elbow into Annie's side just as the woman banged her head against the door. Keeley nearly fell, the pain in her head was so excruciating, but she heard Annie's sharp exhalation behind her and felt her grip loosen and knew her elbow had been well placed. She dragged herself round, her hands instinctively raised into fists, only to see Annie clutching at her side and looking at Keeley in pained accusation.

"Really, dear, you would hit an old lady like myself?" In spite of the sheer ludicrousness of the comment, Keeley couldn't help but hesitate, lowering her hands at the sight of the woman feebly clutching herself.

Then Annie slammed her into the door. Howling with pain and rage, Keeley kicked out, landing a blow on the woman's shin that caused her to stumble. She shoved her as hard as she could, sending her tumbling to the floor, and ran, back through the cottage to the front door, which she knew was unlocked. It also seemed a mile away, though in reality it was just a few feet, and her legs felt like lead. She had reached the porch when she heard Annie behind her, and in spite of herself glanced back over her shoulder, to see the woman close behind her, charging into the living room. Her face was so twisted with rage, she was almost unrecognizable, and she held the vase in both hands high over her head. Her heart thundering against her ribs, Keeley grabbed the door handle, her palms so clammy that they all but slipped off it, and flung the door open just as the vase crashed into the wall centimeters from her head, Annie having flung herself forward wildly in an attempt to prevent her getting out of the cottage.

She stumbled outside and straight into a shocked Ben, Annie screaming in fury behind her.

"It was her—she killed Terry!" she managed to gasp, just as Annie again raised the vase and swung out, so caught up in her rage that she barely seemed to register Ben's presence.

Ben thrust Keeley to one side and out of harm's way, just as she screamed for him to look out; then he tackled Annie, barreling her back into the house. His attack caused her to drop the vase, which landed with a loud thud and then rolled, coming to a stop at Keeley's feet. She looked down as though in a daze, noticing almost dispassionately that it had finally begun to crack down one side, and there was a large chip at the rim.

Ben came back out of the house with Annie, holding her arms behind her in a way that rendered her helpless, the woman now looking confused and sobbing softly. Ben looked grim, but also bewildered; then, as he turned his face to Keeley, his expression changed to one of concern.

"Are you all right?"

Keeley nodded and pointed to the vase at her feet.

"I found the murder weapon," she said.

Later, after Annie had been taken to the station and arrested, then sent to the cells in Derby until she could go before the court for a bail hearing, they sat on the sofa together, Keeley staring out the window without really seeing anything. They were holding hands, although she wasn't sure who had reached for the other first. Ben cleared his throat.

"About earlier," he began.

"It doesn't matter now." She realized it really didn't. Ben continued anyway.

"No, I need to tell you. It was just a couple of dates, back when I was still training and she had just come back from Manchester. Nothing happened between us, I need you to know that."

"Then why didn't you just tell me that earlier?"

Ben looked shamefaced. "Male pride, I suppose. Earlier I felt like you were accusing me of something, and I was just being stubborn. Stupid. I went home and sulked for a bit, and then told myself to get back here and sort things out, before I ended up losing you. Thank God I did."

Keeley laid her head on his shoulder, and after a moment's hesitation, Ben pulled her closer, then began to stroke her hair while resting his chin lightly on the crown of her head.

"I should have known," he berated himself. "Should have worked it out. But Annie Rowland—who would have thought it?"

"Did she say why, in questioning?" Keeley felt an unfamiliar pain slice through her as she recalled Annie's revelations about her mother.

"Not really. She admitted everything, then clammed up. I expect she said more to you? We'll need a formal statement from you, but it can wait until tomorrow."

Keeley let out a sudden sob that startled even herself, and Ben clutched her to him.

"You're in shock."

"It's not that." She recounted exactly what Annie, and Darla before her, had told her. About Donald's affair, and the incriminating letters that described Keeley as their secret love child. Ben was quiet after she had finished, his hand continuing to stroke her hair. When he spoke, he sounded thoughtful.

"Is there any way she could be mistaken? I mean, I remember your dad, and you were the image of him when we were younger."

"She said she had read the letters, talking about the affair, and the baby, and how it had to be kept secret. . . . Wait a minute." Keeley sat upright as her mother's words came back to her.

"Ben," she said urgently, "my mother said she went back to London, that she was there for two months before Dad went back to get her, and I was conceived then. So it couldn't be me, could it, unless she was lying about the dates, but a whole two months would be pushing it."

"She never said who she had the affair with?"

"No. She did say they weren't from Belfrey, although I'm not sure I believe her. But thinking about it, I doubt she would have been happy for me to rent this place from Annie if her husband were in fact my real father."

"Then who? You say Annie was certain the letters were signed by your mother?"

Keeley had a flash of insight and raised her hand to her forehead, the answer suddenly so obvious, it should never have been in doubt.

"From Darla. But she wasn't the only Darla in Belfrey. And I wasn't the only girl born that month." Now she knew why the picture of Donald had seemed so familiar. And Darla Philips hadn't been one to socialize with the locals, so Annie may not even have known her first name, whereas everyone knew Keeley's mother simply by dint of her being the butcher's wife. Her whole being flooded with relief. Annie was wrong.

"Raquel," Ben finished for her. "Raquel is Donald Rowland's love child."

I was right, Keeley thought, *Raquel was involved in all of this, just not in the way I thought.*

"Do you think you should tell her?"

"No," said Keeley firmly. As mean as Raquel had been, Keeley realized she had done her an injustice. Had almost, because of her own insecurity, wanted the culprit to have been Raquel. "There's been enough harm done, enough digging up of secrets better left buried."

Ben nodded, looking thoughtful again.

"So, at the same time your mother was having her own affair with some as yet unnamed person, Darla Philips was carrying on with Donald."

"It looks that way. I wonder how they met? Mrs. Philips was always worse than my mother for acting like she was better than everyone else. Perhaps Donald was her bit of rough."

"It seems," Ben said wryly, "that Belfrey in the '80s was a regular hotbed of vice."

Keeley let out a surprised laugh, and continued giggling as she saw the corner of Ben's mouth flicker in suppressed amusement.

"And they say nothing ever happens around here," she said, to be rewarded with a bark of laughter from Ben. He was still laughing when he took her in his arms and kissed her as though he were a man starved.

"I think I might be falling for you, Keeley Carpenter," he said when they finally broke away from each other. Keeley just stared.

"You do?"

"Yes," he said firmly, then held his hand out to her. "Come on," he said.

Keeley looked at his outstretched palm, bemused. "Where are we going?"

"To bed."

So they did.

BREATH OF JOY

A warming and invigorating exercise that combines breathing with rhythmic movement to charge the entire body with endorphins and positive energy. An excellent antidote to depression and lethargy, and can be used anytime for a quick pick-me-up.

Method

- Stand with your feet hip width apart. Stand tall, but relaxed.
- Inhale and exhale slowly through the nose.
- The inhalation comes in three parts, and each part corresponds to an arm movement. For the first part, inhale up to a third of your capacity while bringing your arms up in front of you.
- Continue inhaling to two-thirds of your capacity, while bringing your lifted arms out to the sides.
- Continue and finish the inhalation, bringing your arms up overhead, reaching for the sky.
- Exhale through the mouth with an audible "ha!" sound, and as you do, bend forward and swing your arms all the way down and back behind you.
- Return to standing. Do this sequence three to five times.

Contraindications

Keep the knees slightly bent if you have any trouble with your knees or lower back. If you have low blood pressure, this exercise may make you light-headed, so try not bending forward too far and performing it more slowly. If you have high blood pressure, migraines, or glaucoma, it is recommended you do not try this practice without first consulting a doctor.

Chapter Nineteen

Three days later, Keeley stood behind the counter of her newly opened café and allowed herself a triumphant smile. It had been a busy morning, as familiar and unfamiliar faces alike had crowded into the Yoga Café. If, as she suspected, a good portion of them were there out of morbid curiosity, Annie's attack and confession being the story of choice in the local and even regional papers, then at least they were eating and drinking as well as feeding said curiosity. Norma and Maggie had been in, of course, oozing false sympathy in a bid to get the details from her. Thankfully, some generous helpings of her summer fruit puddings had distracted them. Diana had been in too, with a small basket of eggs and her timid smile.

It was a beautiful day, the sun high over the dales on the horizon, and her wraps, salads, and smoothies had been as much in demand as her more traditional dishes. The lunchtime rush was slowly abating, and had been so hectic, Megan closed Crystals and Candles early and came over to give her a hand, donning one of Keeley's fresh lemon aprons with the YOGA CAFÉ logo emblazoned across it.

"Duane said he would come in," Megan said now, "along with this new girl he's been dating. I wonder if it's someone from work."

"Maybe," Keeley agreed, doing her best to sound interested. In truth, she hoped Duane had found himself someone nice, and a gym enthusiast with a tan to rival his sounded perfect.

Then the bell above the door sounded, and Duane walked in with a woman who, although certainly glamorous, was definitely not a girl from the center.

"Oh, how rustic," Raquel said with a large, insincere smile, her honeyed tones somehow managing to make the word "rustic" convey all her considerable disdain. Megan's mouth dropped open, while Keeley grinned in surprise. It was perfect, she thought, just perfect.

"I'll just have a cold drink, I think," Raquel said, looking at Keeley in a cool challenge. When Keeley simply beamed at her and made her a fresh orange and lime juice "on the house," she looked a little disappointed. But knowing what she knew, and having spent the last three days being comforted, among other things, by Ben, Keeley could afford to be generous. The couple retreated to a table in the corner, Duane flushing as Megan continued to gape at them.

"How could he go out with *her*?" she said to Keeley in disgust. Keeley shrugged. She actually thought they were well suited, given as they were each as self-absorbed as the other, but didn't want to offend Megan with her appraisal of her cousin.

The bell went again, and this time it was another couple, decidedly more welcome and, Keeley noted with relief, fully recovered from their recent ordeal. Seeing Keeley, Bambi gave an excited woof and wagged his tail furiously, nearly knocking the place settings from a nearby table.

"I'm so glad to see you both, Jack," Keeley said with undisguised warmth. The old man shrugged, but she saw the flash of pleasure in his eyes.

"Well, I'm not keen on all this sort of thing, but I know Bambi here was quite partial to them burgers of yours, so I'll have two of them for him and a pot of tea for myself. Normal tea, mind, none of that herbal stuff."

Keeley prepared his order and then, as everyone was happily eating, there were no new customers, and Megan had gone through the washing up with surprising speed, Keeley decided it was time for a break and sat down with Jack and her own mug of tea. Bambi laid his great head in her lap and looked at her with adoration— or a plea for more burgers.

"He looks so well now," she said, stroking him.

"Aye, he's right enough. Strong old fella. Nearly did for him, that Rowland woman. It's funny, but I always did think there was something not right about her, though I didn't have her pegged down for the murder."

Keeley nodded and sighed. The only blot on her landscape was that she now needed somewhere to live. Annie had been bailed and apparently went to a niece in Devon, and Keeley had packed up her meager belongings and moved them into the apartment at the top of the café.

"You look glum, lass," Jack remarked. Keeley told him about her living arrangements.

"It's not too bad just for me, though it does put paid to my holding classes up there for a while. But I spoke to my mother this morning, and she wants to come and stay. There's not enough room up there for the two of us."

Indeed, she had had to stop Darla from traveling straight up there when she had heard about Annie's attack, reassuring her that both she and the business were fine. Although her mother's concern had touched her, given that it was somewhat out of character, Keeley still wasn't sure how she felt about Darla's confessions of infidelity and wasn't quite ready to deal with it in the flesh. Not to mention the fact that, while their phone conversations may have grown rather more cordial, Keeley wasn't sure that their tentative and reinforced bond would hold up to the strain of being cooped up together in the tiny apartment.

Jack chuckled in sympathy.

"She likes her own way, that one."

"Tell me about it."

"Mark my words," Jack said amiably, pulling on his pipe, "your mother comes back to visit, and there'll be murders."

Recipes from the Yoga Café

TOFU SCRAMBLIES

Serves 4

Perfect for breakfast or a midmorning snack. An alternative to scrambled eggs.

Ingredients

½ onion, chopped

1 tablespoon olive oil

1 garlic clove, crushed

1 red pepper, diced

250 grams firm tofu

1 teaspoon cumin (or turmeric, if preferred)

½ teaspoon black pepper

50 milliliters vegetable stock

Method

1. In a medium pan, sauté the chopped onion in the olive oil on medium heat for about 3 minutes before adding the garlic and red pepper. Continue sautéing until the onion is soft.

2. Crumble the tofu by hand, and add it to the pan.

3. Mix cumin and black pepper into the tofu mixture.

4. Make up the vegetable stock, heat it up, and pour into the pan.

5. Cook until the water is absorbed into the tofu mixture.

6. Add a little salt if desired.

Enjoy!

VEGETABLE MOUSSAKA

Serves 6

Traditional moussaka is meat-based and can be quite high in fat. This alternative is lighter while still retaining the hearty nature of the dish—a great comfort food! If you're not vegetarian but still want a lighter alternative to the traditional dish, substitute 200 grams diced chicken for the beans.

Ingredients

200 grams new potatoes, sliced

2 courgettes, sliced

1 aubergine, sliced

2 bell peppers, sliced

400 grams beans (Italian borlotti beans, also called Roman beans, are the best due to their high protein content

and delicious nutty taste, but if you can't find them, try
cranberry, kidney, or pinto beans)

1 can chopped tomatoes

3 tablespoons fresh basil

2 tablespoons olive oil

1 egg

150 grams plain yogurt

30 grams grated cheese

2 teaspoons grated nutmeg

Method

1. Boil the new potatoes until tender. Preheat oven to 180 degrees C. Grill the courgettes and aubergines on medium heat for 2 to 3 minutes. Grill the peppers on high heat for around 5 minutes, until slightly charred and soft. Add the potatoes, courgettes, and peppers to a baking dish with the beans and chopped tomatoes. Stir well. Add the basil and drizzle the olive oil over everything. Place the dish to one side.

2. Beat the egg. Mix together the yogurt, the egg, and the cheese. When blended spread half the egg mixture over the top of the vegetables. Arrange the sliced aubergines on top of this. Finish by spreading the rest of the egg mixture on top of the aubergines, and sprinkle it with the nutmeg.

3. Bake for 40 minutes or until the topping is golden brown.

TOFU BURGERS

Makes 8 burgers

Use the firmest tofu you can get, add some tasty seasonings, and these burgers make a flavorful alternative to traditional beef burgers.

Ingredients

1 pound extra firm tofu, diced

1 tablespoon cumin

½ teaspoon cayenne

¼ teaspoon sea salt

1 tablespoon soy sauce

1 tablespoon mustard

2 large eggs

½ cup fine bread crumbs

1 onion, very finely chopped

1 tablespoon olive oil

Method

1. All the ingredients except for the oil need to be blended together into one sticky mixture. By far the easiest way to do this is with a blender or food processor! Divide the tofu mixture into eight round, flat patties. Heat the oil in a pan, and add the patties, cooking them on moderate heat for around 10 minutes each, turning once halfway.

2. Serve as you would regular burgers.

SPICY ROOT VEGETABLE CURRY

Serves 6

A great alternative to meat curries, with the root vegetables giving it a homey, wholesome twist. Can be served with rice, couscous, or the bread of your choice, and also works with jacket potatoes as an alternative to chili.

Ingredients

1 garlic clove, crushed

1 tablespoon olive oil

3 cups vegetable stock

4 carrots, diced

For the curry powder (or you can buy a packet and add 2 tablespoons; I prefer garam masala):

   1 tablespoon cumin

   ½ tablespoon turmeric

   ¼ tablespoon ground coriander

   ¼ tablespoon ginger powder

   ¼ tablespoon chili powder (or double for extra heat)

1 cup frozen peas or chickpeas

½ pound sweet potatoes, diced

1 pound turnips, diced

2 tablespoons flour

Method

1. In a medium pan, soften the onion and garlic in the olive oil for around 5 minutes on medium heat. Add the curry powder or spices and stir for 2 minutes. Add the stock and

vegetables and bring to a boil; then simmer on low heat for 45 to 50 minutes, covered.

2. While the curry is simmering, mix the flour with ¼ cup of water. When the flour mixture is smooth, add it to the curry and stir for about 3 minutes to thicken. Serve.

Keeley's Summer Salad Bar

KEELEY'S RAINBOW SALAD

Serves 8

The different colors in this salad signify a variety of fruit and vegetables and therefore a variety of essential nutrients, making this a delicious and super-healthy side, starter, or dessert salad.

Ingredients

2 mangoes

2 avocados

3 tomatoes (preferably vine-ripened, for the best flavor), chopped

1 red onion, chopped

1 bell pepper (any color) chopped

150 grams fresh berries of your choice (strawberries are my
preference)

½ bunch cilantro, chopped

5 tablespoons lime juice

100 milliliters pineapple juice

Method

1. Peel, seed, and cube the mangoes and avocados and place
them in a large bowl. Mix in the tomatoes, onion, bell
pepper, berries, and cilantro. Add the fruit juices to the
bowl, and stir the salad thoroughly.

GREEK FETA SALAD

Serves 6 to 8

Serve this salad with couscous or in a wrap for a healthy
starter or light lunch.

Ingredients

1 teaspoon sugar

200 milliliters olive oil

juice and zest of 3 lemons

1 tablespoon dried oregano

400 grams cubed feta cheese

24 green olives

16 plum tomatoes, chopped

Method

1. Combine the sugar, olive oil, lemon juice and zest, and oregano in a medium bowl. Stir in the feta cubes, and refrigerate to chill. Before serving, chop the olives, and add them to the bowl along with the tomatoes. Stir well. Serve with warm pita and couscous.

ASPARAGUS AND ARTICHOKE SALAD

Serves 6 to 8

A light spring salad that makes a perfect starter or side.

Ingredients

1 large shallot

2 tablespoons lemon juice

2 pounds asparagus

2 tablespoons olive oil

1 cup cherry tomatoes

1 jar artichoke hearts

Method

1. Preheat the oven to 200 degrees C.

2. Slice the shallot and soak it in the lemon juice.

3. Coat the asparagus spears with olive oil, lay them on a foil-lined baking tray, and roast them for up to 10 minutes.

4. Cut the roasted asparagus into chunks, and remove the shallot from lemon juice. Combine the shallot and asparagus with the remaining ingredients in a bowl, and serve as desired.